THINGS I'D RATHER DO THAN DIE

THINGS I'D RATHER DO THAN DIE

CHRISTINE HURLEY DERISO

Mendota Heights, Minnesota

First Edition
First Printing, 2018

Book design by Sarah Taplin
Cover design by Sarah Taplin
Cover images by Pixabay

Flux, an imprint of North Star Editions, Inc.

Library of Congress Cataloging-in-Publication Data
Names: Deriso, Christine Hurley, 1961- author.
Title: Things I'd rather do than die / by Christine Hurley Deriso.
Other titles: Things I would rather do than die
Description: First edition. | Mendota Heights, MN : Flux, [2018] | Summary: "When the two most mismatched seniors at Walt Whitman High School find themselves locked in an aerobics room overnight, their confinement forces them to push past the labels they've assigned each other and they share a night they'll never forget"— Provided by publisher.
Identifiers: LCCN 2018020721 (print) | LCCN 2018027292 (ebook) | ISBN 9781635830231 (ebook) | ISBN 9781635830224 (pbk. : alk. paper)
Subjects: | CYAC: High schools—Fiction. | Schools—Fiction. | Love—Fiction. | Dating (Social customs)—Fiction.
Classification: LCC PZ7.D4427 (ebook) | LCC PZ7.D4427 Thg 2018 (print) | DDC [Fic]—dc23
LC record available at https://lccn.loc.gov/2018020721

Flux
North Star Editions, Inc.
2297 Waters Drive
Mendota Heights, MN 55120
www.fluxnow.com

To Tori and Lisa K. Thank you for sharing your stories with me and for being, well, fabulous.

ONE

JADE

Our last customer of the day flashes me a pinched smile as he limps out of the gym.

Stop thinking about it.

That's been my mantra for the past two weeks. Two weeks of scans and second opinions and hushed conversations about right temporal lobes and . . .

Stop. Stop thinking about it.

Easier said than done as the customer winces in pain as he walks out the door. I give him a sympathetic smile, then blink the moisture from my eyes, hoping he doesn't notice. He would doubtless consider me certifiable for finding his overworked muscles weep-worthy. But the thoughts that I've been pushing down for two weeks come spewing to the surface when I see such a healthy-looking man limping out the door.

A rumble of thunder echoes in the distance.

I jump a little when my boss, Stan, rests his hand on my back. "Got the towels refilled and the machines wiped down, Jade?"

Uh-oh. Does he notice my misty eyes? I have got to pull myself together.

"Yep," I say, my fake cheerfulness now perfected to something of an art form. "Everything except that guy's elliptical. I'll go wipe it down now."

Okay, that's too cheery. I sound downright euphoric at the prospect.

"Great," Stan says, winking at me (which confirms, to my mortification, that, yes, he does notice my tears). "I'll start locking up. Then we can both go home and get a good night's sleep. Time and a half tomorrow, remember?"

"Yeah, that makes it totally cool to have to be back at 5:30 on Labor Day morning," I say, hoping my sarcasm douses his pity. I can take anything but pity.

As I walk from the counter toward the ellipticals, someone suddenly bursts through the door. I glance in the new-comer's direction, then roll my eyes and head back for the counter. Stan never turns late-comers away, so it looks like my work day isn't over after all.

"I'm so sorry," the guy is saying breathlessly to Stan in a light Southern accent. It's Ethan Garrett. We've been classmates since fourth grade—that's when I moved here, to Tolliver, Georgia—but we're just barely acquaintances. He's a nice-enough guy, but his A-list status means we might as well inhabit separate planets.

"I'd forgotten you guys close at six on Sundays," Ethan continues, running his fingers through sun-streaked hair. "Any chance I can squeeze in a quick workout? Twenty minutes tops?"

"No problem!" Stan says jovially.

I press my lips together. Stan won't get stuck staying late, I will. This is why Ethan and I occupy parallel universes: he's clearly accustomed to using his "aw-shucks" charm to ensure the proverbial touchdown in every play of life. (Both literally and figuratively. Of course he's the high school quarterback. Because, you know, nature didn't heap quite enough wonderfulness on him with dimples and natural highlights, so society had to step in and take up the slack.)

"Thanks so much," Ethan tells Stan, then tosses me a dimply "aw-shucks" grin as he heads toward the equipment.

Yeah. Definitely an A-lister.

And which list am I on?

I'm an outlier. Take my academic standing, for example: I make good grades (excellent grades in the subjects I care about), and I have killer one-on-one discussions with my teachers. For instance, Mr. Becker and I once spent a week's worth of study halls discussing whether the ending of *Catch 22* was a massive victory or epic fail. But I'm not a joiner, so I tend to fly under the radar. Whereas my AP classmates' club memberships take up half a page by their yearbook photos, my yearbook photo looks like a mugshot. Not only does the bio space look like a wasteland, but my "vaguely grumpy expression" (Gia's words, not mine. I was going for deep and angsty) suggests homicidal tendencies.

I'm even an outlier in my own family. My uber-outgoing sixteen-year-old brother, Pierce, bears an uncanny resemblance to our dad, with his lanky six-foot frame, chocolatey complexion, tight black curls, and crazy-gorgeous cheek-bones (courtesy of some Cherokee blood that filtered into the gene pool at some point, or so I hear). My eleven-year-old half-sister, Sydney, looks like Lena, my Filipino step-mother, with shiny, ebony hair and naturally pouty lips. Me? Other than my caramel-colored skin and dark curls, I'm told I look like the white lady whose texts and emails I've been ignoring for the past few days. My friend, Gia, jokes that our family portraits look like college recruiting brochures.

And the "diversity" doesn't end there. Let's see: On some Sundays, I'm dragged to Grandma's church, Mount Zion AME, for lots of free-form swaying and hand-clapping, while on others I'm sitting/standing/kneeling ramrod straight and mumbling preassigned lines at Our Lady of Perpetual Monotony. Lena's the Catholic in the family, and I've actually completed most of the sacraments. But I inherited my dad's don't-ask-don't-tell approach to orga-nized religion, and now that I'm old enough to protest, I'm mostly left alone on Sunday mornings to read my novels. Grandma raised Dad, and Lena married him, so they can't exactly rag on me for following his lead of sleeping in. Not that it doesn't keep them from trying.

So how would I categorize myself? Let's just say that there are the Ethans of the world, who have one easy box to check on demographic forms, and there are the African/Caucasian/Cherokee/Protestant/Catholic/Agnostic girls like me. Or, to put it even more succinctly, the Ethans are the stars of the show. The Jades are the extras.

But whatever. Who cares. I've got *real* problems now. My stomach clenches for the four-thousandth time of the day.

"Sorry," Stan tells me as his eyes follow Ethan's trek toward the free weights. "There's always that one straggler, right?"

"Mmm."

"Lock up when he's done?"

I manage a smile. "No problem."

● ● ● ● ●

ETHAN

Whoa. Better make this quick.

I'd planned to run on the greenway today, but as I got in my Corolla and headed for the park, I heard thunder rumbling. So I swung by Regal Gym instead. It closes at six—which, technically, is, like, now—but I figured it was worth a shot to zip in. The worst that could happen is being turned away, right?

I hate inconveniencing the staff, but I can't miss a day of training, even on our one day off from football practice. Coach Davis has been working us hard all summer, but now that the first game of the season is five days away, he's kicked our workouts into overdrive. Hours of side planks, ab crunches, lat pull-downs, and a thousand other forms of torture—in Tolliver's hundred-degree humidity, no less—are officially kicking my butt.

Not that Coach Davis would ever know it. All he gets from me is a crisp "Yes, sir!" and a sharp nod of the head when he bellows his orders. I've got to keep the rest of my team psyched and energized, so no one can see me wilting. My dad loves to tell me how he used to chase the slackers on his team up three flights of stairs to the high school bell tower when he was a quarterback, threatening to use their heads as the bell clapper if they didn't step it up by the next practice. Of course, I'd never follow his lead—generally speaking, my most reliable guidepost in life is to do the opposite of what my dad would do—but I do take my job as a role model seriously, particularly now that I'm a senior. I've got to set a good example.

Still, I don't have as much time for a workout as usual. I promised Brianne I'd drop by at eight, so I'll need to be home within an hour to be able to shower and show up on schedule.

It's just as I'm heading for the free weights that I notice the girl from the front desk walking toward the ellipticals with a cloth and spray bottle. She's shooting me a look. Jade. That's her name. We've been in a few classes together over the years.

I slow my pace and smile. "Hey," I say.

She offers a trace of a smile.

"Sorry I'm keeping you here late," I say, halting my

walk, which forces her to stop as well, since I'm blocking her path.

"No problem."

I study her face. "Really, I can skip the workout today if—"

"It's not a problem," she repeats, glancing over my shoulder at the equipment she needs to clean.

Still, I hover there another second or two. "You're sure?" I persist.

"Yep."

She says it in a fast, clipped voice.

That's the thing about this girl: she can be so intimidating. The look she's giving me now? I used to get the same look in English Lit last year any time I'd get the nerve to speak up. Like clockwork, Jade would turn around and glance at me for just a fraction of a second, like she couldn't quite wrap her head around what a doofus I was. Especially that first day of class, when Mrs. Alexander asked what our favorite book was and my answer was the Bible. Sorry my answer wasn't hipster enough for Jade. But it was the truth.

"Hey, I ran into Calvin today at the grocery store," I tell her, eager to find some common ground.

She stares at me for an excruciatingly long moment, then gives the slowest of nods.

It's only now that it strikes me how lame my comment was. She and Calvin dated for a while, but I heard recently that it fizzled.

"He made the team this year as our kicker," I continue, still aiming for friendly.

Jade's lips tighten as she swallows hard. "That's great," she says, her tone suggesting an epic lack of greatness all around.

I feel my face grow warm as I shift my weight. (Sue me! I was just trying to make conversation!) I consider trying to shift the chitchat to safer ground—briefly, just long enough to salvage this train wreck—but I can't think of anything else to say. Jade and I don't run in the same circles. The only person I ever see her with is her best friend, Gia, another ice queen. I swear, the temperature drops twenty degrees any time you step into their too-cool bubble.

The temperature is practically arctic right now, what with my master stroke of throwing an ex-boyfriend into the conversation, so I guess the best thing to do is abort.

I flash one last smile, then resume walking toward the free weights, my guilt morphing into a touch of indignation: Yeah, I feel bad for keeping Jade here late, but her not-too-subtle little burns haven't been lost on me. (She's got a problem with the Bible? At least I'm not ashamed to claim it.)

Besides, I never turned away latecomers at the auto-parts store where I worked over the summer. Even when I'd been on my feet for nine hours straight, the customers who ambled in at 7:57 p.m. would have sworn I had all the time in the world, that there's nothing I'd rather have been doing than drilling down on the difference between platinum and double-platinum spark plugs. I wouldn't cut my eyes at a customer, even for a split second.

So cut me some slack, Jade, will ya?

I give her one last glance over my shoulder as I head for the free weights, and yeah, my suspicion is confirmed:

She's tossing me another one of those looks.

TWO

JADE

Stan pats me on the back after I return to the front desk. "Promise me a good night's sleep tonight, okay?"

I nod. "I'm good, I'm good," I assure him, wishing I'd waited longer to tell him the news. Granted, he would have needed to know soon; the appointments will probably affect my work schedule, after all. But I'd give anything right now if I could squeeze in just a few more days of normal.

As Stan heads out the door, I plop in the chair behind the counter, reach down to the floor, pull the cell phone out of my purse and text my dad. He's at a continuing-education course in New Orleans with Lena and my little sister Sydney, but only because he'd scheduled it several months earlier—a lifetime ago. Thanks to a handful of mutated cells, he won't be needing continuing-education courses anymore.

Everything OK? I text him.

It's no biggie that he doesn't respond right away; you'd think he was in the Witness Protection Program the way he's so unreachable by cell phone, always accidentally leaving it behind or forgetting to charge it. His pager is much more reliable, but I don't want him to worry that a patient might be having a problem.

I wait a couple more antsy moments (Chill, Jade), then forward the message to Lena. Thank heaven she responds right away.

We're gr8! No worries. Sydney ♥ Bourbon Street. 😑

I curl my lip at Lena's text slang.

Good, I reply. **See you tomorrow.** I refuse to use emojis with Lena. No need encouraging her.

I drop the phone back in my purse but pick it up again when I hear it ping. I look at the text on my screen and smile.

Jay-Shea, I miss you! Sydney writes.

Miss you more, Syd-Kyd! I text back. (My exclamation marks are reserved solely for Sydney.)

Look what I got you! she replies, texting a smiling selfie with a voodoo doll thrust in front of the camera.

Fierce! I respond. **Can I use it to put a hex on Alicia?**

That's the former BFF who's been dissing Sydney since they entered the Ninth Circle of Hell, also known as middle school, a couple of weeks earlier.

Yaaasss! she responds, then follows up with a dozen kiss-blowing emojis.

I send some back. My emoji supply for Syd is unlimited.

My poor baby sister: she's so achingly adorable and smart that she'd gone her whole life without a single hiccup until sixth-grade sadism set in. Suddenly Alicia and her coven are too cool for Sydney, who's still more interested in Barbies than makeup. But I've got my sister's back. I'll always have her back.

I'm still smiling as I drop my phone back into my purse, then gaze mindlessly out into the parking lot. Most of the stores in the strip mall close at six on Sundays, like us. But the anchor store next door, Food Champ, ensures a steady flow of traffic since it's open 24-7.

I'm vaguely aware of Ethan puffing with each rep of his dumbbells a few yards away. He comes into the gym a lot, usually with his girlfriend, Brianne. The other customers' heads routinely spin when their Ken-and-Barbie hotness graces the gym's presence, the couple's studied indifference a testament to years of double-takes. I've had some classes with them through the years, but I don't think I've ever heard Barbie (fine, Brianne) utter a word, either at school or at the gym. She seems to communicate telepathically with Ethan, he obligingly leaning into her urgent eye contact when she has a message to convey. Her puffy, pink lips move, but damn if I've ever caught a word she's said. When she comes into the gym, she flutters her fingertips when I greet her without so much as glancing in my direction. Ethan usually overcompensates with the most humongous smile he can muster, but I dislike him by association. Now, I dislike him even more for keeping me here late.

I glance toward the plate-glass window, then look again. That's weird.

A guy in the parking lot is walking toward the strip mall in fast, jerky steps, wearing a fleece jacket and gloves.

My muscles tense slightly as I lean up and narrow my eyes for a closer look.

The guy's got a buzz cut, and his chin is digging into his chest, like he's freezing cold. He's holding something balled up in his fist. What is that? Something woolen, like a cap . . . As he loosens his grip, still speed-walking, I see that it's a ski mask. A ski mask and gloves in September? When it's ninety degrees in the shade? I stand slowly to get a better look. Hmm. Why is he heading here, toward the gym, rather than the grocery store, which is the only store in the shopping center still technically open? And now that he's opening our door, punching it with the heel of his hand, why is he pulling on the ski mask, adjusting it with a ferocious yank? It's as if . . .

"Get your hands up!"

● ● ● ● ●

My brain does a lightning-quick series of pole vaults to make sense of the guy who has just burst into the gym and pulled a gun from the pocket of his jacket. I never realized until this moment that your brain draws on the sum total of your life experience to process whatever is happening at the moment. And when it clicks through its files in fast forward and finds nothing to serve as a reference point, it goes loopy on you.

That's what is happening to me now. When the robber says, "Get your hands up," I ludicrously associate him with the aerobics instructor who was leading a class just an hour earlier. "Get your hands up!" she perkily instructed, and the hands obediently flew into the air, like mine are doing now.

But this guy isn't an aerobics instructor, and god knows he isn't perky.

I open my mouth, but the question that forms in my head—What do you want?—doesn't make it to my lips. That's another thing I'm learning about unprecedented situations: the different parts of your body all start rocking an every-man-for-himself kind of beat, as if my brain is telling my mouth, "To hell with teamwork, buddy, you're on your own."

I need to pull myself together, so I very sternly inform my various body parts: This guy means business. Shape up! And no, the gym-related pun isn't lost on me.

I know this all sounds like a lengthy process, but these thoughts are sprinting at warp speed through my mind, each fleeting notion imprinting itself on my brain with high-definition clarity. I'm taking it all in: A medium-height guy with a wiry frame. Clear-blue, bloodshot eyes with a tiny V-shaped scar digging into his right eyebrow. Faded jeans slipping down his skinny hips. Dirty and tattered white sneakers. Jittery hands training a gun on me. A gun. Oh my god!

"What do you want?" I finally utter in barely a whisper.

Okay, I can talk. Good to know.

"Money," he hisses.

"Money?" I clarify, and I know that sounds crazy, but I'm really confused, because, seriously, who robs a gym? And it's still light outside, for chrissake!

"Your money! Gimme your money!"

I shake my head frantically. "My money?"

He briefly considers my question, then nods. "Yeah. Your money, too. Then open the register."

Oh, great. I actually *suggested* that he take my wallet.

I nod toward my feet, every muscle in my body shaking. "My purse is on the floor," I say, my voice trembling.

He jerks the gun closer to my face, still clutching it with both of his small, pale hands. "Push it out where I can see it!"

I dig my fingers into my palms, then nudge the purse into the thief's line of vision with my sneaker-clad foot.

"Keep one hand in the air and hand it to me with the other one." He's getting antsier, glancing outside and shaking the gun.

With my right arm aloft, I squat and reach for my purse, cursing myself again for planting this seed. My heart is beating so hard that I'm amazed my fuchsia-colored *Regal Gym: Fit for a King!* T-shirt isn't pulsating.

"Just the strap!" the robber snaps. "Don't touch nothin' but the strap! You try anything, I'll kill you. I swear to god, I'll blow your head off."

I finger my purse strap gingerly and rise slowly with it.

It's as I'm rising that I see Ethan. He's creeping behind the robber, his eyes locking with mine. The robber, still focused on me, is oblivious. I'm almost ridiculously relieved to see Ethan . . .

... until I remember that he's why I'm in this cluster-fuck in the first place.

● ● ● ● ●

ETHAN

Oh my gosh.

Oh my gosh!

Jade's being robbed!

It's taken a second to wrap my head around it, but now the reality is staring me in the face.

Yes, I noticed a guy bursting into the gym after hours, but my mind squandered a few precious seconds trying to muster a reasonable explanation:

He's a customer who forgot something. He's an employee picking up his paycheck. He's a friend of Jade's. He's a stranger who needs directions.

But now I'm cursing myself. Hey, Sherlock, was the ski mask a solid enough clue for you?

I'd just set down a couple of free weights when he caught my attention. Maybe I'm more observant than I'm giving myself credit for, because none of the reasonable explanations I was conjuring could unglue my eyes from the back of his head.

He clearly hasn't noticed me, and something—even at the height of my brain freeze—has compelled me to stay as still and quiet as possible.

But I'm not still anymore. This lunatic's waving a gun in Jade's face, and I'm taking him down.

Okay, Ethan. It's go time. You've got at least half a foot on a guy that you'd swat away like a fly if he were trying to sack you on the gridiron. True, he's got a pistol, but he's probably high as a kite, and you've got the element of surprise. He doesn't know you're going to sneak up on him. Plus, God is with you. He'll be right by your side. "The Lord is my shepherd, I shall not want." You can do this, Ethan. You must do this. Put those zillions of training hours to good use. Channel that pent-up rage you felt when your dad was clocking your mom and you were too little to do anything but cower. Neutralize the threat. Save the girl. Do it now.

NOW!

THREE

JADE

As Ethan closes in on the robber from behind in slow-motion steps, my brain scrambles to take in the scene. For the fraction of a second that the two of us lock eyes, Ethan somehow conveys confidence, signaling he'll get us out of this mess.

But how? By grabbing the robber from behind, running the risk of a stray bullet blasting into my chest? By sprinting out the door and hoping I'm not crumpled on the floor in a pool of blood before help arrives, or that he himself isn't shot in his tracks? My heart sinks as I realize that he's probably not sure of his next move himself.

Again, this sounds like a lingering moment, but it all happens in an instant, because I look away almost immediately to avoid cluing in the robber that someone is about six feet behind him. Ethan, his hair tousled in sweat, holds an index finger to his lips as the robber yanks the purse from my hand. My carotid artery is pulsing so wildly, I wonder if it will explode.

"The register! The register!" the robber hisses, waving

his gun in the general direction of the counter I'm standing behind.

I open my mouth to tell him the register is empty, that most people pay their gym fees through automatic monthly withdrawals, but my brain and my mouth are still out of sync. I guess it's good that I can't form the words, because A) the register, used mainly for the snacks, isn't really empty; and B) the gym's payment structure would probably interest him only if he also happened to be an accountant.

I sense that Ethan plans to make his move—whatever that may be—as I open the register. I force myself not to look at him.

"Now!" the robber roars at me.

My hands tremble as I fumble with the register, then cough loudly as it opens in order to heighten the distraction. Ethan springs in midair, which is when the robber spins around and faces him.

"Freeze, asshole!"

No!

Ethan's hands rise reflexively as he regains his footing. "It's cool. It's cool," he says soothingly.

"Shut up!" the robber screams, aiming the gun at Ethan's forehead, both hands clutching it tightly.

Is this my moment? Do I try to leap over the counter and tackle him? Do I bash him over the head with something? Throw something at him? My eyes scan my surroundings. Nothing's on the counter except a display of snack-bar drinks. Should I throw one of the plastic bottles at his head? It wouldn't be hard enough to knock him out, but maybe it would rattle him long enough for Ethan to wrestle him to the floor.

Or maybe it would enrage him enough to shoot us both dead.

Dead. I could die right now. The next few seconds could be my last moments on earth. The thought catches in my throat as my family parades through my mind: Dad, Grandma, Pierce, Sydney . . . yes, even Lena.

Maybe I should drop to the ground, then shimmy out of sight. But the gym is just one big open area, other than the activity rooms that are yards from where I'm standing. Those rooms might as well be an ocean away, particularly considering all the hulking pieces of workout equipment blocking every potential path. Besides, what's the point of boxing myself in even more?

"Go stand by her!" the robber tells Ethan, jerking his head toward me.

Ethan inches toward the counter, his eyes locked with the robber's.

Robber. That's what I keep calling him. But what if robbery isn't his only motive? I've considered murder, but there are other possibilities as well. My head swims. I feel faint.

● ● ● ● ●

ETHAN

No. No!

How could I have screwed this up? Two lives depended on it, and I couldn't manage to body slam a hundred-and-thirty-pound junkie?

I could have taken him down without so much as breaking a sweat if I'd just committed. It was my split second of hesitation that doomed us. Look at him! His hands are shaking. His watery, blue eyes are bloodshot. Did I seriously believe he'd have the presence of mind to aim and fire a gun in the instant it would take me to bring him down? What a coward I am!

I hate myself even more when I see Jade's eyes. They look like my mom's used to when Dad was waling on her: wide and focused, totally alert, yet full of terror. Her body is taut and rigid, but trembling at the same time.

I swear to God, if this guy so much as lays a hand on Jade, I'll kill him.

Or die trying.

FOUR

JADE

Oh god.

The robber scans the gym and asks me in a growl, "Which of those rooms lock from the outside?"

Um . . .

"Answer me, bitch!"

"All of them," I say breathlessly, although my mind can't process the question adequately to ensure I'm being accurate.

"Key!" he says. The word sounds like shrapnel.

Um . . .

"Key! Key!"

I tremble and nod toward the register. "It's in there."

"Keep your hands up! I'll get it."

He leans over the counter, peers into the register and grabs a key ring, then shoves it in my face. "Which one?"

I fumble until I find one, hand it to him, and fling my hands back in the air.

"It's a master key," I say. "It locks all the inside rooms."

His eyes squint under the ski mask. "If you're lying, I'll blow your head off."

I shake my head as I hear Ethan's staccato breaths just inches away. He's as scared as I am, so why does it feel so comforting to have him close by? I don't know. It just does.

The robber points the gun toward the aerobics classroom. "Move!"

I look at Ethan and he gives me a sharp nod.

I start walking, and the thief gives a quick head jerk, signaling Ethan to follow me. The thief is right on our heels as we begin walking slowly through the gym toward the aerobics room, squeezing past cold, gunmetal-gray pieces of equipment that suddenly resemble torture chambers.

"Make a wrong move and you'll have a bullet in your back," the robber says, pressing the gun into my spine for good measure. Ethan and I stare straight ahead as we walk toward the room that housed the perky "get your hands up!" class just a few minutes earlier. I remember watching the women file out of the room when the class was over, patting their faces with towels and sharing endorphin-fueled high fives. I'd smiled and waved as they walked outside into bright sunshine, into fresh air, into whatever freely chosen activity was next on their list. I want to be one of those women so much, I can taste it. I think I might hyperventilate.

"You sure this door doesn't unlock from the inside?" the robber says as I reach the aerobics room, and I nod, gulping.

The robber grabs a rubber exercise band just outside the door, one of dozens of brightly colored sturdy but stretchy bands tossed in a plastic bin against the wall. I gulp again. Is he going to strangle us with it? Oh god oh god oh god . . .

With the same hand he's using to hold the band, the thief roughly yanks my shoulder, twirling me toward him and almost knocking me off balance. I see Ethan straighten in my peripheral vision, his chest broadening. The thief shoves his gun in his face. "Back off, bitch," he hisses at him.

Ethan maintains a steady gaze, along with his badass posture, for an excruciatingly long moment, staring into the thief's eyes rather than the gun pointed an inch from his face. Stop, Ethan, I beg subliminally. Don't you dare get shot! Please don't leave me alone. Please.

Finally, Ethan lowers his chin, his chest almost visibly deflating, and holds up his hands briefly for the thief's inspection. I try to catch Ethan's eye, but he won't look up.

The thief refocuses on me and jabs the key into my hand.

"Unlock the door," he says, and my breath is coming out in jagged puffs now.

What now? Once Ethan and I are in that room, we've lost any chance of escaping. Assuming we're going to be left alive, that is. Oh god!

Should I thrust the key into the robber's chest? Or better yet, into his eye? Would I be able to stomach it? Would I be able to aim? Would his horrible face, his wild eyes stretched taut by the ski mask, be the last thing I saw before he killed me?

Instead, I numbly unlock the door, more terrified than ever but also incredibly fatigued.

The stress of mentally thumbing through my crappy options is draining the hell out of me.

● ● ● ● ●

ETHAN

As the door opens, the robber abruptly pushes me into Jade, and we both stumble into the room.

The robber follows us in, then flips on the light switch with his gloved hand. "Your pockets!" he says.

What?

"Empty your pockets!"

Jade pats her clothes. All she's wearing is a *Regal Gym: Fit for a King!* T-shirt and a pair of gym shorts. No pockets.

I'm patting myself down as well: sweaty, gray muscle shirt, black gym shorts, no pockets.

"Where's your stuff?" the robber snarls at me. "Your keys, your wallet, your cell phone?"

I toss my head toward the door. "The locker room. In my gym bag."

The robber looks at Jade, who explains breathlessly, "The locker room is still open. I was waiting for him to leave before I locked up."

Before she locked up. She'd have been locked up long before the thief arrived if it hadn't been for me. Not only have I failed to save Jade, I'm the one who got her into this situation in the first place. Jade, please forgive me.

"Which locker is yours?" the robber asks me.

I take a moment to collect my thoughts—who can remember mundane details when a gun is shoved in your face?—then mentally retrace my steps from half an hour earlier. "I just tossed it on the bench," I say, my voice surprisingly steady, the same way it sounded the past couple of times I called 911 on my dad. "The place was cleared out when I got here, so . . ."

The robber considers the information, his eyes narrowed to slits underneath the ski mask. He glances around the room. "Any phones in here?" he asks, though clearly there aren't. The room, about forty by forty feet, features a mirrored wall, posters of perky spandex-clad women, a heart-rate chart, a couple of motivational signs ("No pain, no gain!" and "Strong is sexy!") and a few thin rubber mats stacked against the wall.

"No phone," Jade murmurs.

The thief nods sharply. "Later, muthafuckas."

FIVE

JADE

The robber backs out of the room, the gun trained on me, then slams the door behind him.

I double over, exhaling through puffed-out cheeks. "Oh my god," I gasp, but Ethan shushes me, his eyes still vigilant.

"He's still out there," he whispers.

We hear some clanging right outside the door, then some squeaky noises.

"He's rigging the door with that band to make sure we can't get out," Ethan whispers.

"The band," I repeat numbly.

We freeze in our spots as the noise continues, staring at the closed door as if the aerobics ladies might start wandering in at any minute, grabbing their mats and chugging from water bottles.

After a few seconds, the noise subsides, and we hear the light thud of shoes stepping away. Our eyes are still glued to the door. Another couple of minutes pass before I hear the slight creak of the entrance door. "He's leaving," I whisper, still frozen in place.

Ethan holds up a cautionary hand. He holds that pose, narrows his eyes and whispers, "I think he's gone."

We remain motionless for another moment or two, then Ethan tries the knob. Locked. He backs up several feet, then bolts at full speed toward the door, shoulder first. He rams it as hard as he can. Nothing. He tries it a couple more times, then slaps the door in frustration.

My knees buckle. I think I may throw up.

Ethan rushes to steady me, then lowers both of us to the floor. I feel like a noodle, slithering downward inch by inch.

"It's okay," he says softly. "He's gone now."

We both sit there rigidly, our backs against the wall. We stare straight ahead, too shell-shocked to speak. The rumbles of thunder overhead grow closer. We're presumably breathing, but I've never felt so deathly still in my life. My eyes don't even blink. Neither of us moves a muscle for . . . what? One minute? Five? Ten? My freaked-out brain has lost all concept of time.

After a while of stunned silence, it occurs to me that, despite having known Ethan for years, I've never really talked to him other than welcoming him to the gym or asking to borrow a pencil in class. Our school, Walt Whitman High, is pretty small—maybe a hundred and forty people in our entire senior class—so everybody knows everybody else, especially those of us with gag-inducing bumper stickers. *My Kid is an Honors Student (subtext: And Yours Isn't!)*

But what do I really know about Ethan? Let's see:

- I think he lives with his mom and has a vaguely shady dad.

- He belongs to the trendiest church in town, one of those nondenominational God-is-awesome types. (T-shirts are involved, which is how I know; branding is huge at this church.)
- He's always organizing Jesus-y things in school, including some gathering at the flagpole every morning.
- He actually produced a PowerPoint presentation, along with a couple of YouTube videos, when he ran for student council last fall. (My best friend, Gia, and I got serious snark mileage out of this. He won anyway.)
- He's got the world's snottiest girlfriend.

That's it. That's what I know.

In other words, it would be less awkward to be locked in a room with a complete stranger than someone you supposedly know but don't really.

The fact that I'm now pondering this awkwardness I guess signals that my shock is somewhat subsiding.

But a quick glance around the stark, harshly lit room reminds me of our sucky circumstances, including the thought that the robber could make a return appearance.

"What if he comes back?" I say.

My words, coming out of the blue after so many moments of stark silence, startle even me. It's like starting a conversation with a stranger on an elevator.

But Ethan ups the awkwardness ante by actually taking my hand. He looks at me and squeezes it gently. "He's probably just a junkie looking for a quick fix. My church ministers to that type all the time."

I look at him evenly. "Looks like that's going well."

Ethan studies my eyes for a second, then nods.

So much for my comic relief. I thought a nice chuckle might break the tension, but sarcasm apparently isn't Ethan's thing.

"Jade?" he says.

"Yeah?"

"Do you mind if we pray?"

● ● ● ● ●

ETHAN

I know I'm going out on a limb.

Jade no doubt has me pegged as a Jesus freak and is *way* too cool for things like prayer. I think she and her weird friend Gia are atheists.

But Jade's scared. No telling how long we might be stuck in here, and I feel the need to comfort her. Maybe this is a way to introduce her to Jesus. Maybe this is all part of His plan.

Still, I have no idea how Jade's going to react when I ask to pray. She might say something snarky to try to make me feel ridiculous. But I'm not ashamed to claim my Christianity. And if a door has just creaked open that might lead her to Christ, well, that's always a chance worth taking.

But I guess my worries are unfounded, because when I ask if I can pray with her, all she says is . . .

"Okay."

Her lashes flutter a little as I stare at her for confirmation.

"Okay?" I repeat.

She laughs a little. "Sure. Why not."

Thank you, Jesus! Please don't let me screw this up.

I move to my knees and gently pull Jade into the same position. Then I take both of her hands and close my eyes.

"Dear Jesus," I pray, "we just love you so much and are so grateful that you've kept us safe during this challenging time. We ask that you continue to keep us safe and that you shower your many blessings upon the man who was desperate enough to put us in this unfortunate situation. Please, Lord, help him find the true path to redemption by knowing the light and the love of your word. Help me help him by sharing your word and spreading the awesome news that all sins are forgiven in your name, that all wrongs can be made right and that eternal salvation awaits all who trust in you.

"Jesus," I continue, "we just praise your name and thank you for every minute you've given us on this beautiful earth, knowing this life is only a foreshadowing of the eternal paradise that awaits those who trust in your name." Pause. "In your name we pray." Another pause. "Amen."

I savor the moment, not moving a muscle. Finally, I softly exhale and let our hands fall apart, my breathing steadier than before.

"Thank you," I tell Jade earnestly. "I know you're not a believer, but that helped me."

SIX

JADE

I bristle. Not a believer? What the hell does Ethan know about me?

Whatevs. Ethan isn't bothering to pause to notice my reaction to his smarmy statement. After a quiet moment drinking in his superiority, his eyes begin scanning the room.

"You're sure there's not an extra key in here?" he asks.

I glance around and shake my head. "The manager and assistant manager have master keys, but the one in the cash register is the only one I've ever used."

"And you were telling the truth when you told the robber there's no phone in here? Not anywhere?"

I look at him evenly. "Yeah, there's one in a secret panel in the wall." He gives me such an intense, hopeful stare that I instantly regret being a smartass. "I'm kidding."

He swallows hard. "I don't know that this is the best time to joke."

I press my lips together. "Yeah, well, I don't know that six p.m. is the best time to come to a gym that closes at six p.m."

He sets his jaw. "I asked permission. The manager said it was fine."

"Yeah, well, the *manager's* not locked in a room with you, now, is he? I'm thrilled the *manager* was cool with you screwing up my schedule, because I'm thinking that right at this very moment, the *manager* is—hmm, what's the word that comes to mind?—fine."

Ethan considers my words, then his face falls. "I'm so sorry."

I sigh, exasperated. Yes, I wanted the satisfaction of retracing our steps and reminding Mr. Wonderful how we got in this mess. But the sadness in his eyes doesn't make me feel any better. I don't want Ethan to feel guilty. He has nothing to feel guilty about, other than coming to the gym at closing time; which, granted, isn't normally quite as consequential as it happened to be this time. For better or worse, we're in this together.

The rumbling thunder comes closer, closer, closer, and a steady rain begins thrumming on the roof.

I say in barely a whisper, "Just so you know, this isn't your fault, you dope."

His green eyes flash at me. "So now we're name calling?"

My jaw drops. "You called me an atheist."

His brow crinkles. "Aren't you?"

I put a hand on my hip. "You know nothing about me! But thanks for self-righteously judging me and believing the crap that you good 'Christians' spread around the school.

Oh, but you're not gossiping, right? You just need to know who to feel superior to."

He gives me an inscrutable stare. "I'm sorry you feel that way."

"I'm sorry you act that way," I fire back, but my shoulders droop when Ethan squeezes in his lips and lowers his eyes.

"I'm teasing," I concede. "Well . . . kinda."

More silence.

"So," I finally say, "are you gonna pray, like professionally, after you graduate?"

He narrows his eyes. "Pray professionally?"

"Preach. You know: be superior on a full-time basis," I clarify, tossing him a playful smile. He smiles back, thank heaven. Pun intended.

"I want to study engineering, assuming I can get a scholarship," he responds.

"Well, duh, your scholarship's in the bag," I reply. The bio next to Ethan's photo in the high school annual looks like a novella of honors, awards, and club memberships.

"Hope so," he says simply.

I'm about to mention that my dad got his undergraduate degree in biomedical engineering, but I freeze as the reminder of my dad also reminds me of his current location—New Orleans—which makes my heart sink.

I drop my head and groan.

"What?" Ethan prods.

I sink to the floor again and squeeze my hands against

my scalp. "I figured Dad would head this way when he realized I should've been home by now and he couldn't reach me on my cell phone."

Ethan's face brightens. "Yeah?"

"But my parents are at a CE course in New Orleans through Labor Day tomorrow."

His brow furrows.

"Continuing education," I clarify.

"So your dad is getting his degree?"

I stiffen slightly. "He has a degree. Several, actually. He's been practicing dentistry for twenty years."

"Oh, right. Sorry. It's just . . . I thought he was, like, a dental assistant or something."

Okay, this is just getting worse.

"He's an endodontist," I say in a tight voice. "That's a dentist with extra training. A specialist." Asshole.

"Right, right," Ethan responds obliviously. "But there are other kids in your family, right? Surely one of them will—"

I bite my bottom lip and shake my head before he can finish. "My sister's in New Orleans with my parents. Pierce is home, but he'll probably figure I'm spending the night with Gia or something." My eyes widen. "But your family . . .?"

Now Ethan is the one shaking his head before I can get my hopes up. "I told my mom I was going for a run in the park. And I was going to, but when I heard thunder, I headed here instead."

"But when you don't come home?"

Ethan shrugs. "Mom will be frantic, but I doubt she'll be able to guess where I am."

"Our cars?"

"But nobody knows to look here. Besides, Food Champ is open 24-7. Nobody will notice our cars unless they're looking for them."

Ethan stands up and begins pacing, glancing anxiously around the room. "Don't you guys have a panic button or something?"

I raise an eyebrow. "So you think this is a good time to use it?"

He tosses me a look of mock delight. "Joke! Wonder of wonders: I got it this time. Am I finally becoming hip enough for you?"

I lean back against the wall and press my knees against my chest. "I don't think it's really hip to use the word 'hip.'"

He shoots me a glare. But despite his best efforts, his face crinkles into a smile.

"You are high-larious," he says, then plops beside me, his sweaty thigh brushing lightly against mine.

We sit there for a while, then I give a low whistle. "Wow. Robbed. That's intense."

Ethan nods. "I was gonna jump him, you know. I had at least six inches on him. If I'd tackled him just a split second earlier . . ."

I nod. "That would have made a much better story than this one."

He laughs lightly, splaying his fingers over his face.

Rain is still falling, the gentle patter rocked by the occasional rumble of thunder.

"I wish I could have saved you," Ethan says softly.

I smile wistfully. "Well, I'm alive, so consider me saved. Oh, wait, did you mean the churchy kind of saved?"

He chuckles. "No, I meant the keep-you-from-being-locked-in-a-gym kind of saved."

I smile lightly, then we sit there another few minutes. With no watch, no window, and a still-scrambled brain, I'm more disoriented about the time than ever. Have another three minutes passed? Fifteen? I don't know. I just know that Ethan is seeming slightly less like a random guy on an elevator than he did before. I wonder if he's thinking the same thing about me. Although, Jesus, he knows enough about me to call me an atheist? Not that I'm necessarily offended. It just blows my mind how effortlessly Walt Whitman High School manages to put you in a nice, neat box.

I shake my head slowly, peering at the ceiling. "Saved. It's just so damn presumptuous."

Ethan's eyes narrow, seemingly in search of context. Then he says, "Oh, you mean the churchy kind of saved?"

"Yeah," I say, shifting my weight to face him as I warm to the subject. "I mean, you seem like a good guy—granted, you'd rank higher on my list if you'd tackled the thief—but a nice person. I mean, including the robber in your prayer? Nice touch, dude."

"Um, thanks?"

"But going around *saving* people? I mean, who are you to declare people deficient enough to need saving?"

He shrugs. "Everybody needs saving. And it doesn't mean you're deficient. It just means you're lost."

"Says you," I say, jabbing the air for emphasis. "God, that certainty. Certainty about something that nobody can know for sure. And no matter how humble you try to seem, if you think you have all the answers, then you stop asking questions or being interested in what anybody else has to say. No offense, but you come off as incredibly self-righteous and superior."

Ethan cocks his head. "So if you ask for directions and I know the way, I should keep my mouth shut so I don't run the risk of looking superior?"

I swallow patiently. "In the first place, nobody's asking you people for directions. You just assume they're lost and butt in by telling them which direction you think they should be going. A little presumptuous, don't you think?"

"You people," Ethan repeats. "Nice."

"In the second place: You think you know the directions, but I'm not so sure. If there's a god, maybe what he really values is people keeping an open mind and thinking for themselves, rather than walking in lockstep on whatever arbitrary path was identified as the 'right' one over two-thousand years ago in some little Arabian desert."

Ethan eyes me quizzically. "So you *are* an atheist?"

I huff. "I'm somebody who doesn't have all the answers,"

I say testily. "And whether you want to believe it or not, so are you."

He ponders my message for a moment, then says, "Wanna play Twenty Questions?"

• • • • •

ETHAN

"Seriously? You consider Miley Cyrus an actress?"

See? This is what I mean by Jade acting like every thought in my head is hopelessly lame.

"Why not?" I respond. "She had her own show."

Jade snorts. "So did Lassie."

"Yeah, well, you didn't guess the answer. I win."

"But you gave me misleading information!"

I shrug. "Art's subjective. Deal with it."

Jade tosses her hands in the air. "Art? Oh my god. Plus, you answered yes when I asked if she was hot?"

Another shrug. "I think Miley Cyrus is hot."

"Geez. Who else do you think is hot? Indira Gandhi?"

"Can't place her off the top of my head," I say, just to mess with Jade, then eye her warily. "But I think *you're* hot."

Oh gosh. Did I really just say that?

Jade's cheeks flush.

I grin. "You were totally fishing for that compliment."

Jade gasps. "I totally was not!"

"You're very cute," I say, then decide since I've gone

this far down the road, I might as well go another mile or two. "So why don't you ever date? I mean, other than what's-his-name."

Jade crosses her arms huffily. "What's-his-name?"

"Calvin. The guy you broke up with. I never see you with anybody but Gia."

She squeezes her eyes shut, then pops them open like she can't believe I've just said what I said, which basically was just stating a few facts. I laugh, leaning lower and closer to see her face better. "Your cheeks are the color of your T-shirt."

"Whatever," she snaps, smoothing the hot-pink shirt.

I'm still studying her eyes, intrigued by how freaked out she is. "So why don't you date?" I persist.

She opens her mouth to respond, but all she manages are sputtering sounds.

I mouth *wow*. "You can go on for hours about religion but you can't stand twenty seconds of conversation about yourself?"

She waves a hand dismissively. "All the guys in our school are morons."

I emit a low whistle.

"What?" she challenges.

"I dunno. I'm just thinking you sound a little, um, what's that word . . . superior."

Jade cuts her eyes at me. "Well, if my standards were as low as yours . . ."

My back suddenly stiffens and and I clamp my lips shut.

Jade searches my eyes. "Sore subject?"

But I'm not budging. There's no reason to rag on Brianne.

Jade rubs the back of her neck. "Lighten up, will ya?" she says. "The whole school worships your beloved Brianne. How much adoration does she need?"

I dig my nails into my palms. "Nobody's asking you to adore her," I say in a steely tone. "Just not to take cheap shots, that's all. And nobody worships her."

Jade raises an eyebrow and drops her jaw. "You're sure we're talking about the same girl?"

I roll my eyes. "If you must know, she actually takes a lot of crap for being pretty."

Jade rests her chin on her knuckle in mock-enlightenment and nods slowly. "Ahh, it's a bitch to be beautiful, huh? Tragic, really. Maybe she should start a support group."

I try to hold a steely gaze—seriously, people can trash me all day long, but leave my girlfriend alone—but I finally smile in spite of myself. "You could join it," I insist.

"Yeah, I have an entire room in my house filled with my pageant trophies."

I wrinkle my nose. "You are so full of crap acting like you aren't pretty."

"Right," Jade says, curling her lip. "Besides, you know Brianne is a total bitch to me, right?"

Now my jaw drops. "She totally is not!"

"Oh, please. She totally is."

"Wrong! She says she spends her whole life overcompensating because people always assume she's a snob." I intertwine my fingers loosely over my knee. "I kinda know the feeling."

Jade *hmphs.* "In the first place," she says, "if the way she acts is what she would consider overcompensating, she's the least-convincing actress on the planet." Pause. "And that includes Miley Cyrus."

I chuckle in spite of myself.

"And in the second place—"

"You and your places," I mutter, smiling.

"In the *second* place," Jade continues, "my heart just bleeds for you two having to take the time to toss crumbs to your admirers. Do the paparazzi stalk you on your dates?"

I drop my head and smile, still kind of annoyed but accustomed to the crap that comes with being a quarterback dating a cheerleader. People assume our lives are perfect. People are delusional.

"Now *you're* blushing!" Jade says. "So you can't take it either, huh? Talking about yourself?"

"According to you, I'm my own most fascinating topic of conversation. Not to mention the most fascinating topic of conversation to my legions of fans. You should consider yourself lucky to be locked in a room with me. I might even sign an autograph before the night's over."

Jade pretends to swoon, then we sit with silly smiles pasted on our faces as the rain falls harder.

"I know why you don't date."

"What?" Jade says, then huffs indignantly and says it again: "What?"

"I know why. You and Gia—you're like . . . a unit. You're always together. Like you're each other's bodyguards or something. You're both such cute girls, but you give off these vibes like, 'Move along, folks, nothing to see here.'"

"What are you talking about?" she says, all faux-incredulous, like this is news to her. Please. She knows her reputation. She built her reputation, whether she wants to believe it or not.

"It's like you're in your own little world," I continue. "This really smart, too-cool bubble. It's intimidating."

Jade blushes.

"That's crazy," she says, her voice softer than I expected. "In the first place, it's not a crime to have a friend."

"Here we go with the 'places' again," I say with a groan.

"And in the second place," she continues, "I have lots of friends."

"Name one who's not Gia!"

Pause.

Long pause.

"Just an observation," I finally say, still trying to keep things jokey.

As long as we're sparring playfully, I'll give as good as I get.

Except Jade is suddenly biting her lip, looking hurt. I swear, if I've hurt her feelings, I'll never forgive myself.

● ● ● ● ●

JADE

I'm so irritated with myself right now that I settle into a silent funk. How ridiculous of me to feel defensive.

But my sullenness eventually gives way to righteous indignation. "So I hang around a lot with my best friend," I tell Ethan sulkily. "That makes me different from ninety percent of the school population how?"

He gives me a cautious glance. "I didn't mean to hurt your feelings."

"Who said anything about hurting my feelings?" I snap, throwing my hands in the air. "But why does it matter to you who I hang out with? And why are you even noticing?"

He lowers his eyes, swallows hard, and nods. Damn. He looks sad again.

"Just for the record," I continue, hoping to cajole him onto jokier ground, "it doesn't exactly do wonders for your ego when you find out your first real boyfriend is gay."

He steals a glance at me. "Calvin's gay?"

I wince. "I thought everyone knew that. Everyone except me, of course."

"I didn't know," Ethan says.

I squeeze in my lips. "Mind keeping it on the down-low? I don't like blabbing other people's business."

"I don't gossip," Ethan says earnestly.

"Of course you don't."

Annoyance flickers in his eyes. "What does *that* mean?"

I sigh. "It was a compliment."

He holds my gaze. "You were making fun of me."

"I was not," I insist, though I really kinda was. I guess his Mr. Perfect routine is wearing a little thin, particularly considering how many times he's inadvertently insulted me in the past half hour. What business does he have declaring Gia and me a unit? Granted, she and I spend a lot of time together. But we get each other. Gia, natch, was right there to pick up the pieces of my sliced and diced ego when Calvin dumped me, just like she's been since we were kids. Plus, she's insanely funny and irreverent (she's the confirmed atheist, by the way) and we both know that we're just marking time in high school, waiting out the cliques and airheads and stoners and holy rollers.

"I don't think you realize how hard it is for me," I blurt, surprising even myself. "Let's see: I'm too white for the black crowd, too black for the white crowd. Every day feels like a test of loyalty, like I have to prove myself and help people figure out which box to put me in: 'Are you one of us or one of them?'"

My answer, incidentally, is always the same: Nope. I don't belong anywhere. I'm "other" on every checklist. Thanks for asking.

I squeeze my nails into my palms, already regretting my TMI moment.

"That must be really tough," Ethan says simply, and damned if his earnestness doesn't make me feel more hopelessly exposed than ever. Why in the world did I go down that road? The last thing I want is for anyone to feel sorry for me. Dad, who grew up here in Tolliver, can offer up some legit stories about racism—like the time the local police picked him up on suspicion of burglary, a charge that might have stuck had he not lucked out by having twelve-hundred witnesses that he was elsewhere. (The crime was committed when he had happened to be giving his high school valedictory speech.) Or the time Dad told his school counselor he wanted to be a dentist, and she informed him the degree wasn't offered at Tolliver Technical College. Or the time he stopped his car to help a lady stranded on the side of the road and she threatened to mace him if he came one step closer. Or the zillions of times he's been pulled over for Driving While Black.

Dad tells me all the time how much things have changed since he was a kid, how lucky Pierce and Sydney and I are to live in a more tolerant and enlightened day and age, and who am I to argue? Hell, all I have to do is listen to Grandma's stories about our ancestors' slave days to know I'm living large. But still . . .

My life can feel so lonely sometimes.

Gia's enough of a nonconformist to understand me, and she's too big-hearted and open-minded to assign me to a box. I love her for that. We are *so* moving on the instant the buzzer rings on high school.

My stomach muscles suddenly tighten.

I *was* so moving on. Now? Who knows.

Stop thinking about it.

The air suddenly feels heavier. Must be the storm.

I jump a little as I realize that Ethan is gently taking my hand in his.

"I really am sorry I hurt your feelings," he whispers.

I consider his words, then manage a weak smile.

"Sorry I hurt yours, too," I say. "Good for you for not gossiping. Really."

He squeezes my hand as we listen to the steady rainfall, which is growing more hypnotic by the minute.

My eyes are heavy, but my body is still on high alert. "You think we'll be stuck in here all night?" I ask Ethan softly, our intertwined fingers now dangling together.

"Well, since you refuse to press the panic button . . ."

I try to laugh, but my gaze falls and Ethan leans in closer. "Hey," he says, releasing my hand and lifting my chin until we make eye contact. "It's gonna be alright. I've got your back, okay?"

SEVEN

JADE

Our eyes stay locked for a long moment.

"Green," Ethan says, more to himself than to me.

"What?"

"Green. Your eyes look blue from a distance, but up close, I realize they're green."

I smile. "Like yours."

He considers my words, then shakes his head. "Nah. Mine are like the color of, I dunno, Brussels sprouts. But yours . . . yours look like the ocean."

Still staring. Still smiling.

As the moment lingers, Ethan's gaze shifts slowly from my eyes to my lips. I can feel his warm breath on my face. We're already pitched toward each other, and it feels so natural to let gravity keep prodding us forward . . .

Except that it *isn't* natural. My muscles tense as I remind myself that Ethan has a girlfriend. Even if he didn't, we clearly have nothing in common. We're stuck in a room together, both scared shitless. Nothing would be more awkward than to let ourselves get carried away. I clear my throat and stiffen my back.

"Mind if I do some yoga?" I say, averting my eyes. "I gotta stretch."

Ethan clears his throat, too, then nods. "Stretch away."

I definitely need some space right now, and who knows, yoga might help untangle my intestines, which, come to find out, tie themselves in knots when a gun is shoved in my face.

I stand up, kick off my tennis shoes, grab one of the mats against the wall and drop it in the middle of the room.

My yoga routine is pretty basic—mountain, sun salutation, cobra, the poses you learn in the starter classes—but I like how one move morphs into the next, my breaths synchronized with each motion. I know it sounds pretty New Age-y, but I started a class with Lena a couple of years earlier, and what do you know, I loved it. Maybe it helps that talking isn't allowed during yoga.

I realize as I move from one position to the next that Ethan is gazing at me. Not in a creepy way, just a mindless kind of way. Duh. How stupid that I misinterpreted his vibe a couple of minutes earlier. He wasn't complimenting my eye color; he was passing the time. He wasn't thinking about kissing me; he was staring at the only other face in the room. He's looking at me now because what else is there to look at in here?

"Hey," I say to him between moves, assuming the no-talking rule is optional for people in hostage situations. "You know what else I was thinking?"

"What?" he responds.

"Your prayer earlier?" I say. "That whole 'please keep us safe' deal?"

He laughs lightly. "Yeah?"

I inhale, exhale, then move from the tabletop pose to downward dog, an inverted *V*-shape, which means I'm now looking at Ethan from upside down, staring at him between my legs as my curls dangle from my ponytail.

"Well," I say, "according to you, God knows everything, right?"

"Right."

"And he can do anything he wants to do, right?"

"Ah, the classic 'omniscient/omnipotent' paradox," Ethan says.

"Ooh, impressive words for a jock," I say, then exhale through an *O* in my mouth as I walk my feet toward my hands.

"I've been down this road a few zillion times," Ethan says.

I curl my body up vertebra by vertebra, until I'm upright again, then splay my arms and upper back skyward.

"So let's suppose you're a dad," I say, holding the pose.

"Okay . . ."

"And your kid is in trouble. He's trapped somewhere and he needs your help."

"Oh, this is so abstract," Ethan teases as I relax my position and settle back beside him on the floor. "Your hypothetical intellectualizing is blowing my mind. This is too deep for my jock brain."

I wrinkle my nose at him. "My point," I say, "is that if God knows we're stuck here, what's the point of prayer? Why do we have to beg him for help? Wouldn't he be motivated to help us just because he loves us and we're in trouble? I mean, would you expect your kid to beg you for help if he were trapped?"

Ethan looks at me patiently. "I wasn't begging. I was reminding God I love him and trust him."

"Why should he need reminding? He knows everything, right? And he knows your heart. Is he, like, a narcissist who needs constant adoration? You know . . . like Brianne?"

He cuts his eyes at me, but he's not pissed this time; I can tell. "I'm just talking to God," Ethan says. "I love him, and he comforts me, and I want him to know it. It's a relationship. That's what God is about. That's all he wants from you, too, by the way: a relationship."

I shrug playfully. "I'm kinda Catholic."

He eyes me suspiciously. "You *so* are not."

"I so kinda am! I've been through sacraments and everything! Some kind of veil was involved, as I recall."

"Yeah, well, just because I walk into a ballet studio doesn't make me a ballerina. Haven't you just spent the past hour trying to convince me there's no God?"

"Just challenging you to think," I clarify.

"Yeah, Catholics are all about thinking for themselves."

I point at him. "Superior! Superior!"

"I'm cool with Catholics," he insists. "But the formality . . . I dunno. I prefer stripping it down."

My jaw drops. "Your church looks like Disneyland!" I say, recalling a couple of visits with friends that involved a stage, sound system, live band, and IMAX-quality videos. "It's like a Broadway production! 'Stripping it down.' Right."

Ethan shrugs. "If I never stepped foot in a church again, it wouldn't change my relationship with God."

I snort.

"What?" he asks.

I press a knee gently toward my chest. "That's not the vibe I get from the Jesus freaks in school. I mean, that crowd—your crowd, I guess, no offense—that crowd doesn't make religion seem personal at all. It seems like it's mostly for show. Let's just say your church seems awfully cliquish."

Ethan scoffs. "It's non-denominational! It's open to everybody!"

"Blah, blah, blah. That's what you say, but your pews somehow manage to magically get filled with people who look and act like you," I say.

He looks genuinely stunned. "Which is how?"

I tap my fingers on my knee. "Popular. Awesome. Fake-humble. Status-conscious."

He winces, feigning a kick to the stomach. "That is cold, Jade Fulton."

"The truth hurts, huh?"

We smile at each other playfully.

"I don't mean to sound bitchy," I say after a long moment, sounding more wistful than I intended. "I shouldn't judge. I just *feel* so judged. Kinda chaps my ass."

He considers my words, then says, "I can't speak for anybody besides myself, but I never mean to judge." To my surprise, his voice breaks, and suddenly, he has tears in his eyes.

He swallows hard, then says, "I'm the last person to judge."

EIGHT

JADE

Another clap of thunder rocks the room, but I don't notice this time.

I lean closer to Ethan, studying his eyes intently. "What?" I say softly.

He shakes his head quickly and his eyes fall. "Nothing. Stupid."

I'm trying to make eye contact, but he won't let me. "Me?" I prod. "I'm stupid?"

He shakes his head again, still looking at his hands. "No. It's stupid that I'm . . . getting emotional, or whatever."

I touch his hair, and he finally meets my eyes. "It's okay," I whisper.

"Sorry," he says, shaking his head with his eyes still downcast. It's just . . . my family's so screwed up that it makes me feel screwed up too, just by association, or because of the genes, or whatever. I hate it comes across that I'm judgmental or superior or whatever, but I guarantee you, that's the opposite of how I feel."

"Oh, Ethan."

The rain is pounding overhead, and after another jolting thunderbolt, the electricity flickers.

I glance anxiously at the ceiling. This room has no windows. If the electricity shuts off, we'll be in total darkness.

But after a couple of flickers, the lights stay on. I exhale heavily.

"You got a lighter, by any chance?" Ethan asks, his voice steady again.

I lift my arms and glance at my T-shirt and gym shorts—now the sum total of my possessions. "Do you think maybe I keep one in my sock?"

Oh, good. He's smiling. But his eyes are still moist.

I swallow hard. "I'm sorry I was snarky."

His fingers dangle over his knees. "It's okay. The way you were describing the Christians at school? I know some of them fit that description."

I shake my head. "I was just being a—"

"No, I get it. I get that. But a lot of people don't have what you have. And don't get me wrong, I'm glad that you have it. But for me, God isn't a luxury. I really need him . . . ya know?"

My eyes search his, but his glance skitters away again.

"You've got this great family," he continues. "Your mom's on the school board, your dad's a dental assistant . . ."

"Dentist," I correct him again, but this time, my tone is soft. "Endodontist, technically. And it's my stepmom, not my mom, who's on the school board."

"Oh, she's your stepmom?"

"Duh. She's Asian."

"And you're . . ."

"Not Asian."

He smiles sheepishly, but his eyes are sparkling. "Sorry I'm not up on my ethnicities. You just look really exotic."

"Yeah, I get that a lot."

Sigh. I hate to sound overly sensitive, and I guess people mean well, but "exotic" tends to be the go-to compliment when people don't know what else to say about my what-the-hell appearance, or are fishing for information about my DNA.

"Anyway," Ethan continues, "your family looks so together. Sure you can take religion or leave it. You've got everything."

My hands tighten into clammy fists. That's approximately a hundred and eighty degrees off the mark—particularly with the news about Dad—but I'm more interested in Ethan's situation right now than mine.

"So what's the deal with your screwed-up family?" I ask him softly.

His eyes fall again. "My dad's an alcoholic, he left my mom and me when I was ten. But he still lives right down the street. Lucky me," he says sardonically. "Love it when he shows up drunk at my games and blesses me out for every mistake I make. He does it right after the game so he'll have an audience; he loves looking like a big man in front of everybody. He's the real athlete in the family; he knows how it's supposed to be done."

Ethan's expression hardens. "Asshole," he says softly.

I swallow hard. "I'm sorry."

"You know what's ironic?" he continues. "My football stats already put his to shame, and I've only just started my senior year. Yet he rubs my nose in every trivial error I've ever made in a game. I made forty-three completions in a single game last fall—forty-three!—and all he could talk about afterward was my 'shitty' release."

He glances at me apologetically. "Sorry about the language."

I smile sadly. "It's okay."

"My release was unshitty enough for forty-three completions," he mumbles mostly to himself, tossing a hand in the air, "but whatever."

I laugh lightly, and Ethan's face softens. Then he laughs a little, too.

"I can't win with him," he continues as the rain pounds on the roof. "When I do something right, Dad acts like I'm full of myself and need to be knocked down a peg or two. When I do something wrong, he acts like I'm a disgrace to the family name. Me the disgrace. Right."

I fumble with my fingers on my lap, not sure if it's a good or bad thing that I've prodded Ethan to crack open this door. He seems to want to talk about it, but maybe he'll regret it in retrospect. It's hard to bare your soul. Or at least I assume it would be, since I'm never quite able to do it.

"He got my mom pregnant in high school, then spent the next ten years using her as a punching bag," he continues, and I wince. "I always tried my hardest to take the hits for her, but she got knocked around plenty."

His eyes turn stony again, and I squeeze my arms together, chilled. What kind of monster hits a defenseless woman and little kid? I don't think I've ever heard my dad so much as raise his voice.

"I don't know why Mom put up with it," Ethan says, his voice sounding hollow and far away. "He never even managed a steady paycheck, and whatever he made, he drank away. Mom's the one who got some training and kept us on our feet. She's a medical transcriptionist."

I nod, touched by how clearly proud he is.

"And the women! Dad always had girls on the side. His big-man talk is just a front; if he's not getting a constant infusion of praise by some chick, his ego bottoms out."

I feel a stab in my heart thinking of my dad, the most principled person I've ever met. Even when he had to deal with the biggest flake on earth—my mother—he was never anything but respectful. He never uttered an unkind word about her, even when he gathered me sobbing from the front-yard stoop, awaiting the visits that never came.

"And the ultimate irony?" Ethan continues. "Dad left Mom! Granted, he moved just down the street—close enough to constantly monitor our comings and goings, like we're his property or something—but as many times as I begged Mom to leave him, he finally saved her the trouble."

He snorts ruefully. "Get this: She still cooks for him. He trots over to the house a couple of times a week for supper, and Mom never turns him away. Even takes casseroles to his trailer! She says he's more like her kid than her husband—well, her ex—which I guess explains why I've always felt like an adult."

I lean a little closer to Ethan. "I'm really sorry."

He stares straight ahead, then shrugs. "It's okay. I don't want anybody's pity. I just wonder . . . if I had a *real* dad—I mean, a decent one—would I need God so much? And if not, what does that say about my faith? It makes it pretty self-serving, don't you think? I'd like to think my faith would be strong no matter what my life was like, that even if it was perfect like yours, I'd still embrace God's word. But . . ."

Another thunderbolt shakes the room, and this time, the electricity goes off. The room is pitch black, and the hum of an air conditioner goes eerily silent.

I gasp a little and feel Ethan grab my hand.

"It's okay," he murmurs, but I feel nauseatingly, excruciatingly un-okay.

"I'm sure it'll come right back on," Ethan says.

"Why do people only say 'I'm sure' when they're not sure at all?" I whisper, clutching his hand tighter. I shut my eyes and inhale deeply through my nose.

The rain, heavier now, pounds on the roof.

"I'm sure we'll be fine, with or without electricity," Ethan says, and god, his voice sounds incredibly comforting.

"How long do you think we've been in here?" I ask.

"Nine days. Maybe ten or eleven."

A smile inches its way up my cheeks. "I don't know that this is the best time to joke," I say, imitating his low Southern drawl.

"Ooh, nice accent," Ethan says. "So now I'm a dumb jock, a Jesus freak, *and* a redneck?"

"If the shoe fits," I tease.

We sit in the darkness for a while, then I yawn and stretch my arms. "Man, it's exhausting to be robbed."

I hear Ethan pat his lap. "Wanna crash?" he says.

"Seriously? You think we might actually be able to sleep?"

"Well, our options are pretty limited. We can always pray some more."

I laugh, then he laughs, which makes me laugh more, and pretty soon, we're doubling over in the pitch-black aerobics room.

"Hey," I say giddily, "what do we do when we have to pee?"

"Don't remind me, 'cause I kinda do."

I sputter with more laughter.

"Surely there's a leftover water bottle in here," Ethan says.

"Not on my watch. Besides: A lot of good that would

do me. Particularly considering I'd be operating in total darkness."

"Then just, I dunno, think arid thoughts."

I laugh again lightly, then kinda-sorta take him up on his offer by feeling out his shoulder and resting my head on it. My head on Ethan's shoulder. Jesus. What a surreal day it's been. As cozy as it feels, I don't think I could have brought myself to do it with the lights on. But somehow, in the darkness, it feels okay. Good, even.

Ethan runs his fingers through my ponytail and starts singing softly:

Jade, you made my life complete the day you flashed your smile so sweet.

I smile. "Is that a real song?"

"Mmm," Ethan says, then continues singing as my eyelids flutter.

Jade, you laid your sweet soul bare and taught me what it means to care.

What do you know: Maybe I really can fall asleep while being held captive in an aerobics room, my head propped on the shoulder of a guy I'd barely exchanged ten words with before now.

"You have a pretty voice," I say sleepily.

He's still running his fingers my hair, the rain now a gentle patter.

A few moments pass, then: "Ethan?"

"Mmm?"

"I'm sorry about your dad."

"Mmm."

"Do you hate him?"

"Nah. I love him. Crazy, huh?"

"Nah."

Pause.

"Ethan? What you said before? About my life being perfect?"

"Yeah?"

My eyes are closed as I murmur, a hair's breadth away from deep sleep, "My life's not perfect."

● ● ● ● ●

ETHAN

The world has never seemed quite as still as it does at this moment.

Jade's fallen asleep. I gently ease her head from my shoulder to my lap and touch the curls that spill over my legs.

I'm beat too, but my adrenaline is pumping way too hard for me to sleep. That thief has the key to this locked room; he could come back at any minute. Do I think he will? Nah. I know his type: a jittery junkie looking for a quick fix. But it's possible. I need to stay on high alert, like I used to after Dad would finish throwing Mom across the room and tear off in his rusty old pickup truck, headed for a bar to down a twelve-pack.

I was pretty sure that when he eventually made his way back home, he'd stumble to his bed and pass out—and that was the case, nine times out of ten. But Dad was nothing if not unpredictable. I think he liked to keep Mom and me on our toes. Maybe he'd come back four hours, or six hours, or two days later. Or maybe he'd come back in five minutes, still raging and wondering if Mom had some guy stashed away in the closet who'd pop out as soon as he thought the coast was clear.

What a joke. The last thing Mom ever wanted was another man in her life. And Dad's the one who had a never-ending string of women. Projection, my psychology teacher called it. Anyway, he kept us on edge by constantly switching up his brand of crazy.

So I learned to stay vigilant.

I finger Jade's ringlets as I cradle her head in her lap, coiling the loose curls around my index finger in the pitch-black darkness.

That's weird that her mom's not really her mom. Who knew? The mom—well, the stepmom, I guess—is always so cheerful when I see her in the lunchroom collecting canned goods or whatever other fundraiser she's organizing. And the dad, he always seems to be in the middle of volunteer projects too, greeting everybody with a friendly, booming voice and a firm handshake.

True, it always struck me as weird that Jade was an atheist—okay, fine, not really an atheist, but kinda—considering that her parents are in the middle of every good cause in town. But on the other hand, it just seemed like more evidence of an awesome family, one where everybody gets to be real and authentic.

I wonder who Jade's real mom is. I wonder what's up with that.

I wonder if maybe I'll be able to fall asleep after all . . .

NINE

JADE

It's the whoosh of the air conditioner rather than the flood of light that startles me awake.

But now that my eyes are open, I squeeze them shut again to protest the sudden transition from total darkness to bright fluorescence.

I lift my head from Ethan's lap—whoa, my head was in his *lap*? When did that happen?—and notice that he's rousing, too, his back against the wall and his head slumped to one side. His eyes flutter open.

"The electricity's back on," I say.

Ethan winks at me sleepily. "Thanks, Captain Obvious."

I wrinkle my nose at him, stand up, put my hands on my hips and look around.

"It's not raining anymore," I say. "Oh, sorry. Was that too obvious for you?"

"Duh." Ethan yawns and stretches his arms.

"How long do you think we've been in here?" I ask.

He shrugs. "Long enough to give serious consideration to your question."

My brow crinkles. "What question?"

He stands up and stretches some more. "How we're supposed to pee."

I rub my palms together. "I know *how*. I just don't know *where*."

He sweeps his arm across the room. "What you see is what you get. Looks like the mats are absorbent."

My jaw drops. "You have got to be kidding."

Ethan shrugs. "Desperate times call for desperate measures."

I consider his words, biting my lower lip, then conclude, "I'm not that desperate yet."

Still, we're both staring at the mats.

"Hey, you know what I read recently?" I say. "I read that some diseases—like, intestinal diseases or whatever—can be cured by fecal transplants. Transplanting someone else's poop into your GI tract. Something about getting the healthy bacteria to repopulate."

Ethan winces. "Why are you telling me disgusting things?"

"I dunno. It's kinda related. In the category of 'things I'd rather die than do.'"

"Meaning you'd rather die than pee on a mat?"

I shrug. "I guess we'll find out."

He rubs his hands together. "It would be really helpful to stop talking about it."

"Right," I agree. "Change of subject. How about this: What would *you* rather die than do?"

Ethan settles back on the floor as he considers the question, and I sit by his side, leaning against the wall. "What I'd rather die than do, huh?" he says. "Hmm . . . I dunno. I'd rather die than hurt somebody's feelings?"

I curl a lip. "Oh, please."

He tosses me a fake sneer. "Too churchy for you?"

"Too precious. Honest: What would you rather die than do?"

He thinks for a few seconds, then tosses a hand in the air. "Umm . . . get stung by a jellyfish?"

My jaw drops. "Wuss!"

"Gimme a break. It hurts."

"For, like, four seconds!" I say. "Shorter than that if you rub wet sand on the sting, or better yet, just get right back in the water. You can't take a little jellyfish sting?"

He looks at me evenly. "Okay, how's this: I'd rather die than play this stupid game."

I stick my tongue out at him and we smile, Ethan's lopsided grin crawling back up his face.

"But not before you enlighten me with your brilliant answer," he says. "You're up: What would you rather die than do? No gross answers, please. And nothing that reminds me I have to pee."

I inhale deeply, then exhale through an *O*-shaped mouth. "Well . . . I have this thing about belly buttons."

"What?"

I scrunch my face. "Belly buttons. I can't stand the

thought of mine being touched, or touching somebody else's. Even lightly. Even accidentally. I just can't stand it. So that's it: I'd rather die than have my belly button touched."

Ethan considers my answer.

"Now that I've told you," I say gravely, "I'm afraid I'll have to kill you."

He nods. "Because I'll devote the rest of my life to trying to touch your belly button?"

"Because I've planted the seed and there's even the most remote possibility this will come up again. That's how freaky I am about my belly button."

"Don't some medical procedures involve needles in your belly button?" he asks.

I cringe, burying my face in my hands. "Stop it, stop it," I moan. "I truly can't stand it. See, this is why I have to kill you."

He laughs. "But aren't you planning to be a doctor? Which might involve, I dunno, contact with a belly button?"

I cock my head and study his Brussels-sprout eyes. How did Ethan know I wanted to be a doctor? And how did he know Lena's on the school board or that Dad is, as he so quaintly calls it, a 'dental assistant?' And how did he know Gia is my best (okay, fine, *only*) friend? I had no idea he knew anything about me, much less cared. I feel so weirdly touched that my stomach clenches. But I press in my lips and manage a weak smile. "Not a problem. No medical school for me. My plans have kinda changed."

He studies my face. "Why?"

I shake my head and stare at my lap.

Ethan leans closer. "Why, Jade? What's going on with you?"

BANG!

TEN

ETHAN

Jade and I jump. Then . . .

BANG! BANG! BANG!

Our eyes lock.

"Police!" a voice barks from the entrance.

We're still frozen in our spots.

"Police! Anybody here?"

Jade grabs my hands. "It could be the robber," she whispers, her heart pounding. "He has the key."

I hesitate for a second until we hear another voice calling out: "Ethan?"

The voice is female and frantic.

I squeeze my eyes and whisper thanks to God. "Brianne," I call. "Brianne!"

I jump to my feet, pulling Jade along. "Brianne!" I yell again, rushing to the door and pounding on it. "We're in here, in here!"

We hear a rush of footsteps, then rustling sounds at our door.

"Brianne?" I call again.

"We're coming, we're coming!" she calls. "The door's

rigged with something, but we're getting it. Hurry, Officer, please!"

Then, another voice on the other side of the door: "Jade?"

I look at Jade, whose face melts into a smile of relief. "It's my boss," she tells me, then yelps, "Yes, Stan! I'm in here, too!"

Still another voice: "Hang tough, Jade!"

Jade clutches her heart. "Pierce?" she calls.

"Yeah, we're almost in."

Jade bounces on the balls of her sock-clad feet, both of us beaming. We hear a key turn in the door, then . . .

"Ethan!"

Brianne runs in first, her blonde hair in a floppy bun. She's wearing a T-shirt and shorts, looking frenzied and ecstatic at the same time. She throws her arms around my neck and gives me a passionate kiss. A long, passionate kiss. A kiss that finally makes the police officer clear his throat.

I gently pull her away and mouth, "I'm okay."

The police officer is holding a gun, as is another one scanning the gym from the doorway. Jade's boss and brother rush into the room.

"Are you okay?" her brother asks breathlessly as he sweeps her into a hug that lifts her off the ground.

Jade nods, gulping hard.

The officer in the doorway is communicating with another on a hand-held radio, their scratchy correspondence indicating no backup is needed.

"What time is it?" Jade asks Pierce, who is still squeezing her tightly against his side. He looks disheveled—jeans, wrinkly T-shirt and tousled black curls—but relieved.

"Around two a.m.," he says. "Probably closer to three by now."

"How did you find us?" Jade asks him.

Pierce nods toward Brianne, whose arms are dangling behind my neck. "She got the ball rolling," Pierce says.

Brianne nods and gazes at me. "I've been looking for you for hours."

I glance at Jade, and we lock eyes for just a second before she looks away.

"If we could ask you both a few questions," one of the officers says to Jade and me.

"Bathroom break first?" I ask, and when the officer nods, I bolt toward the door.

Yes, I desperately have to pee, but this moment is not lost on me. I can walk out of this room any time I want.

I'll never take that for granted again.

● ● ● ● ●

JADE

". . . So we'll be in touch."

"You think you'll catch him?" Ethan asks the officer, all of us sitting around the table in Stan's office. I'm squeezing my arms together to ward off the chill that's kept me shivering since we sat down half an hour earlier. Ethan tosses me an occasional glance, his arm draped across Brianne's shoulder. At one point, I catch her peering at me as she kisses his hand. It's the only time I can remember her looking me in the eye.

"We'll certainly do our best," the officer tells us. "In the meantime, you'll need to contact your wireless provider, your bank, your credit card companies, the DMV. . ."

My head is swimming. My most personal stuff—my cell phone, my driver's license, my goddamn lip gloss—is in the hands of a thief. I've never felt so violated. I shiver some more, then scan the room and look away when I notice Ethan's eyes on me. Brianne has followed his gaze and is staring at me again. God! I've gone my whole life trying to blend in and suddenly feel like a neon arrow is pointing at my head.

"We can go now?" Brianne asks the officer.

"Yes, ma'am."

She jumps up and pulls Ethan's hand. He hesitates, then gets out of his chair and lets her tug him toward the door. Just as they're walking out, he turns toward me.

"Hey, Jade?"

I glance up. "Yeah?"

"I . . . I'm sorry."

I smile and shake my head. "No apologies."

He's still lingering, resisting Brianne's tug. "Come to my church some time?" he asks me. "As my guest?"

I swallow hard and am hugely relieved that Brianne

has impatiently pulled him along before I can answer. I blink the moisture from my eyes, then chide myself for being so ridiculous.

I've just shared the most intense experience of my life with Ethan—a guy I cheated death with, a guy I shared some of my deepest insecurities with, a guy whose lap I used for a pillow just a few minutes earlier—and he's giving me the kind of elevator speech he'd give to anyone who crossed his path.

I've never felt quite this lonely in my life.

Because Ethan just tossed me a crumb.

ELEVEN

ETHAN

I wish Brianne would give me some space.

The police suggested that both Jade and I collect our cars later rather than drive home alone. I don't know why; I'm fine. And frankly, I'd rather be by myself right now.

Even though it's Brianne's car, she's asked me to take the wheel—says she's still a nervous wreck—and she's nuzzling me as I head toward my house in the dark. She does this a lot when I drive, and considering she has to practically sit on the gearshift console to do it, it's not particularly safe or comfortable. I hate having to maneuver past her thigh every time I need to switch gears.

But I don't say anything. I never say anything, and considering she just got me rescued, this probably isn't the best time to start. Still . . .

I couldn't help noticing how rude she seemed to Jade. What was that all about? Or is Jade right, that Brianne always acts that way and I've just never noticed?

I don't know, but I'm doing a slow burn just thinking about it. Not even bothering to give Jade the time of day after what she'd just been through? Curling her lip at her? Unbelievable. I stare straight ahead with a steely gaze.

"So what did you two do all night?" Brianne asks, nuzzling even deeper into my chest.

I swipe a lock of her bun out of my face and refrain from rolling my eyes. "Trying not to get killed was pretty high on our list," I say in a tight voice.

She huffs. "What did you do for the eight hours you were locked in? You knew you weren't going to get killed when the robber left."

"We didn't know anything," I respond, slapping my wipers a couple of times to clear leftover raindrops from my windshield. "All we knew is we were trapped."

She considers my words, then lifts her head and kisses my cheek. "Not anymore. Thanks to me."

I manage a smile. "Yeah. Thanks to you." I flick on my blinker and turn right on the wet pavement. "You were great."

And she was. Brianne told me back in the gym that she'd driven house to house when she and Mom couldn't figure out where I was. I'm as reliable as clockwork, so they knew something was up. They paced around hoping I'd show up any minute. But after a while, they started working the phones, calling my friends, my coach, my dad . . .

It was close to eleven when she and Mom called the cops, and by that time, Brianne had decided to go looking for me herself. She drove through the rain to a dozen or so spots—the park, the high school, the auto-parts store, every fast-food joint in town—before she thought to check the Regal Gym. When she spotted my car, she called the cops and begged them to break down the door. But there was no sign of forced entry, so she had to cool her heels for another forty-five minutes while the cops called the manager and waited for him to show up with a key.

She was amazing, and I appreciate it. But how does she think we spent the past eight hours? Comparing calculus notes?

Still, I won't rock the boat. I never rock the boat. I've spent my whole life trying to steady the boat. That's what I do.

"So you aren't going to tell me?"

I glance down at Brianne, her cheek still pressed against my chest. I'm so tired and my brain is so fried that I can hardly see straight, much less focus on a conversation. "Tell you what?" I ask, and this time, my irritation clearly seeps through.

Brianne notices and pulls away, then looks at me through narrowed eyes. "You're not going to tell me what you've been doing for the past eight hours?" she says in a tight voice. Great. She's mad.

I take a deep breath and keep staring straight ahead, the streetlights seeming to stretch into a single blurry line on the nearly deserted road. "What I've been doing the past eight hours," I repeat in a monotone. "Hmm. Wondering if the thief was coming back, and if so, what I would do about it. Wondering how long I'd be locked in that room. Wondering how long I could go without peeing."

Silence fills the air before Brianne finally responds. "And Jade?"

Now, I do roll my eyes. "Pretty much the same thing. You'd be stunned how limited your options are in a locked room."

I still feel her gaze boring into me. "My point exactly," she says icily.

My eyes narrow. "What are you implying, Brianne?"

She crosses her arms. "That girl has always had a crush on you."

I toss my head back and laugh out loud. "What?"

"Oh, duh, Ethan! This isn't exactly breaking news. You think I don't see how she looks at you when we go to the gym?"

I press my lips together. "You are way off the mark."

"Then why did you invite her to our church?" Brianne says, her hands flying in the air.

I squeeze the steering wheel harder. "Don't you want everybody to come to our church?"

I hate that I'm just now realizing the answer: no—an answer that confirms everything Jade thinks. Cliquish. Status-conscious. Fake. But *no* is Brianne's answer, not mine.

"She's not even a Christian!" Brianne spews, as if this is a good reason to want someone not to come to church.

"Aren't she and Gia, like, atheists or something? Or whatever that witch religion is called? Such freaks!"

I crack my window for a shot of cool air to keep my head from exploding.

"You don't know anything about Jade," I say simply.

Or maybe me, either, for that matter. Right now, I feel like I have a lot more in common with Jade than Brianne—and I like her a lot better, truth be told.

The ultimate irony is that Jade's not the one with a crush.

I am.

● ● ● ● ●

JADE

"What do you mean, you're not telling them?"

I roll down the window of Pierce's car, then wince at the blast of thick, damp air and roll it back up. The hum of his engine and the chirp of crickets are the only sounds on the rain-slickened street.

"I mean it," I say testily. "And neither are you. Dad's got enough going on right now."

Pierce shakes his head incredulously. "So at the dinner table, rather than saying, 'Oh, by the way, Jade was robbed and locked in the gym overnight,' I'll just mention how I did on my biology test?"

"It was no big deal," I mutter.

Pierce is silent, but I sense him tensing. With a jerky motion, he turns on the radio, way too loud, and we listen to Logic blasting few seconds. *I'ma show 'em how to act, I'ma show 'em how to act* . . .

Then, just as jerkily, Pierce snaps the music off.

"Jesus, Jade, Dad's not dead yet."

Dead. I don't think anyone had actually used that word yet. But there it is. There's no wishing this away any more.

Eight hours of emotional overload suddenly spew out of me like a volcano. I start heaving in sobs.

Pierce glances at me anxiously, then pats my arm. "Sorry," he murmurs. "It's okay."

But there's no stopping me now. I cry for a good five minutes, alternately wailing and gulping in gasps of air. Pierce pats me occasionally but otherwise lets me cry. I guess the alternative would be making a beeline for the psych ward.

At some point, Pierce fumbles in his glove compartment and produces some kind of dust rag. "It's all I've got."

I grab it gratefully and blow my nose.

"Sorry," I say after a few moments, my breaths still ragged but my freak meter now considerably dialed down. "Guess I needed to get that out of my system."

We drive in silence for a couple of minutes.

"Has she contacted you lately?" I finally ask.

"Who?"

He knows who.

"Mom," I say.

Pierce's knuckles blanch as he squeezes the steering wheel tighter. "Mom contacts me all the time," he says in a clipped voice, his sparkly, ebony eyes staring straight ahead. "I live with her."

Okay, yet again, he's refusing to go there. When Mom—our *real* mom—started contacting us a few weeks earlier, Pierce told me he blocked her, and he hasn't mentioned her since. But I guess I assumed that his curiosity would have won out at this point.

Whatever. I get it, I really do. Pierce was only four, a full eighteen months younger than me, when Dad married Lena, so I don't think he remembers our mom. And I guess he can't remember his life without Lena.

But I do. So how do I feel about Mom? I'm not sure. But I haven't blocked her.

"What's Ethan like?" Pierce asks, the abrupt segue a clear sign that mom discussions are off limits.

I ponder how to respond, then just shrug. "A typical dumb jock," I say.

Okay, I was aiming for glib, but my stomach clenches. Ethan, I've discovered, is a lot of things, but dumb isn't one of them.

I bite my lip to ward off a fresh wave of tears.

TWELVE

JADE

"You weren't going to tell me?"

I rub my eyes and squint against the sunlight flooding my room.

I sit up in my bed, still dressed in the gym T-shirt and shorts I collapsed in a few hours earlier. Or at least I guess it's been a few hours.

"Dad?"

He flings his big, strong arms around me. "How could you not have called me? What were you thinking?"

I melt into his arms for a few seconds, then untangle myself. "When did you and Lena get back?" I ask. "I thought your plane wasn't due until this afternoon."

"It's five-thirty," Dad says. "We've been home for an hour."

I shake the confusion from my head. "Five-thirty p.m.?"

He nods and my eyes widen. "Work," I say. "I was supposed to be at work at five-thirty this morning."

"Apparently you get the day off after spending the night locked in the aerobics room," Dad says, easing me back against my pillow.

I roll my eyes and moan. "I told Pierce not to tell."

"Because why?" Dad demands. "Because your parents might not be interested in knowing you were held at gunpoint and locked in a room overnight?"

"It was nothing," I mutter, shaking my head. "*Pierce.*"

Dad sighs and presses a cool palm against my cheek. "Thank god you're okay. And it wasn't Pierce who told us, by the way."

I lean up on my elbows. "Then who?"

"Who haven't we heard from?" he says. "Let's see: There was the call from the police—that's always fun—and Gia, and, what's his name? Ethan? Along with about forty other people. Apparently, the word's spread on Facebook. Promise me that next time you get locked in an aerobics room overnight I'll be the first to know?"

I peek at him and wrinkle my nose. "I didn't want you to worry."

He looks at me sternly and pulls me to a sitting position. "Jade LaShea Fulton: I am your father. And until I draw my last breath, you and your brother and sister will be my top priority. You can't blow me off that easily."

His face softens into a smile. "Pierce said you swore him to secrecy," he says. "But no worries. Finding out from a reporter was much more exciting."

"A newspaper reporter?" I clarify.

"Oh yeah, him too," Dad says. "Plus reporters from two local TV stations."

I squeeze my eyes shut. "This is going to be on the news?"

"It's already on the internet," Dad says. "But that's good. The more coverage the story gets, the higher the chance of finding the scumbag who robbed you. The police have already released security footage from the parking lot."

"Good," I say, my voice steely. "I can't wait to stare into those creepy eyes again and make sure that asshole's goin' down."

Dad winces. "Language?"

"My bad," I say unconvincingly.

Dad laughs. "I guess you're entitled. Jade, I'm so sorry for what you went through. And I'm so proud of how brave you were. Mom is too."

A cloud of confusion drifts through my brain. Dad's always respected my decision to call Lena by her first name, and that's what we call her when we talk about her. Well, it *was* what we called her. Until Dad's glioblastoma diagnosis, at which point he flipped the script. All of a sudden, she's Mom. Sorry. I can't get with the program overnight. Complicating matters further, of course, is the fact that another woman who calls herself Mom is suddenly on my radar. But of course, Dad doesn't know that. Just one more secret I'm keeping to minimize the stress in his life.

"Where is Lena?" I ask, reverting to our "before" pattern, which I greatly prefer.

"At the grocery store, stocking up on all your favorites. I told her we already have all your favorites in the house, but I guess a night locked in a gym calls for eight gallons of fudge ripple rather than one. We might have to buy another freezer to store all your ice cream."

"Now, that's a plan I can feel good about."

Dad smiles, takes my hand, and says, "Hey, Jade, one more thing."

Oh god.

I swallow hard. "Yes?"

"I went public with the sale of my practice. There's an article in today's paper."

My eyes flood with tears. Dentistry is what Dad does. His routine is as predictable as the sunrise. He's the most steady and competent man I know, striding quickly from his office to an exam room with his white coat flapping, but always making his patient feel like he has all the time in the world.

"Does the article mention the cancer?" I ask, my voice quavering.

Dad nods. "Word was already getting out, and I'd rather people know the truth than think I'm stumbling around drunk or something."

He's smiling, but I can't smile back. A tear rolls down my cheek and Dad brushes it away with his thumb.

"This is our stuff," I say bitterly. "It's too soon for everybody to know our business."

Dad sits silently as my mind screams the words I'm actually thinking: It's too soon to leave the land of denial. Can't we wish away the cancer for just a few more days? Or pretend that a miracle cure will fall from the heavens just in time to save him? It's too soon for our world to disintegrate. That's what it feels like: disintegration. The actual news a couple of weeks earlier—well, the confirmation of the news—was something of an explosion. But since then, it's been a quiet, slow disintegration, like one little chunk of our lives after another is just . . . dissolving. Like Dad's mind and body will dissolve.

Dad hugs me, holding me so tightly that I can feel his heart—his strong, steady heart—beating against my chest.

"Everything sucks," I murmur, and he strokes my hair.

I peer at my framed list of quotations on my bedside table as Dad caresses me. Every year for my birthday, he jots down a famous quotation in my card, then teaches me about the person who said it. For my eighteenth birthday last week, he compiled all the quotations and framed them, maybe figuring he wouldn't be around to add to the list anymore after this year. Quotation number eighteen, the last one, is from Thomas Fuller: "It is always darkest just before the day dawneth." I stare at the words until the tears completely blur my vision.

"It'll be okay," Dad says into my ear.

Every other time he's told me that, he's made sure it was true.

But he can't this time.

•　•　•　•　•

Dad and I are still clinging to each other when Pierce saunters into my bedroom biting an apple and says, "Think the gym will pay you overtime for last night?"

I laugh in spite of myself.

"Is she awake?" I hear Sydney call excitedly from the hall, then she sprints into my room. With a running leap, she springs onto my bed and wraps her skinny arms around my neck, her silky, black hair splaying across my face.

"Oomph!" I say with a laugh as she squeals, "Jay-Shea!"

After smothering me with kisses, Sydney coos, "Tell me everything about being held hostage."

I spend the next fifteen minutes giving the broad strokes: guy in ski mask sticking a gun in my face, me volunteering my wallet (groan), Ethan sneaking up behind him, Ethan's football experience being a total bust.

Dad, Pierce, and Sydney have sprawled in various positions on my bed as I finish the story.

"So," Pierce says as I wrap it up, swallowing the last bite of his apple. "If anybody's wondering, I had an eventful day yesterday, too. The McDonald's drive-thru screwed up my order."

We laugh and throw pillows at him and his apple core.

It feels good to laugh. We won't be together much longer.

But we're together now.

● ● ● ● ●

ETHAN

"Honey?"

I groan, blink several times, then squint against the glare of the sun. I feel like I've been asleep for all of fifteen minutes.

"Honey, supper's almost ready."

Supper?

I look at the clock on my bedside table, then do a double-take and bolt out of bed.

"It's six o'clock p.m.?" I ask my mom, who nods nervously, chewing her lip.

"Why didn't you wake me?" I say, my hands flying in the air. "I'm supposed to be at practice!"

Mom shakes her head and places her hands over my cheeks. "Honey, *honey*," she says. "Coach Davis understands! He said to take all the time you need . . . as long as it's not longer than twenty-four hours."

She tries to cajole me into a smile, but I'm frantic. I can't stand being late. Have I seriously slept the whole day?

"Mom, sorry, I gotta get dressed and head out."

"Ethan! I was kidding about the last part! The coach really did say to take all the time you need."

"I don't need any time," I mutter. I feel bad for snapping at Mom—she was up until five in the morning, too, and my ordeal has no doubt been harder for her than it was for me—but seriously, she knows I can't miss practice.

She couldn't have jostled me awake? I fling open a drawer and grab a shirt.

"Honey, you can't go!" Mom wails. "It's Labor Day. The coach said probably half the team is out of town. And I've made supper. Brianne is on her way."

I shake my head, trying to dislodge the thoughts in my sleep-muddled brain. "Brianne? Why?"

Mom pulls a lock of dark-blonde hair behind her ear. "Honey, she's been a nervous wreck all day. It's killed her not to be able to talk to you. I kept telling her you needed your sleep—"

"Why was she calling you?" I ask, more irritated than ever, but still fishing around for my clothes.

"Your cell phone's gone," Mom reminds me. "Besides, I didn't mind Brianne calling me. I knew how upset she was. And, praise the Lord, Ethan, she's the one who found you."

"Hee-ro!"

Mom and I both jump, startled, and look toward my bedroom door. Dad is sauntering in, already bleary-eyed from what I'm guessing has been a steady diet of Budweiser starting at, oh, eleven or so this morning.

"Go on in the kitchen, Mel," Mom scolds him. "Supper'll be ready in a minute."

"Gotta salute our hee-ro!" Dad says, then slaps the heel of his hand against his forehead, which grows longer by the day as his hairline recedes. "Yeah, boy. Hee-ro!"

I suck in my lips but continue collecting my workout clothes.

"Saw the security footage of your attacker on the news," Dad says. "Musta been all of, what, five foot six? Maybe a hundred and ten pounds soaking wet? Bet you were shakin' in your boots."

I refuse to glance his way, but in my peripheral vision, I can see Mom wagging a finger at him. "Mel, get in the kitchen!" she repeats. "I made meatloaf, your favorite."

"I can't salute our hee-ro?" Dad says, swaying on his feet. "It's not every day you come across a high school quarterback who can't manage to take down a hundred-pound pansy."

"A pansy with a gun," I add under my breath, then hate myself for dignifying his stupidity with a response. Why in the world do I feel the need to grovel for his approval?

"That's it!" Mom tells him, aiming for stern though her voice is still cajoling. "I'm wrapping up your supper to go, mister. I'll fix some for Byron, too."

"Ooh, Byron wants our boy's autograph!" Dad says of his drunkard brother.

"Well, he'll have to wait," Mom replies, ushering Dad out of the room.

Dad takes a stab at staying put, but he's in no condition to resist. He lets Mom lead him down the hall, and I hear her sing-song voice imploring him to leave me alone as she wraps up his dinner.

I steady myself on the open drawer, squeeze my eyes shut, then give a sharp nod and finish getting dressed. I've tolerated Dad's crap all my life. No need for today to be any different. Still, I feel my heart pound against my shirt as Mom shoos him out of the house.

I run my fingers through my hair, then step into the bathroom and brush my teeth. I hate being late.

When I rush into the kitchen, Mom is slinging meatloaf on a plate. "You gotta eat!" she says.

"No time, Mom."

"Ethan! I won't let you leave this house without eating!"

She looks like she's on the verge of tears. This is yet another familiar stage in her dances with Dad. It takes all of her energy to deal with him and stay calm in the process, so once he's finally out of her hair, she kinda falls apart. She looks so small standing in front of me on the faded kitchen linoleum, her Georgia Bulldogs T-shirt swallowing her petite frame. I know she needs me now, but my adrenaline's pumping in anticipation of showing up late for practice.

But Mom comes first. Now's the time for my part in the dance, when I play her knight in shining armor and stay strong enough for both of us until she has a chance to replenish her stamina. Dealing with Dad is a tag-team operation.

I pause for a moment, then sigh heavily as she puts my plate on the kitchen table.

"You do not have to go to practice tonight!" she insists, taking a fork from the drawer with trembling fingers and handing it to me.

"And you don't have to put up with him," I mutter, stabbing a bite of meatloaf.

"What?"

I glance at her.

"You heard me, Mom," I say softly. "Why do you put up with him?"

My brain is clearly still fried from the past few hours, because I never ask obvious questions like this.

Mom pulls up a chair beside me and rests a hand on my shoulder. "Honey, your dad's got a good heart," she says, and I actually snort. Yeah, my brain is definitely still fried.

"He's your dad," she says, moving her hand to my knee and patting it absently. "And he don't mean any harm, honey. You know that. He's just mouthing off." She pauses, then adds definitively, "You gotta respect your dad, son."

I shift in my seat to face her. If we're finally going down this road, by god, she'll have to say whatever she says looking me straight in the eye.

"He doesn't respect us," I remind her bitterly. "He sure as hell doesn't respect you."

Her blue eyes skitter away. "Honey, I can't defend your dad," she finally says in a small voice. "It's just that . . . I understand him. He does what he knows how to do. He acts like he knows how to act. I can't blame somebody for doing all they know to do."

I keep staring at her, but she won't look at me. Finally, I turn back to my plate and continue eating, my teeth chomping furiously.

"Honey, how would he know any different?" Mom asks me softly, staring at her lap. "Your grandpa was the same way. Both your grandpas."

Okay, here's my opening. I spin around again to face her. "Right," I say. "Your dad was a drunk, too. But you rose above your raising. Why couldn't Dad? Why do you always let him off the hook?"

She considers my question, looking like she's shrinking into her tiny frame. I know my questions are hurting her, and I can't stand hurting her. But it's out there now. My mind is rattled enough to finally choke out the questions I've been holding in for years.

"Honey," Mom says, "women are stronger than men."

Then, she quickly qualifies her response: "Most men, that is. *You*, honey, you're just amaz—"

I hold up my palm to cut her short. As much as I hate Dad's crap, I hate Mom's condescension even more.

Besides, what's the point? This conversation is going nowhere. Dad will never change, and neither will Mom.

I stab another piece of meatloaf and resume eating, my jaw clamping with each bite.

If I'm lucky, I'll be out the door before Brianne gets here.

THIRTEEN

JADE

"Jade LaShea!"

I glance over my shoulder and see Gia speed-walking down the hall.

Damn. It's only an hour into the school day, and I've already run a gauntlet of questions and double-takes. Most of the questions are about Ethan's and my now-infamous overnighter in the aerobics room, but the news about Dad has prompted a whole parallel-universe set of comments, especially from my teachers. I might as well be walking around in my underwear.

"Could you return a phone call?" Gia says with a raised eyebrow as she approaches me, swishing a lock of dark hair off her shoulder.

"Sorry," I say, feeling dozens of eyes plastered on me as our classmates file to their second-period classes. "My phone was stolen."

"I called your landline. Over and over and *over* again."

I shrug. "I'm sorry, Gia. I slept 'til dinner time. It was a pretty intense day."

Gia's eyes turn doleful. "Jade, your dad . . ."

I nod. "Sorry I didn't tell you. I just couldn't quite . . ."

"I get it," she says.

I hope she means it, because that's not the only secret I've been keeping from her.

"But you know you can always talk to me," she says.

"I know," I say, then tug her arm in the direction of our next class, figuring I'll attract less attention walking than standing still. And I really do feel bad. I've been an open book to Gia since we met in fourth grade, gushing about everything from crushes to my dreams of being a multitasking novelist/neurosurgeon. But what can I say? I've never had such crappy news to share.

"That whole robbery deal," Gia says as we walk. "I don't even know where to begin. And then you don't return my calls?"

"Look, if I'm ever locked in an aerobics room again, you'll be the first to know," I say. "Oh, wait. I actually promised the same thing to my dad."

I slow my pace as we approach our English Lit class, the doorway clogged with comers and goers.

Just as the doorway clears, I notice Ethan bolting toward me.

"Jade!" he calls.

He's with Brianne, and as he approaches she tries to pull him away. He casts her an annoyed glance. "Hold on," he mutters, gently yanking his arm free.

"We'll be late," she says, her voice tight.

"Jade, I've been trying to call you," he tells me, bobbing his head to see me through the crowd.

"Yeah, I pretty much just slept all day."

"But you're okay?" he says, a hint of urgency in his voice.

"She's fine," Brianne responds, tugging on him again.

"Brianne!" he snaps.

She drops his arm, her hands flying up dramatically. "Fine!" she says, then walks on without him, her floral perfume lingering in the air.

"You're sure you're okay?" he asks me again, inching closer, and I nod.

"And your dad," he continues. "I heard about your dad. I just can't believe . . ."

"Yeah, thanks," I murmur, letting the flow of the crowd push me further into the door. I lock eyes with Ethan for a second before he's swept back into the hall traffic.

"Thank you," I repeat, my words swallowed by the crowd noise.

I dig my nails into my palms.

Gia is asking more questions as we make our way to our seats, and I'm responding with vague "mmms," "rights" and "sorries."

Why do I feel so prickly? This is crazy. Of course Gia's worried about me, just like I'd be worried about her. I guess my guilt is getting the best of me; at this point, it's my little secret that the joint future she and I have been planning all through high school has abruptly splintered apart. We spent our entire junior year nailing down college choices, imagining ourselves sipping lattes in Boston Common, throwing a Frisbee in Harvard Yard, or, okay, studying under the arches at the University of Georgia if our Ivy League aspirations fell through. But wherever we went, it was a given that we'd go together and be roommates; I mean, how could we trust anyone other than each other to appreciate an *Inbetweeners* marathon on a slow weekend?

I cringe. *Inbetweeners* marathons. *I know why you don't date . . .*

Yep. When Netflix bingeing with the good ol' BFF ranks high on the social calendar, it's a safe bet that your idea of a wild and crazy time is a game of Words with Friends.

But that was then. This is now. It's irrelevant that Gia and I apparently used to freeze other people out with our "intimidating" vibes, because our paths have just officially diverged. She'll be going off to college soon, and I'll be staying home to take care of my dad. I wouldn't miss a moment of his last days on earth, and with medical bills and his suddenly-AWOL salary, tossing Frisbees on the quad is definitely not an option. It's been real, Gia.

Still, it's not fair to her that my guilt is coming across as irritation.

"Jade?"

I glance up, startled, at Mr. Finch, who obviously has called my name more than once.

"I'm sorry," I say, smoothing my shirt. "What?"

"I was just noting that you seem to be the elephant in

the room," Mr. Finch continues. "May I say on behalf of the class how sorry I am about your dad. He's a wonderful dentist and I know the whole community shares your family's sadness."

I slink lower in my seat and feel my neck grow hot.

"And also on behalf of the class," he says, "I extend my heartiest congratulations on enduring a grueling experience over the weekend. I think I speak for us all when I say—"

"Details!" a guy named David calls from the back of the room, his hands cupped around his mouth for maximal amplification.

The class laughs and offers some tepid applause, Mr. Finch waving his hand halfheartedly to regain control.

"Yes, details!" another classmate calls out.

The class laughs some more, and some of the clapping grows animated. A guy behind me even contributes a pinky whistle.

I swallow hard and feel the walls close in on me. How do I get out of this? I'd suddenly rather—I dunno—get stung by a boatload of jellyfish than endure another microgram of attention.

My face grows hotter and I wonder if I might hyperventilate, or even throw up. (How'd that be for the latest chapter in my life-turned-good-story?)

Gia turns around and glances at me, then glances again, wide-eyed this time. My panicked eyes lock with hers for a second.

"Uh . . . if I may," she stammers, addressing the whole class.

She gets up and walks to the front of the class, her skinny jeans and boots giving her a lithe, slinky vibe.

"Jade has been rendered speechless by her ordeal," Gia says, and the class laughs nervously. "But luckily for us all, she's appointed me as her spokesperson. I'm sure you've all heard by now that Jade single-handedly wrestled the thief to the ground, disemboweled him, then forced him to use his own intestines as a jump rope for an impromptu workout. They were, after all, in a gym."

The class laughs some more, and I find myself laughing, too. The knot in my stomach starts to loosen, and I feel my shoulders relax.

"I will be handling Jade's press from this point forward, so please refer all requests for interviews, autographs, photo ops, Oprah specials, and memoirs to *moi*." Gia bows extravagantly, then returns to her seat amid scattered, good-natured applause. A guy named Victor tosses her an admiring hand horn, and she flashes him a discreet peace sign in return.

A couple of moments pass before she turns to face me, and by the time she does, a decade's worth of love and appreciation is oozing from my pores.

The flicker in her eye makes it clear she reads my eye contact loud and clear: *Thank you, world's coolest BFF. I heart you.*

I definitely have some explaining to do to her—about

why I've shared every detail in the world with her since fourth grade yet couldn't quite bring myself to tell her that my dad is dying; about why I was too simultaneously numb yet amped yesterday to return her calls; about not having the foggiest clue how my future will unfold other than that part about our plans being shot to hell; about feeling vaguely embarrassed when I saw her this morning, because I'm suddenly excruciatingly self-conscious that we've somehow become a unit.

Well, maybe I'll skip that last part. It's not her fault I've become glued to her hip. How's that for a coward's strategy to avoid rejection? Never, ever put yourself out there, and freeze everyone else out in the process. I'm not just holding myself back; I'm holding Gia back, too.

As much as I heart her, I think it's best for both of us if we broaden our horizons a bit.

Speaking of which . . .

I lean forward and tap Gia on the back. She tilts her head in my direction.

"Hey, spokesperson," I whisper. "Wanna go to the football game Friday night?"

● ● ● ●

ETHAN

Ordinary differential equation: no partial derivatives.

Partial derivative: single variable. Got it.

Not.

Who am I kidding? It's only second period, and my concentration is already shot. I couldn't wind down last night after football practice; my coach and teammates were ribbing me about the robbery just like my dad did, though they at least pretended to be kidding. The morning so far has been filled with smart-ass remarks from guys saying they wished they could have traded places with me—references to Jade that I shut down real quick.

The bell rings and I breathe a sigh of relief. My friend, Brent, gets up from the seat beside mine, hoists his backpack onto his shoulders, then lingers at my desk, no doubt expecting us to walk together to our next class like we always do.

But I just keep sitting there. I'll wait 'til the room thins out before getting up.

"Ya okay?" Brent finally asks.

"Yeah," I respond without looking up. "Why wouldn't I be?"

Brent shrugs. "You look like you've got somebody in a chokehold."

I glance at my clenched fists laying on top of my desk and force myself to loosen my grip.

"I'm good," I say, then rise from my seat and grab my backpack.

"Dude, you're sure you're okay?" Brent says as we leave the room, leaning into my ear for as much privacy as possible in a crowded hall.

"Yeah," I say, then purse my lips as I see Brianne rushing toward me. We don't have any morning classes together, so once we finish our prayer session at the flagpole before school, we usually don't see each other again until lunchtime. Unless she's tracking me down. Like now.

"Hey! I'm so glad I found you," she says, nudging Brent out of the way.

"Hey," I say, glancing down the hall and wishing I could just keep walking.

Her brows weave together. "Are you okay?" she asks, her blue eyes searching mine.

"Yeah." I'd be a lot better if everyone quit asking me that. "I'm late. See you at lunch."

"Ethan!"

Her expression freezes me in place. "You barely said two words to me at the flagpole," she hisses.

"Hey, bro," Brent says, tugging lightly on my arm. "I really need those notes."

Brianne doesn't even glance his way; she's still too busy shooting me death rays with her eyes.

"Gotta go," I tell her, then continue down the hall with Brent. I feel Brianne's glare boring in my back as we walk.

"Thanks," I tell Brent under my breath. He's been around Brianne and me long enough to know when I need an emergency evacuation.

"What's up with you two?" he asks as we hang a left toward our class.

I shake my head wearily. "She was waiting for me at

my house after practice last night," I tell him. "I told her I just needed to crash. Guess she's pissed."

A few people call out to me as we continue walking, mostly guys talking good-natured smack about my night in the gym, but Brent manages to ward them off with a friendly smile and keep us moving.

"She's pissed?" he repeats. "So even being held hostage doesn't earn you a good night's sleep?"

I smile ruefully. Yep, Brent knows Brianne only too well. As good a friend as he is, I'm usually as defensive with him as I am with everyone else if he disses her. Not that he ever insults her or anything; he's too nice a guy for that. He'll just toss me a heads-up every once in a while if he thinks she's being too clingy. Like now.

Only this time, I don't have the energy—or, okay, fine, the inclination—to defend her. I stayed up all night tossing and turning, and now I'm running on fumes.

"Hey, Ethan."

I do a double-take at the guy who's just passed me, then reach out and touch his arm. "Pierce."

He turns around.

"Yeah," he says with a smile. "How's it going?"

"Good, good," I tell him, people still jostling past us. "How's Jade?"

"She's good," Pierce says. "She's here today. Our parents offered to let her sleep in, but . . ."

"Yeah, I saw her earlier," I say. "I'm so glad she's okay. Will you tell her I . . ."

Tell her I what?

Tell her I apparently am looking for any excuse to talk about her? Tell her I'm pathetically psyched to see her brother in the hall because it's a connection to her? Tell her I can't stop thinking about her?

"Tell her I said hi?" I continue weakly.

I sound ridiculous, particularly considering that Pierce is bobbing his head trying to maintain eye contact because people keep filing past us.

"I'll tell her," Pierce calls to me over their heads, then waves and folds back into the traffic.

"That's Jade's brother?" Brent asks me as we continue walking.

"Yeah."

"He's a really nice guy," Brent said. "We play soccer together. Hey, did you hear about their dad?"

"Yeah, I—"

"Hey, Garrett, I heard you scored some brown sugar over the weekend. Sweet!"

My eyes flash at the source of the voice: a guy named Austin Lewis from my chem class who I barely know. Then I lunge at him.

"Dude," Brent says, pulling me back.

Austin jumps back and throws his hands in the air. "It was a joke, Jesus!"

Brent jerks his head, signaling him to keep moving, which is a stellar plan considering that my adrenaline is practically spewing out of my ears. Brent still has his hands full holding me back. My heart feels like it'll burst out of my chest.

"It's cool, it's cool," Brent murmurs in my ear, which reminds me of when I said the same thing to the robber. In neither case was anything remotely cool.

"I'm okay," I finally tell Brent. He loosens his grip but still eyes me closely. I feel other eyes on me as well.

Austin has already moved on, so there's no chance of me going ballistic, but the onlookers seem prepared for anything. Would I actually have hit him if I'd had the chance? I dunno. But I've never been so tempted.

Our second-period teacher, Miss Hawthorne, comes to the door of her classroom and anxiously waves her hand to move everyone along.

"Sure you're okay?" Brent asks me nervously as we walk inside, my pulse still slamming against my neck.

"Yeah," I say unconvincingly, dropping into my seat with a deadweight thud.

Then I grab a pencil from my backpack and snap it in half.

● ● ● ●

I glance at my watch. Football practice starts at four, so I have less than an hour, but I'm eager to squeeze in a visit with Pastor Rick. I hop in my car for the ten-minute drive when the dismissal bell rings.

He called me last night after practice, making sure I was okay after the robbery and reminding me his door is open any time if I need to talk. This seems like an excellent time to take him up on his offer. He's been my lifeline too many times to count in the six years since I've joined his church.

My mom and grandparents still go to First Baptist, but when the fire-and-brimstone sermons started giving me panic attacks, Mom agreed to let me try out the new nondenominational church with a couple of friends. I was hooked right away: the blue jeans, electric guitars, amazing outreach, informal Bible study groups, sermons based on love instead of fear. And Pastor Rick. He and his wife, Stacey, look like a couple of teenagers themselves, totally cool and relatable. When I confided in them one Sunday about my dad's latest drunkfest, they reminded me that 'in the wilderness, the Lord your God carries you, as a father carries his son.' That's the day I really felt it: that I *do* have a loving and awesome father, a message I want to spend the rest of my life sharing.

But my head has been such a jumble of confusion for the past couple of days that I desperately need to touch base with the closest thing I have to a father here on earth: Pastor Rick.

I drive up to the church, a modern, single-story, angular building with lots of natural light—none of the stained glass or steeples I grew up with—then pull into a parking spot. I glance at myself in the rearview mirror, noticing my eyes are pinched and my neck tensed. Geez, I really need to grab some *Z*s at some point.

I run my fingers through my hair, take a deep breath, and head for Pastor Rick's office. I tap lightly on his door.

"Yep!" his cheerful voice booms on the other end.

I creak the door open. "Pastor Rick? You got a minute?"

"Ethan! What a nice surprise," he says, waving me in.

"Sorry to drop by unannounced."

"Hey, there's nobody I'd rather see," he says, rising and extending his hand. After I shake it, he sits back down and waves me into the chair across his desk.

"So how's it going, buddy?" he asks, leaning back and propping sneaker-clad feet on his desk. "You sounded a little shaky on the phone last night."

I shrug. "It's been an intense couple of days."

Pastor Rick studies my face a few seconds, then takes his feet off the desk and leans into his elbows. "Tell me what's going on."

I stare at my hands, folded in my lap. "Just . . . I've had a lot to think about recently."

Pastor Rick holds his kind, steady gaze. "Shoot."

I shift my weight uneasily. "Well . . . I mentioned to you on the phone how the robbery made me feel kind of like a phony."

"Because you couldn't control the situation?"

"Yeah. I mean, when I think of the times my teammates have lifted me on their shoulders for winning a football game, yet I couldn't overtake a guy half my size . . ."

"Yet you came out alive," Pastor Rick says, arching his brows. "Talk about the ultimate victory."

I purse my lips. "Nothing about that night feels victorious."

Pastor Rick leans in even closer. "Sometimes the most heroic thing you can do is walk away."

I snort ruefully. "My dad called me a hero. Sarcastically, of course."

His unrelenting eye contact forces me to meet his gaze. "Yet you know the truth."

I nod uneasily, then let my eyes fall again. "That whole 'truth' concept . . . That's been tripping me up, too."

The pine trees outside his office window rustle in a breeze.

"Care to elaborate?" Pastor Rick asks, his tone as genial as ever.

I sneak a glance at him. "The girl I was locked in the gym with? Jade?"

He nods.

"She and I did a lot of talking that night. I mean, what else was there to do, right?"

I feel my cheeks flush at my awkward choice of words. I've spent forty-eight hours trying to tamp down rumors, and here I go inadvertently planting a seed. I squeeze my hands together tighter.

"Anyway, Jade is . . . I guess you'd say she's agnostic. But she's a great person."

Okay, how pretentious did that sound? Jade would call me out immediately: Is there any reason an agnostic shouldn't be a great person? And lucky her that I've given my stamp of approval! Still, I keep plowing ahead.

"Anyway, she asked me a lot of questions and challenged

a lot of my beliefs. I thought, 'Great. This is an awesome opportunity to witness.' I even wondered if the two of us being stuck in a room together was part of God's plan. But I've really been chewing on some of the things she said."

I glance at Pastor Rick for a sensitivity check. I'm well-versed in all the talking points used to defend things like Creationism and the Rapture to non-believers. But didn't Jade have a point that no real growth or insight can take place when you approach every conversation as if you already have all the answers?

"Care to share any examples?" Pastor Rick asks.

I shrug. "Like why we should have to ask for God's help if He already knows everything, or whether Christianity is really as inclusive as we like to believe. Nothing I haven't heard before, of course but, I dunno, I guess something about being locked in that room made me more—"

"Ethan, the Bible teaches us that 'the one who doubts is like a wave in the sea, blown and tossed by the wind,'" Pastor Rick says softly.

I furrow my brow and ask, "But shouldn't our beliefs be able to withstand some scrutiny? The Bible is inerrant, so examining our beliefs more closely should *strengthen* them, right?"

He nods eagerly. "Absolutely, Ethan, absolutely. And good for Jade for encouraging you to step outside your comfort zone and think of things from someone else's perspective. We could all use more practice doing that."

But how much practice do we get in an echo chamber?

Sure, my fellow churchgoers and I talk to each other a lot about our faith, and even our doubts, but we all share the same general mindset. Most people I know think pretty much like I do.

"On the other hand," Pastor Rick continues, "remember what Jesus told Thomas: 'Blessed are those who have not seen and yet have believed.' Ethan, Satan will throw every trick in the book at you trying to rattle your faith."

Is he implying that Jade is an instrument of Satan? No. I don't accept that.

And what exactly is the upshot? He *does* want me to examine my beliefs or he *doesn't*? I have a sinking feeling that I know the answer.

"Mark my words, you will encounter many nonbelievers in your life," Pastor Rick says. "You can't let a single conversation with an atheist knock you off course."

My muscles tense. In the first place (here I go with Jade's places) I never said Jade was an atheist. And in the second place, I vaguely resent Pastor Rick for suddenly seeming to fear I'm about to tumble over to the dark side. I've committed my life to Christ and spent the past six years working my tail off for this church. Haven't I established my bona fides? And shouldn't I be able to explore some of the nuances of my beliefs without being scolded not to let my faith falter? I mean, c'mon: God is the way, the truth, and the life; surely He can handle a few questions from a confused teenager, right?

That thing Jade said in the gym—that if it were my kid,

I wouldn't expect a constant pledge of loyalty—it kinda stuck. I'd want my kid to come to me with any doubts or confusion, and I wouldn't judge him for asking questions.

"Ethan," Pastor Rick continues, "I want you to remember: It's when you're feeling the weakest that God is holding on to you the tightest."

I nod and even manage a smile. If I'm being totally honest, I'm a little frustrated by the platitudes. Still, this is the most comforting thing I've heard today.

FOURTEEN

JADE

"You're going where?"

I plant a hand on my hip. "The football game. Should we alert the paper about this breaking development in our family as well?"

Lena presents a palm in surrender. "It's fine, honey. I'm just a little surprised. You've never been interested in football before."

I turn back toward my bedroom mirror, sit in my chair, and spritz cucumber-melon-scented moisturizer into my hair. "I just thought it would be fun," I mutter as I scrunch my curls, still sounding way too defensive to pull off the casual vibe I'd aimed for.

But, geez! Why is everyone making a federal case about my going to a high school football game? Isn't that what teenagers do? It was bad enough to have Gia practically check me for delirium when I suggested that we go. (Just an idea! No biggie!) Now, Lena's acting like I've just told her I'm joining the Peace Corps and moving to Tibet.

Still, I'm trying my best to dial down my attitude. Lena's really knocked herself out for me all week—buying my favorite foods, spending hours at the cell phone store re-placing my SIM card, standing in an insanely long line at the DMV to deal with my stolen driver's license—so I've definitely got to cut her some slack. And I will. Right after she stops grilling me about a stupid football game.

"Fun's good," Lena says, nodding agreeably as she leans against my doorway, her jeans hugging her impossibly narrow hips. "So you're gonna go cheer on Ethan?"

I roll my eyes and drop my jaw. "I am going," I say slowly, "because I am a normal teenager doing a normal teenage thing."

And really, that's all I want anymore: normal. I've barely even given Ethan a second thought all week. I all-but-blew-off the private Facebook messages he's sent, responding with smiley-face emojis to his occasional "Everything OK?" queries. What else is there to say? I don't even know the guy, for crying out loud. Suddenly we're best friends just because we were locked in a room together? Suddenly the reason I'm going to a high school football game is because I spend every minute of my life obsessing about him?

Please.

"Got it," Lena says. "I just thought, I dunno, I think he's a nice guy, is all. I was really impressed with how he's called to check up on you."

I eye Lena warily. "Called who? Ethan's called you?"

Up shoot her palms again. Another surrender. "No big deal," she says. "He's just called to make sure you're okay."

Dad suddenly pops his head in my doorway. "You're talking about Ethan?" he asks. "Yeah, he called me, too. Seems like a really nice guy."

I'm trying to absorb the weirdness of Ethan calling to check up on me—what is he, my guidance counselor?—when I spot the bulky metal contraption Dad is discreetly trying to shield from view.

"What's that?" I ask him.

"This?" Dad says breezily, pulling it closer. "It's one of those highly technical medical devices they call a walker."

I stare at him.

"Honey," Dad says, "it's no big deal. My balance has gotten a little iffy, so the physical therapist recommended I go ahead and start using it, just to be on the safe side."

I blink back tears. "The physical therapy is supposed to keep you from having to use it."

Dad approaches me, limping more noticeably than ever. When he reaches me, he touches my hair with his right hand, steadying himself on the walker with his left. "Physical therapy isn't going to cure me, honey. You know that. All I care about at this point is having as much quality of life as possible, and if that means using a walker, well, that's fine with me."

I dig my nails into my palms. It is not fine with me. It's not fine that a cold, ugly, clunky contraption now stands between me and my father. And not just any father. I know I'm biased, but truly, mine has always blown the curve for other dads. My father is energetic and athletic and amazing.

He should be on the tennis court right now after ten hours on his feet treating patients. *That's* normal, dammit. I just want normal.

But I swallow hard. "Okay," I say.

Dad holds my gaze. "You're sure you're okay?"

I nod briskly. "Yeah. Everything's cool."

Dad smiles, Lena winks at me, and they leave me alone in my room.

I take a deep breath, then stare back into my mirror and start brushing mascara on my lashes. I've never bothered much with makeup before, but what the hell, I'm broadening my horizons, right? Besides, mascara offers great motivation not to cry. One little pity party, and splat, there goes your mascara all over your cheeks. I'm tired of crying.

My sister, Sydney, suddenly swoops into my room and plops onto my bed.

"I'm going to a sleepover at Alicia's tonight," she says, her pixie face beaming.

I narrow my eyes and turn to face her. "Alicia? She's been horrible to you lately."

"Not anymore," Syd says, shaking her head. "That was all, like, a big misunderstanding."

My brow is still furrowed. "She's been dissing you every day at the lunch table," I remind her slowly.

"No, truly, we've totally made up."

I bite my lip. "Syd, this sounds shady to me."

"She apologized," she insists. "You know things are always weird at the beginning of the school year."

"O-*kay* . . ."

"Everybody's gonna be there," Sydney says, her eyes sparkling.

"Casey and Charlotte?" I ask, referencing yet two other "friends" who've been dissing her lately.

"Yes! And this new girl named Rhee. Isn't that the coolest name? It's short for Rhianna, or Rhiannon, or something."

Sydney peers at me closer, then coos, "Ooh, Jay-Shea, your makeup! You look so pretty!"

"Can you handle my beauty?" I tease, waving my mascara wand through the air.

Sydney jumps up and runs over to me. "Put some on me! For the sleepover."

I raise an eyebrow. "Uh, that's not happening."

"Please, Jay-Shea? All my friends are wearing makeup now."

"Yeah, Syd, about these friends . . ."

"Sydney! Time to go!"

We both glance at the door as Lena calls her from the bottom of the stairs.

Sydney bounces lightly on her feet. "Gotta go."

She waves, then bounds toward the door.

"Syd," I call, and she turns back around.

"If you're not having fun," I intone, "call me."

"Okay, okay! But it's all cool. Really."

As she zips out of the hall and disappears down the stairs, I resist the urge to call out to her one last time.

"Please let them be nice to her," I whisper under my breath, then catch my reflection in the mirror and smile self-consciously. I'm sure Ethan would want to know who exactly I'm praying to.

But then I shake the thought from my head. Who cares what he thinks? Anyone who would date Brianne isn't exactly high on my credibility list.

And so what if I'll be on his turf tonight? He doesn't own the school. The guy who will just happen to be on the field for the game I'm just happening to go watch, even though I haven't been to a football game since I quit the marching band two years ago. Nothing weird about that, right?

A text pings. I pick up my cell phone and peer at the screen.

If your dad is making you and Pierce block my calls, I'll see him in court!

I stiffen. When I finally replaced my cell phone yesterday, I saw that I had forty-seven texts and a least a dozen missed calls from her, none of which I responded to. She's really picking up the pace.

I guess I actually should have blocked her, like Pierce did. Absorbing the gut punch of my dad's glioblastoma diagnosis, then getting locked in a gym overnight, kinda crowded out the breaking news of my AWOL mom suddenly popping back into my life.

Still, I squint, lean in closer, and reread this particular text. Most of her correspondence up to this point has been of the "Hey, Baby Girl, call me!" variety. I guess when deadbeat parents drop back into your life after years of being MIA, they try to act super-casual, like they've just been away for a weekend or something, to dial down the awkward quotient. I'd gone years without so much as a visit, a call, a card, and then she pops up out of nowhere acting like a neighbor wanting to borrow a cup of sugar?

Pierce didn't even bat an eyelash, blocking her after the very first message. But even though I haven't responded, my curiosity has won out over my resentment. Mom? My mom? She wants to see me? I don't even know where she lives. I wouldn't know what she looked like if I didn't see her pictures at Grandma Stella's house and constantly hear from her side of the family how much I look like her. But she's suddenly trying to bounce back into my life? What the hell?

But now, she's sounding hostile rather than friendly. And she's threatening to mess with Dad. That'll happen over my dead body. I'm guessing Dad is oblivious to this blast from the past, and that's just the way I intend to keep it.

My stomach tenses as I type out the first text I've ever written her:

What do you want?

I gaze at the words for a moment . . .

. . . then hit "send."

● ● ● ● ●

ETHAN

"So I want you to go out there tonight and kill 'em!" Pause. "Now, let's bow our heads in prayer."

I try to look casual placing my fingers over my mouth as I lower my head, anxious to camouflage my smirk.

That sentiment—"Let's kill 'em! Now, pray!"—is classic Coach Davis. Actually, it's classic every coach I've ever known.

What kind of spell did Jade place on me last weekend, making me rethink things I've taken for granted my whole life? Why do all the balls in my life suddenly seem tossed in the air?

Right now, it's Coach Davis' order to 'kill 'em.' I don't want to kill anybody. And who cares about the outcome of a stupid game? If years of training are all but useless in real-world situations, what's the point? I feel like turning every trophy I ever won into scrap metal.

"Hey, Ethan."

I glance up at Brent as I tighten the laces of my cleats. He waves me over, so I get off the bench and approach him, our other teammates rustling around as we await the coach's signal to hit the field for kickoff.

"Um," he says in a hushed voice, leaning into my ear. "Everything okay with Brianne?"

My eyes narrow as I clutch my helmet tighter.

"Yeah. Why?"

"No reason."

Brent tries to avert his eyes, but my gaze stays locked on his. "What's going on?" I ask, my voice steady and quiet.

He shrugs, then swipes his long, brown bangs from his forehead. "Just . . . I've heard a few things."

I suck in my lips. Do I really want to hear this, particularly right before a game? Ever since Brianne and I started dating, I've made a commitment to ignore gossip. And there's always plenty of gossip where we're concerned. I have no idea why. Okay, fine, she's really pretty, and I guess we rub a lot of folks the wrong way. People tend to pile on the snark, especially when we have the temerity to do things like run for student council.

But whatever. We can take it. We both know that scholarships are our ticket out of Tolliver, so a few snickers and smart-ass remarks won't knock us off course. I've had plenty of practice letting gossip roll off my back.

Still, this is a little different. Brent's a real friend. He's not the kind to talk trash just to knock me down a peg or two. And he's clearly reluctant to speak up.

I deliberate for a moment, then prod him along with my eyes. "Just spill it, bro."

He glances around the locker room warily as teammates continue brushing past us, their shoulder pads clonking against ours.

"It's probably just bullshit, man," Brent says, his brown eyes oozing pity. Geez, I hate pity.

"Spill it," I say, trying to sound friendly. "We don't have much time."

He looks around one last time, then leans in again. "Jocelyn told me after school that Brianne and Craig Cooper might have something going on."

I force myself not to react.

"But like I said, it's probably just trash talk."

I nod stiffly. Now I'm the one avoiding eye contact.

"Jocelyn thinks Brianne's just trying to make you jealous. Payback, I guess. Brianne thinks something happened between you and Jade last weekend."

I give him a level stare. "Nothing happened."

"Totally," Brent says, holding up a palm. "I know that. Everybody who knows you knows that."

I seethe. Everybody except the person who's supposed to know me best.

"Hey, man," Brent says, studying my eyes. "You didn't hear it from me, right? Jocelyn would kill me."

I snort. "Isn't this the point? Isn't it supposed to get back to me?"

Brent shrugs, then lowers his eyes. "I'm sorry, dude."

I nod, then jump a little, startled, as the coach blows his whistle. A burst of adrenaline surges through my veins. Time to hit the gridiron and crash through the stupid sign Brianne and the other cheerleaders spent the afternoon spray-painting for us. Now there's an excellent use of people's time.

Well, who's more stupid? Brianne for painting it, or me for crashing through it like some ridiculous poser? Everything suddenly seems so pointless.

Still, I'll make it through the game. I'd never let my team down. But what bothers me the most as I trot onto the field . . .

. . . is that the story I just heard doesn't surprise me one bit.

FIFTEEN

JADE

"There's Ethan. Number twelve."

I shift my weight on the bleacher and tsk. "Why would I care?"

Gia turns to face me, her hand dangling outside the popcorn box. "Why wouldn't you care?"

I shrug impatiently. "Everybody keeps acting like I'm Ethan's new BFF just because we spent a few hours locked in a room together."

Gia's brow crinkles. "Who is acting that way?"

Okay, she's right. I keep overreacting any time Ethan's name comes up, and I seriously have to chill. I swirl the Coke in my red Solo cup and take a sip.

But I still feel Gia's eyes boring into me. "You fell for him that night, didn't you?" It's a statement, not a question.

I roll my eyes and keep looking at the field, the crackly voice of the announcer piercing the night air over loudspeakers.

"You did!" Gia says. "Omigod, why didn't I get that right away? You fell for Ethan Garrett."

I squeeze my eyes shut and shake my head slowly. "You are so insane."

"Insanely accurate? God, I was an *idiot* not to get that right away."

"There is nothing to get," I say through gritted teeth.

Gia's brows pop up and she gasps. "Did you make out?"

"What?"

"Or . . . more? Whoa, Jade, no wonder you've been so weird since that night."

"Will you shut up!" I glance around nervously. People are all around us, but, thank heaven, nobody seems to be paying attention. "You are a maniac! Nothing happened! Got it? You think I'd make out with a dumb jock?"

My stomach tightens. That's, like, the hundredth time I've called him that this week, and it sticks in my throat a little more each time, mostly because it's not true but also because it makes me sound so . . .

What's that word, Jade? Superior?

Gia studies my face, her pretty, gray eyes accented with winged, black eyeliner. "You know you can tell me anything."

I nod. Okay, Gia, where would you like me to begin? Let's see: My dad is dying; we've covered that one, right? But did I mention that since I don't want to leave his side, I'm skipping the whole roommate plan next year? Oh, and speaking of the fam, my birth mom, who's suddenly popped up out of nowhere, is meeting me for lunch Sunday, though— surprise—I'm the one who has to drive ninety miles to make it happen. Oh, and all these weird, conflicted feelings

I have about Ethan? Do you have a spare hour or two or twelve so I can drill down on those?

Right. I can tell Gia anything. Anything except everything.

"There's nothing to tell," I say in a small voice.

She stares at me a minute longer, then sighs.

Our eyes drift back onto the field as Calvin nails a field goal. Woot.

My cell phone pings. I take it from my pocket and peer at the screen.

Sooooo sorry, Baby Girl gotta reschedule our lunch Sunday. I've been crazy busy lately. But we'll make it happen SOON. Can't wait!

It takes a couple of minutes to pry my gaze away from the screen. It's a sudden breeze that jolts me out of my freeze frame. I put my phone back in my pocket and squeeze my arms together, then glance at Gia. Good. She's concentrating on the game.

Damn. Have my eyes really just filled with tears? I actually thought the mother who blew me off fifteen years ago might be reliable? That I'd seriously let my heart skip a beat at the thought of seeing her again? I am a major-league fool.

I'd even rehearsed the lie I'd tell Dad and Lena when it was time to slip out of the house Sunday: "Gotta work on a chemistry project at Gia's. See you in a few hours."

A few hours! As if the flake who gave birth to me had any intention of penciling in "a few hours" for me! I'm nothing to her. I never have been. Why in the world would I have allowed myself to think differently? Why, oh why, was I stupid enough to respond to her text? Congratulations on serving yourself up for rejection yet again, Jade.

I dig my nails into my palms. If Gia notices my misty eyes, she'll no doubt manage to shake the truth out of me, and I'm not ready to go there yet.

"So," Gia finally says, still staring at the field while she pops more popcorn in her mouth. "I've been reading up on glioblastoma, and there's all kinds of exciting research going on."

"Gia, please let's not talk about it now."

"No, I just was going to say I'm getting the idea that it's not nearly as hopeless as—"

I shoot out of my seat. "I gotta get some air."

She looks at me quizzically. "We're outside."

I flap my hand in front of my face, glance at the people sharing our bleacher, then turn right and bolt past them, forcing a domino-effect knee squeeze.

"Hey!" Gia calls, then jumps up and follows me, prolonging the knee squeeze.

I reach the aisle and start trotting down the stairs, not sure where I'm going but feeling too light-headed to trust myself for long on steps.

"Jade!" Gia is calling after me.

As I reach the bottom of the bleachers, I glance at the cheerleaders and notice Brianne glaring at me, her eyes cut to extra-narrow slits thanks to her tight, ribbon-bedecked cheerleader ponytail. Oh, get over yourself, Pom-Pom Girl.

Maybe her recent round of glares is intended to make up for years' worth of zero eye contact. I consider holding her gaze for a second, but roll my eyes instead. I turn around and head for the back of the bleachers, still clutching my Solo cup.

"Will you wait up!" Gia says, but I'm not waiting, I'm walking as fast as I can without sloshing my Coke.

"Hey, Jade."

I glance toward the voice and see a group of girls sitting under the bleachers a few yards away in the dark. I squint to make out who they are, then realize they're my kinda-sorta acquaintances from my freshman-year stint in the marching band. They're clarinet dropouts, too.

"Hi," I say, walking toward them. "Not sure this is the best view of the game."

The girls laugh, and one of them, Deirdre, motions toward a spot on the ground, my invitation to join them.

"The refreshments are better on this side of the stadium," she says, and as I settle onto the damp grass, she lifts a fleece jacket to offer a peek of a bottle of rum.

"Want some?" she asks.

What the hell. I'm broadening my horizons, right? I nod, and Deirdre pours some into my Coke.

"Jade!" Gia hisses, catching up with me and slinking to the ground in her skinny jeans. "What is *up* with you?"

"Hi, Gia," one of the girls says, and Gia offers a grudging wave.

"You're drinking rum?" Gia asks me incredulously as Deirdre replaces the cap on the bottle.

"Want some?" Deirdre asks her.

"Yeah, could you pour some into my popcorn, please?" Gia snaps.

The girls laugh. "You can get a soft drink at the concession stand," one says. "Or drink it straight from the bottle."

"Mmm. Livers are highly over-rated." Gia casts me a what-the-hell glance.

For some reason, her prissiness motivates me to take an extra-long swig from my cup.

Yuck.

But, like I said, what the hell. I take another swig.

"You don't drink?" Deirdre asks Gia, sounding stunned. Gia gets that a lot: her atheist label seems to prompt lots of other labels people consider vaguely related; ones like alky, boozer, stoner, partier—things that are laughably off the mark. Gia's favorite is Satanist. ("You'd think those geniuses might deduce that if I don't believe in God, chances are low that I believe in Satan," she quipped once.)

But rather than waiting for Gia's answer, Deirdre seems to abruptly remember that I'm the celebrity du jour. "Oh, Jade, tell us about your night in the gym!" she says, leaning in for my campfire story.

"It was . . . a night in the gym," I say, then take another sip, which prompts Deirdre to unscrew the cap again and refill my cup. I smile at her.

"Held hostage in a gym, *so* random," another girl muses. "And with Ethan Garrett."

That name, I've suddenly decided, is code for "time for another swig."

"Will you at least slow it down?" Gia mutters, and I toss her a blasé look.

"Did you make out?" Deirdre asks me. "I've heard Brianne is crazy jealous of you."

"She should be," one of the girls says with a sniff. "You're way prettier."

"Please," I say.

"Oh, by the way, sorry about your dad," the redhead says, and I'm grateful that this parenthetical shout-out— now seemingly obligatory wherever I go—is out of the way.

"Tell us about the robbery," Deirdre says, and damned if that doesn't suddenly sound like a perfectly fine idea.

I start from the beginning: the guy in the parking lot catching my eye as he clutches a ski cap on a ninety-degree day; the gun in my face, followed by my invitation to take my wallet along with the money in the register; Ethan sneaking up behind him but getting foiled in mid-pounce; my yoga in the aerobics room; the electricity flickering off; the discussion about how to pee (well, we knew how, we just didn't know where) . . . the whole nine yards.

The girls laugh, insert questions and refill my cup as the story progresses, and pretty soon, I'm leaning back against my elbows in the grass, sitting up occasionally only to take another swig from my cup. As I careen from one rollicking detail to the next, I consider the possibility that I'm the greatest storyteller who ever lived. The possibility alone emboldens me to add new depth and detail to the story, and the more the girls laugh, the richer my tapestry becomes.

Tapestry. Isn't that a funny word? The kind of word you would never use (or at least I would never use) except as a metaphor? And isn't that weird when a word becomes much more common as a metaphor than as whatever it originally defined? I digress a few moments to elaborate on that particular thought, and though the girls look a little confused, they're still laughing.

Well, Gia's not laughing. Gia, I decide on the spot, is a killjoy. This in itself is weird since she's so funny, but there you have it: She's *tsk*ing and frowning at me, and I think this is the very definition of a killjoy. I think if you look in the dictionary under "killjoy" this very moment, you'll see Gia's scowling visage.

Visage. That's a funny word, too. I wonder if that's the kind of word the average person knows. People tell me I have an off-the-charts vocabulary, courtesy of my hyper-articulate dad, and I'm sure I sometimes come off as a know-it-all. But truly, I'm so unclear on which words are considered show-offy that I usually don't realize I've stumbled into esoterica until I get a quizzical glance, at which point I quickly try to dumb things down.

Dumb things down. Now, there's a stupid expression.

Dumb was never meant to be a verb, and if you're making things dumber, shouldn't you be dumbing something up?

And killjoy: Has there ever been a more literal noun than that? Nothing graceful or nuanced about it, just a clunky, literal word. And shouldn't it be joykill? Joykiller?

I wonder why they don't call murderers guykills.

I wonder how close Ethan and I came to being murdered by a guykill that night in the gym. Was the thief really just a junkie in need of a quick fix, or did he contemplate killing us? Whatever his intentions might have been, I felt damn close to death that night, *damn* close. I tell the girls this now.

Someone refills my drink, and soon after this, I think, "Why am I just leaning back on my elbows? Why don't I lie down completely in this moist, cool, delicious grass?"

So I do. I lie down, giggling as my drink sloshes on my shirt, and stare up at the bleachers.

The other girls are laughing at me (well, all except Gia, of course) and I think, "If it's this easy to get a laugh by lying down, why didn't I think of it a long time ago, especially since lying here is such a squishy delight?" This strikes me as a profound thought.

"I love rum," I say aloud, something else that strikes me as profound, which is when Joykill Gia snatches my sloshing cup out of my hand and pours it on the ground.

Wasn't that rude?

But it's okay, because although my sense of time is getting a little wobbly, I'm aware at some point that my cup has been refilled. Or maybe it's a new cup, because it has Coke in it along with rum. So maybe somebody brought me a new Coke. Wasn't that sweet? It's so sweet, I want to cry. And I need to thank whoever put a new Coke in my hand, and I need to thank whoever topped it off with rum, because I've decided that what I said before about loving rum is really, really true, and omigod, I love these marching-band dropouts *sooo* much. I truly do. I tell them that now.

I decide "squishlicious" would be a good word to describe cool, moist grass in which one lies. I make a mental note to find out how to have this added to the dictionary. I ask one of my fellow marching-band dropouts to remind me to do this, and then say "I love you" again when she promises she will.

My biggest laugh of the night comes, improbably, when I ask the question I least intend to be funny:

"Is this what it feels like to be drunk?"

● ● ● ● ●

"Nooo!" I shake my arm loose from Gia's grip and give her an exaggerated pout. "I wanna watch the rest of the game!"

I have no memory of moving from the squishlicious grass behind the stadium to the front of the bleachers, but here Gia and I are, standing just a few feet from the cheer-leaders as the last seconds of the fourth quarter tick by. I don't know where my fellow band dropouts are. I miss them.

"If you don't call him, I will," Gia says.

By the time she says this, I've forgotten who "he" is and what we were arguing about.

Oh, yeah. She wants me to call my brother. She says I'm too drunk to drive home, and the game is almost over. Gia's dad is picking her up and could give me a ride home, but do I really want him to see me this way? This is what she asks me in a very scold-ey tone. I'm inferring the correct answer is no.

Gia's on her phone now.

Dammit!

"Hi, Pierce, it's Gia. Listen, sorry to bother you, but do you think you could swing by the football field and pick up Jade?"

"Gia!" I squeal.

"No," she continues, "she's got her car, but I don't think she should drive."

"Gia!"

"No, no, she's okay. She's just . . . long story. But you can be here in a few minutes? Great."

She ends the call and looks at me evenly. "Friends don't let friends drive each other crazy."

The stadium buzzer sounds.

"Gia," I moan again, but I'm too mellow to really protest, and at least she called Pierce instead of my dad, but still.

I gaze out onto the field. "Who won?" I ask.

"The other guys," she says, and my eyes fall on jersey number twelve. Ethan is taking his helmet off, his head hanging dejectedly as the coaches wave cupped fingers to corral their teams. The cheerleaders and some spectators file onto the field in the players' direction. I notice Brianne walking toward Ethan, her cheerleader ponytail bouncing perkily.

Then I notice someone else. A big, balding and burly red-faced guy has charged Ethan like a bull. I can't hear him from where I'm standing, but he's clearly pissed, jabbing his finger in Ethan's chest. Now he's kicking the ground around Ethan's feet. And all the while, he's practically spitting in Ethan's face, his face contorted with rage.

That's when I tear onto the field. I don't remember forming the thought; I just take off running, running as hard as I can toward Ethan, my arms pumping and my heart pounding. I hear Gia running behind me and calling my name, but there's no slowing me down.

I barrel into the red-faced man, butting my chest against his and almost knocking him backward.

"Leave him alone!" I scream.

The man's jaw drops.

"I mean it! Keep your goddamn hands off of him!"

I feel Ethan gently grab my arms from behind.

"It's okay, Jade," he says in my ear.

But I'm still chest-butting the man, sputtering with rage and trying to yank my arms free.

The crowd stares at me, mouths agape.

"Jade, Jade," Ethan coos in my ear. "Cool it. It's okay."

My eyes lock with the red-faced guy—Ethan's father,

I've already deduced. "Don't you ever touch him again," I say, my voice dripping with venom.

His dad is still too astonished to react. He just stands there looking dumbfounded.

"It's okay, it's okay," Ethan is saying.

A coach steps between the man and me. "Game's over, Mr. Garrett," he says. "You win some, you lose some. We'll get 'em next week. Time to go home and sleep it off."

He pats Ethan's dad on the back, then he glances at me. "That goes for you, too, young lady."

The onlookers are still frozen in stunned silence, but within a few seconds, people start breathing again. Mumbles begin churning through the crowd, then one person changes position, then another, then . . .

Then back to normal. It's like the pause button has been deactivated. Everyone's moving around again.

My hands start shaking. Ethan turns me around and tips my chin until our eyes lock. "What was up with that?" he asks, trying to sound playful.

"I . . . I . . ."

I suddenly realize Brianne's face is inches away from mine. I try to stammer out an apology—that's the right response, I guess, but my head is spinning and I really don't know what to say, and I can't form words anyhow, so I just stand there dazed for a minute, then . . .

"Come on, Jade."

It's Gia, pulling me toward her. I let her take my trembling hand and lead me away.

• • • • •

ETHAN

My dad glares at me one last time for good measure, his beer breath wafting through the muggy night air, then lets my Uncle Byron lead him away.

But it's Jade I'm focusing on. My eyes follow her as Gia guides her off the field.

I want to run up to her and . . . and what? Thank her? Console her? Confront her? I could smell alcohol on her breath. Maybe the stress of the past few days has taken more of a toll than even she realizes.

But "confront" isn't the right word; it sounds too aggressive. Still, she's been avoiding me all week, and I have this intense need to connect with her, to make sure she's alright and maybe even to give myself a quick reality check. We really did bond that night in the aerobics room, right? Not in any of the tacky ways our immature classmates keep suggesting, but on a human level. That was real, wasn't it?

I was starting to wonder, based on how she's been treating me like a stranger the past few days. But this . . . this was real. She truly cares about me. Why else would she have charged my dad like a crazed bull? Why else would she be defending me so passionately?

Yes. Our bond is real.

But right now, I can't do anything but watch her walk

away. She's made it clear she needs her space. I know all too well what it's like to have that need blown off, so if anybody should respect that, it's me. Still, my eyes follow her until the very last second that Coach Davis rounds us up to head back to the locker room. I hear my teammates snickering; I guess the rumors about Jade and me will be kicked into high gear from this point on. But I couldn't care less.

The last thing I notice as we leave the field is Brianne. She's been standing by my side the past five minutes, but I haven't registered her presence. But now, as my gaze flickers her way, I see her curl a lip and glare at me. It's the kind of expression that in the past would have prompted me to rush to her side to explain, to apologize, to reassure, to cajole, to whatever. But right now, all I feel is indifference.

I wipe my sweaty forehead with the back of my hand, then turn away and trot off the field with my teammates.

● ● ● ● ●

"Well? Are you coming or not?"

I crook my elbow in my open car window, the breeze billowing against the side of my face.

"Coming where?" I say listlessly to the voice on the other end of my Bluetooth.

"What?" Brianne responds. "I can barely hear you."

I consider closing my window to minimize the noise, then decide against it.

"Listen, I'll see you later, okay?" I say without bothering to raise my voice.

"What?!?"

Her voice is plenty loud.

A couple of my teammates told me in the locker room that they'd seen Brianne leave the field arm in arm with Craig Cooper. I don't know what kind of reaction they were expecting, but I barely batted an eyelash.

I don't know what kind of response Brianne is expecting now, but her tone suggests she's definitely falling short of perky.

"Get your ass to the Pizza Palace right now!" she hisses, and I smiled ruefully. So our regular Friday-night routine is supposedly still on?

"I'm really beat, Brianne," I say. "I'm gonna go home and crash. But you have fun. Bye."

I tap the button on my steering wheel, disconnecting the call. Whoa, this breeze feels incredible.

The phone immediately rings again, and I consider ignoring it. But I don't want to do that. I don't want to be with Brianne anymore, but I don't want to be immature about it. The last thing I want is more game-playing.

"Why are you acting this way?" Brianne asks over the Bluetooth, her voice shrill. "Does this have something to do with your precious Jade? And how insane is she, causing a scene at the game? I mean, I knew she was weird, but I didn't know she was psycho. God!"

"Gotta go, Brianne. Have fun at the pizza place."

"Ethan!"

Sigh.

"Yeah?"

"Are you mad because I left with Craig Cooper? I was just catching a ride!"

I tap my steering wheel idly. "No, I'm not mad. In fact, I think we should see other people."

Silence.

Then *sniff, sniff, sniff.*

"Please don't cry, Brianne." I'm trying to sound sympathetic, but the only thing I'm feeling is fatigue.

"I love you, Ethan!" she sobs, her voice a volcano of despair.

I sigh again. I should be able to say it back. I've *been* saying it for over two years, and if it actually was love, I should still be feeling it, right?

I don't know. I don't know anything anymore.

"Is something going on with you and Jade?" she says through more tears.

"No."

"Don't lie to me!"

"I'm not lying, Brianne."

"Ethan, come see me right now! Either you come here or I'm coming to your house."

"Please, Brianne, let's just—"

"I spent five hours searching for you in the rain last weekend! And I'm the one who got you rescued! It's because I love you, Ethan. Baby, I love you so much, my heart hurts. I don't know what kind of number that robbery did on you, but we've got to get back to where we were. And

I don't know what you've heard about Craig and me, but please don't believe any stupid rumors. We're just good—"

"Brianne, can we talk later?" I say wearily. "I really need a good night's sleep."

More sobs.

"I'm not trying to hurt you," I say calmly. "It's just, the jealousy and the game-playing, I don't think it's healthy. It's not good for either of us."

"I love you, baby." Now, her voice sounds weak and defeated. Which is more than I can bear.

I run my hand roughly through my hair, then without even making a conscious choice, turn the steering wheel left instead of right at the intersection.

Brianne's right: She did spend hours in the rain looking for me. I have been in love with her for years, whatever high school love might mean. And yeah, although I'm seeing Brianne more clearly lately—and not necessarily liking what I'm seeing—I have a lot more context than the average person. Her dad's a womanizer, and her mom is always pushing her to lose weight and earn more ridiculous plastic tiaras in beauty contests. It's a lot of pressure. I get that. It doesn't excuse rudeness, or possessiveness, or over-the-top jealousy, but Brianne and I have a lot in common. And we've been there for each other.

Whatever the cards hold for our relationship, it shouldn't end with a phone call. That's just not right.

"It's okay, Bree," I say soothingly. "I'm on my way now to the Pizza Palace."

She sighs heavily.

"So we're okay?" she asks, her voice trembling.

"We're okay," I say weakly. "But, Brianne, our relationship, we've got to get more mature about this if we want it to last."

"Anything, baby," she says. "Anything you say. Just hurry, okay?"

SIXTEEN

JADE

I prop up on an elbow and cup my hand over my eyes.

"What the hell?"

I squint and see Pierce opening my blinds, flooding my room with late-morning sunshine.

I squeeze my eyes shut, moan and flop back down.

"Wanna tell me why you got drunk last night?" he asks, then plops down on my bed.

I peek at Pierce through a single eye. "Thanks for picking me up."

"So should I gather the family for an intervention?"

I sigh heavily and sit up. Whoops. It takes a couple of seconds for my brain to catch up and settle in my cranium. That's a new sensation. I press my fingers against a throbbing temple.

"I'm fine," I say.

"Drunk is not fine," Pierce says, his long, curly lashes rimming disapproving, dark eyes.

"I was not drunk. I had *one* rum and Coke."

"With, like, forty refills, according to Gia. And you could barely walk to the car. Oh, and apparently you started a fight with somebody on the field? What were you trying to do, cram a lifetime of delinquency into one night?"

I moan and drop my head back. (Oops. My brain and cranium still aren't quite syncing up.)

"I have to be at work at one o'clock," I mutter. "Are you ready to clear out, or do you have, like, a couple of bodyguards waiting to haul me away in a van?"

"Not this time," Pierce says, leaning closer. "And I'm cutting you some slack, considering you got robbed last weekend. But, Jade, I swear to god, if this happens again I'm telling Mom and—"

"Good plan," I tell him, scrambling out of my covers, which entails nudging him unceremoniously off the bed with my feet. "Now, out."

But once we're both on our feet, I spontaneously reach out and touch his arm. "Hey, Pierce?"

"Yeah?"

"That's for having my back."

"Yeah, don't push it," he says, and we share a smile.

I'm not quite used to this role reversal. Ever since Mom—our real mom—bailed on us, I've been extra protective of him. He cried himself to sleep in my bed every night for weeks after she left, sucking his thumb and calling out for her in his dreams. He asked me once if we could knock on every door in the neighborhood to see if she was there. When he got an oversized Christmas present when he was three, he expected her to pop out of the box. Pierce doesn't remember any of this (or so he claims) so he pretends that being abandoned while still in diapers is a non-issue. His whole life seems to be devoted to that proposition: Of course he charmed our stepmom the instant he met her, kicking off a lifelong lovefest. Of course he's awesome at sports, making every soccer goal look fluid and effortless. Of course he's the funniest guy in his class. His science project of determining which teacher was the most sleep-inducing became an instant legend. But to me, he's still the kid with a thumb in his mouth crying himself to sleep. And now, here he is rescuing me from aerobics rooms and being my designated driver when I get trashed at a football game.

"Jade, if you need counseling, I could give Mrs. Esbell a call," he quips, referencing our most sleep-inducing teacher.

"Yeah, pencil it into my study hall period, will ya?" I respond as I good-naturedly shoo him out of the room.

I close my door behind him, then lean against it and exhale through puffed-out cheeks.

No intervention is necessary, because I will never let myself lose control like that again. How can I ever face any of the people who saw me last night? I can never face the marching-band dropouts who had the pleasure of hearing me wax poetic about adding new words to the dictionary. I can never face the spectators who saw me stumbling around the bleachers. And I can never, ever face those who beheld my *pièce de résistance*: going off on Ethan's dad after the game.

My knees bend and I slither to the floor, holding my face in my hands. Stupid, stupid, stupid! My profile wasn't quite high enough as it was? I really had to invent a new reason to get people talking about me? I can only imagine the stories that are already circulating. Maybe the rumor mill has transformed my rum and Coke into cocaine by now, or maybe my tirade at Ethan's dad has morphed into a YouTube-worthy beat-down. Oh, and the best news of all: Those snarky insinuations about my falling for Ethan during our overnighter? There's a chance, just a chance, that the gossip would have started to die down, were it not for my virtuoso performance last night in fanning the flames. Fanning the flames? I practically started an inferno.

Stupid, stupid, stupid!

Maybe I can join the witness protection program.

Knock, knock, knock.

"Pierce, please, not now," I moan.

"It's Sydney."

I look up abruptly. "Syd?"

"Yeah."

Her voice sounds small and sad, a distinct departure from her usual rocket-fueled exuberance.

I stand up, open my door and sweep her inside with a wave of my arm.

"What's up?" I ask gently.

She peers at me for a moment, then dissolves into tears, her pixie face crinkling like a leaf.

"What?" I prod.

She rubs her eyes with her knuckles, choking on jagged little sobs.

I close the door behind us, then guide her gently to my bed. I lean back against my pillow and sweep her into my arms.

"Alicia?" I deduce.

She nods, sniffling.

"Tell me everything."

Syd whimpers for another moment or two, then says, "Everybody hates me."

"Okay, that's not true." I hold her tighter, stroking her silky hair. I wonder if she can feel my heart beating through my shirt. If those little snots hurt my baby sister, so help me, I'll pulverize them.

"When I got to the sleepover yesterday," Sydney says, still sniffling, "we started playing some games."

That's never good. Not in sixth grade, anyway.

"Yeah?" I prod nervously, bracing myself for the worst.

"We sat in a circle and took turns saying who our best friend is," Sydney says, her voice sounding smaller and smaller as I nestle her head in my arms.

"That's a spectacular idea," I say drolly, hating Alicia already. Well, hating her *more*.

Syd turns to face me, her face crinkling into a new wave of tears. "I'm nobody's best friend."

She starts sobbing again, her breaths a series of little hiccups, and I hug her closer.

"Casey said she was Charlotte's best friend," Syd tells

me through her sobs, "and Charlotte said she was Casey's best friend. I wasn't surprised, although I thought they both might pick me. Then Carmen said she was Louisa's best friend, and Louisa said she was Rhee's best friend. Which made me feel bad for Carmen, but then Louisa said, well, really Carmen and Rhee and Alicia were *all* her best friends. Then Rhee said the same thing: that Carmen and Louisa and Alicia were all her best friends."

Okay, my head is seriously spinning.

"Then it was my turn," Syd continues earnestly, "and I said, 'You're all my best friends.' But Alicia said I had to pick, and I could only pick one."

Alicia is Satan incarnate.

"So I said Alicia," Syd says, her brows an inverted *V*, "and I thought Alicia would say me, because, you know, we really are best friends—at least I thought we were—and since I was the only one nobody had picked so far, I thought for sure . . ."

My body tenses, and Sydney presses her face into my chest for a new wave of tears.

"But she said Rhee!"

Sniff, sniff, sniff.

What a nest of vipers.

"And then," Sydney cries, and omigod I'm not sure if I can take this, "Alicia said we were gonna go around the circle giving 'best' awards—like best smile, best hair, best clothes, best whatever."

Okay, now my blood has reached a full boil.

"And I'm the only one who didn't get any 'best' awards!" Sydney sobs, her breaths more jagged than ever. "And when Alicia got to 'best eyes,' she said, 'Sydney, you don't count in this category, so don't feel bad that you won't win it.'"

My eyes narrow into slits. "You don't count?"

Sydney nods. "Alicia was like, 'I have hazel eyes, and Casey has blue eyes, and Charlotte has brown eyes, and whatever, but . . .'"

"Yes?" I say, my voice clipped.

"She said my eyes have no color. And that no color doesn't count."

Sydney crumples in my arms. I let her cry for a moment, then turn her shoulders, forcing her to look at me. I gaze into her sparkling onyx eyes—perhaps the most beautiful eyes on the planet—and lower my chin until our gaze is level.

"Here's the thing," I tell her slowly. "Do you know what black is?"

Sydney shakes her head, trembling.

"Black," I tell her, "is the absorption of *all* colors. Black isn't nothing. It's everything."

My ceiling fan clicks rhythmically overhead as she absorbs my words.

"I hate my eyes!" she finally wails in response. "They're ugly!"

I sit up straighter, forcing her to straighten up, too. "What's ugly," I say, "is so-called friends trying to tear you down."

Geez! Why was I stupid enough to think Sydney would be spared this kind of shit? I guess it's because I've always sized her up as the golden girl: gorgeous, sweet, smart yet innocent. Surely life would never heap on her the kind of social slings and arrows I've been dodging all my life. Yes, she's mixed too, but in such an adorable way that I ridiculously considered her racist-proof. She's even the golden child in our family, the one whose mother didn't abandon her.

But how naive of me. My poor baby sister.

"Sydney," I tell her, lifting her chin with my index finger. "Do you think I'm pretty?"

She nods, her chin quivering.

"Well, you know what?" I say. "Then I am pretty. That's how much your opinion matters to me. You know me inside and out, so if I'm pretty to you, well, case closed. I'm pretty. Now, listen to me: You are beautiful."

"Thank you," she says in a small voice. "But you really are beautiful."

I sigh. There's so much more I want to say to her: that Sydney's "friends" are snakes, that she's got to wise up and become a better judge of character, that the only way other people will value her is if she values herself.

But all of this will have to wait, because it's now that she lobs her most heartbreaking disclosure of all:

"What made me saddest of all," Sydney continues, her voice still shaky, "is that Rhee asked me what it's like to have a dad who's dying."

Her watery eyes search mine.

"Jade, I don't want Daddy to die."

•   •   •   •   •

ETHAN

"I just think it's too soon."

I glance at Brianne for just a second before returning my eyes to the road. "You don't have to go," I remind her.

She flings her blonde ponytail off her shoulder. "I'm thinking about you, Ethan," she assures me. "You might get post-traumatic stress going back so soon."

Right. She's thinking about *me*.

Yes, after a long talk the night before, I've reluctantly agreed to recommit to our relationship. But I've also committed to a new set of ground rules: I'm no longer going to let myself be pushed around. I'm no longer putting up with irrational jealousy. I'm no longer adjusting my comings or goings to accommodate Brianne's insecurities—and that includes my trip this Saturday afternoon to Regal Gym.

Before, I would have backed down right away in the face of her sulkiness. But this time, I didn't skip a beat: Yeah, that's where I'm going. See ya.

Her reaction was stunning. She immediately cut the crap and said, "Of course, go wherever you want." And not in a snide, pissy way, but in a way that made me realize I have a lot more power in this relationship than I ever realized. Maybe the more I respect myself, the more she'll respect me.

Not that she's magically transformed. Her sudden jolt of maturity didn't stop her from inviting herself to come along, and now it's not stopping her from nagging me in the car. But I'm breathing easier realizing that things will be different from now on. They have to be.

And if Jade happens to be working at the gym today?

Good. I need to reassure myself that she's okay. I've backed off calling and texting her; the last thing I want to do is make another person feel crowded. But the way Jade confronted my dad at last night's football game? Whether she wants to admit it or not, I know for sure now that the bond we formed that night in the gym wasn't one-sided. She felt it, too. I don't know what that means, or why I feel so protective of her, but I hope she is working today. I want to see her. And if that's a problem for Brianne, well, it's her problem.

True, I haven't been back to the gym since the holdup, but that's only because of my football schedule. I have a get-right-back-on-the-horse kind of mentality.

I pull into a parking space and turn off my ignition.

"You're sure?" Brianne repeats, and this time, I don't even bother to respond.

As we walk toward the door, my heart rate quickens, not because of post-traumatic stress (whatever that is) but because through the window, I can see Jade behind the counter. I wonder fleetingly if she'll be embarrassed to see me—that scene last night was intense—but I'm too excited to care.

I hold the door open for Brianne, then follow her inside. As we walk to the desk to scan our cards, I notice Jade dropping her chin and pushing a lock of hair behind her ear.

"Hi," she says weakly, and Brianne breezes past her without so much as a glance.

"Hi," I respond buoyantly, over-compensating. Then . . .

"Brianne," I call, still planted in my spot as Brianne filters into the gym.

She turns around and looks annoyed.

"Jade just said hello to you," I say.

Brianne's jaw drops subtly. "What?"

"I said Jade just smiled and said hello, and you didn't even acknowledge her."

Now, Brianne's jaw drop is dramatic. "What?"

I shrug. "Maybe you didn't hear her. But now that I'm pointing it out, I'm sure you want to say hello."

I notice Jade swallowing hard in my peripheral vision.

Brianne blushes but maintains a steely gaze. She considers my words. "Hello," she finally intones, looking at me instead of Jade, one eyebrow arched dramatically.

She stands stone-still for a minute, then jerks her head around and walks to an elliptical, her hands clenched into fists.

Jade presses in her lips as I continue hovering at the desk.

"I'm sorry about that," I say softly.

"About what?" she asks, clearly trying to seem casual.

I think for a second, then say, "You told me how snooty Brianne is. I'm really embarrassed to say I never noticed. I mean, she can be really nice when she—"

"Right, right," Jade agrees eagerly, too eagerly.

"I mean, that's not okay with—"

"It's cool, Ethan, really, it's cool." She nods for emphasis.

I run my fingers through my hair.

"Jade, about last night . . ."

"Ethan, I am so sorry about that. I don't know what came over me. I was such an idiot."

I step closer to her. "I really appreciate it. I mean, coming to my defense like that."

She waves a hand through the air. "It was nothing. Just me being over-sensitive. Making a scene made everything worse. Although I'm pretty sure I had your dad shaking in his shoes." She laughs at herself. I love the way she can laugh at herself.

"Can we just forget it?" she asks.

I smile. "That's the thing: I can't forget it. I don't want to forget it."

She drops her eyes and digs the toe of her sneaker into the carpet.

"Please, Ethan," she says, still looking down.

I stare at her a little longer, then nod. "Guess I'll go grab a quick workout," I say.

She nods.

"But I'll keep an eye on the front desk in case anybody robs you."

She smiles. "Yeah, but you've perfected that whole tackling-bad-guys-from-behind move by now, right?"

I return her smile. "Yeah. I've got your back."

Jade's ocean-colored eyes shine. "Have a good workout."

I linger just one minute more. I don't want to walk away.

But I finally do.

"See you around?" I say.

Jade's staring at her shoes again. "Yeah," she responds. "See you around."

SEVENTEEN

JADE

"Crossword puzzle?"

Dad nods and I hand him the newspaper. I pick up a copy of *Us* magazine and absently thumb through it as we sit in his neurologist's uber-chilled waiting room.

I skip to the last page of the magazine and ponder who wore it best (Blake Lively or somebody I've never heard of), the most challenging thing my brain can handle on this Thursday afternoon. Almost a week has passed since my meltdown at the football game, and it's taken every ounce of energy I can muster to render myself invisible in school. Gia has done a stellar job running interference for me, going so far as to plant a couple of rumors about herself to deflect attention from my notoriety ("Did you hear I've decided to drop out of school and become a tattoo artist?") It's an apt reminder that if you're going to be joined at the hip with a friend, it's cool for the friend to be willing to take a bullet for you.

I've gotten particularly good at dodging Ethan in the halls, and neither he nor Brianne have come back to the gym since Saturday, so my strategy of running out the clock seems to have some traction.

"Five-letter word for youngest Kardashian sister? Second letter 'h'?" Dad says without looking up from his puzzle, and if that doesn't add insult to injury, I don't know what does, because he knows I know the answer and hate myself for knowing it.

"I dunno," I murmur, and Dad nudges me playfully.

I laugh, then feel the familiar knot in my stomach that accompanies my seemingly inevitable mental calculations.

In this case: How much longer will Dad be able to fill in a crossword puzzle?

I inhale deeply and remind myself what I told Sydney the other day, that none of us knows how long we have to live, and rather than wasting time or energy thinking about the future, we should focus on enjoying the present. Yep. Words to live by.

I force my gaze back onto Blake Lively's picture.

Today's actually not a total bust. I was able to talk Lena into letting me take Dad to his doctor's appointment. The two of them are insanely committed to the fantasy that they can spare my siblings and me of any direct dealings with Dad's disease, so Lena's been doing backflips trying to do everything herself, a real challenge particularly considering that Dad's seizures have forced him to quit driving.

But I don't have the patience for martyrs, and I told Lena so. Between Dad's chemo, radiation, and checkups, we need all hands on deck. Lena's kinda getting with the program. We're all getting with the program. Actually, I guess we're all kinda making up the program as we go along.

So here we are, me squeezing my goose-pimpled arms together as I contemplate Blake Lively's fashion sense and Dad filling in the crossword squares, lowest-common-denominator pop culture answers notwithstanding.

A nurse opens a door and says, "Dr. Fulton?"

Dad smiles and lifts himself up, clutching his walker for support. I'm half out of my chair, not knowing how to help.

"Want me to come?" I ask him softly.

"Nah," Dad says. "Catch up on your Kardashian news so you can help me with my crossword puzzles."

I wrinkle my nose at him and watch him walk through the door as the nurse holds it open.

I sit back down and squeeze my hands together. Should I have insisted on going with him? Dad is sure to sugar-coat whatever the doctor says, and we need real information. And did he need help getting to his feet a few seconds ago? Should I have offered him my arm, or steadied the walker for him, or . . .?

I don't know, I don't know, I don't know. I don't know how to help my dad. I don't know why my dad got cancer. I don't know why it's so friggin' cold in this doctor's office. I don't know anything.

"What do you know."

I glance up and see Ethan smiling at me.

My jaw drops in surprise. "Um, hi," I say. "What are you doing here?"

"Bumped my head at football practice," he says. "It was nothing, but the coach insisted I get it checked out."

"And?"

"I just checked in. Mind if I wait with you?"

"Sure." I nod toward the seat Dad was using, and he sits down, threading his fingers together. He glances at me, then does a double-take. "Hey, are you cold?"

"I'm fine," I say, but he's already taking off his letter jacket.

I try to wave it away, but he's handing it to me, insisting, and after a couple of seconds, I rest it over my shoulders. Whew. That's much better.

"Thanks," I say. "You're sure you're not cold?"

"Nah." He's wearing a grass-stained Walt Whitman High T-shirt, his muscles bulging underneath.

"Who are you with?" I ask, then feel my face flush. "I mean, you didn't drive yourself here with a concussion, did you?"

"Yeah. I only passed out a couple of times on the road."

He's giving me such a stoic poker face that I hold his gaze for a second. Then that lopsided grin starts crawling up his face.

"I don't know that this is the best time to joke," I scold playfully, and he laughs.

"My mom's parking the car."

"Ah. Well, I hope your head's okay. Hey, want me to pray for you?"

He laughs some more. "That would be nice, actually."

I pull his jacket tighter around my arms and smile. "I wasn't making fun of you," I say.

"Like hell."

I laugh. "A swear word! From you?"

"A biblical word," he corrects me. "Now, where's that prayer you promised me?"

"God, next time you want to knock some sense into Ethan's head, please make sure he's wearing a helmet."

"It wasn't God knocking my head; it was a linebacker," he says, his Brussels-sprouts eyes glimmering.

A couple of new patients filter into the room and wander over to unoccupied chairs.

"So why are you here?" Ethan asks me after a moment.

"My dad."

"Oh."

Pause.

"I just . . . I can't tell you how sorry I am about your father. I tried to call you a few—"

"Right. I know. Thanks."

Ethan stares at his intertwined fingers. "What I said that night in the gym, about your life being perfect? That was stupid. Nobody's life is perfect."

I offer a small shrug. "It's okay."

"No," he insists. "It wasn't okay. That's what pulls people apart from each other, or keeps them from ever coming together in the first place: assumptions. Ridiculous assumptions. Judgments. Like you said."

An overhead television in the room is tuned to a sunny lady giving us sunny news about migraines.

"The game we were playing that night in the gym," I say tentatively. "What you'd rather die than do?"

"Yeah," Ethan says, leaning into his elbows.

"I think my dad would rather die than do this disease." My throat catches on the words. I blink back tears.

"But he won't," I continue in barely a whisper. "At first he said no to chemo, no to radiation, no to all of it. He knows the deal with glioblastoma, and his is extra aggressive. He knows the treatment will probably make him sicker than the disease. So what's the point, right? But he's pushing ahead for us, for his family."

My words hang in the air as the sunny migraine lady keeps yammering.

The nurse appears in the doorway and calls another name. Another patient treads to the door, treads to whatever news or diagnosis or treatment he's about to receive. I wonder fleetingly what that patient's story is. I wonder a lot about people's stories these days. Ethan's right: Nobody ever has it as easy as people assume.

"My dad gives me a different quotation every year on my birthday," I tell him, "and this year, it was from Thomas Fuller. 'It is always darkest just before the day dawneth.'" He framed the whole list this year. I think he assumes we're at the end of the line."

A tear spills down my face, and Ethan plucks a tissue from a box on the end table. He hands it to me, his eyes searching mine, and I blot it against my cheek.

"Did you know my dad completed his residency while raising two little kids all by himself?" I ask him, my voice wistful. "My mom flaked on us—after they split, she kinda drifted in and out of our lives for a couple of years, then fell off the grid entirely—so my dad was doing everything single-handedly: changing diapers, making dinners, everything, all while getting his training in endodontics. I mean, of course, my grandma was there every step of the way (my *sane* grandma, the one on my dad's side) and he married Lena when Pierce and I were still pretty small. But he had a hell of a load for a while there. And you know what? He was always in a good mood. Always."

"That's amazing," Ethan says. "Seriously."

"It just kills me," I continue, "that all of his hard work, those long hours, those killer exams—he was laying the groundwork for what we have now. And just when he could take a breather and start to enjoy it . . ."

My eyes mist up again.

"I hate that your mom bailed on you," Ethan says.

I tap my fingertips together. "She's actually been popping back up on the radar lately. She started texting Pierce and me a few weeks ago. Just out of the blue. Years of crickets, then, 'Ta-da!' Pierce blocked her right away, but . . ."

"So she wants to see you," Ethan says, which you'd think would be a good guess.

"Nah. She said she did, but when I made a lunch date with her, she blew me off."

Ethan winces. "I'm so sorry."

I shrug. "I was a moron for texting her back. I guess I was just more curious than anything."

Ethan shakes his head, his eyes somber. "Of course you were. She's your mom."

I purse my lips. "Moms can be highly overrated."

He nods. "Dads, too."

"Yeah. Sorry yours sucks."

Ethan drops his chin and laughs.

"But you've got a great mother," I venture. "I mean, she's hauling you around town with your concussion, so I'm assuming she's a stand-up kinda gal?"

"Yeah, she gets bonus points for that," Ethan says, still grinning.

"And I definitely hit the jackpot with my dad, right?"

Ethan nods. "For sure. And now you've got *my* dad under control, so good job with that."

I laugh, but then the knot settles back into my stomach.

"My dad really is incredible," I say softly, my smile dissolving. "Sometimes I think I'd rather die than watch him suffer." I spend a silent moment contemplating that sentiment, then nod. "Yeah. I think I'd rather die than that."

Ethan is shaking his head, trying to lock eyes with me.

"No," he says. "You can't think like that."

I manage a weak smile. "Don't worry. I'm not gonna jump off a cliff or anything, but—"

"But nothing," Ethan says. "You've got too much to live for to talk like that."

Another patient gets called from the waiting room. This one is in a wheelchair.

Ethan moves closer. "Let's play a new game," he says. "Things we'd rather do than die."

I look at him evenly.

"I mean it," he says. "That's how everybody should be thinking: What would I rather do than die? Any of us could die at any minute, right?"

I shrug, and he grows more animated: "I mean, we could've died the other night in that gym, right? The thief could've shot us. I felt close to death."

Yeah. Me, too.

"So your dad's situation?" Ethan continues. "It's horrible. It's awful. It's so, so sad. But when it comes right down to it . . ."

"Yeah?"

"His situation is everybody's situation. He just has some advance notice, which, I dunno, might be some kind of blessing in disguise. But any one of us could be dead by tomorrow."

"Thanks for cheering me up."

Ethan smiles his lopsided grin.

"We should all be thinking of what we'd rather do than die," he says, "because any of us can die at any minute."

"Have you considered turning your sentiment into a country music song?" I quip. "Or maybe a bumper sticker?"

I glance at him for a sensitivity check. I default to humor when things turn heavy (thanks for the practice, Birth Mom) but the last thing I want is for Ethan to think I'm making fun of him.

He tosses me a smile (whew) but then turns somber again. "Remember, Jade: Your dad's life isn't your life. Just like my dad's life isn't my life." His eyes fall. "I have to remind myself of that sometimes."

Now, I'm the one trying to hold his gaze.

"Do you need me to rough him up some more?" I ask faux-solemnly. There I go, scurrying back to my comfort zone. But it's okay. Ethan gets me. Another grin spreads across his face.

"I'll put my money on you any day," he says. "Hey, are you coming to the game tomorrow night? It's at home."

I lower my head and splay my fingers loosely over my mouth. "I think I'll do the football fans a solid and stay home."

"Come!" Ethan prods. "Come watch me play. Come kick my dad's sorry ass. Please?"

I laugh into my fingertips, then say, "Another cuss word! You, Ethan Garrett, are full of surprises."

And there's that lopsided grin again. "You have no idea, Jade Fulton. You have no idea."

● ● ● ● ●

"You are. You're smiling."

"I told you, I'm not smiling," I tell Dad as I drive home from the doctor's appointment. Yes, it was incredible reconnecting with Ethan again—I'm thinking a long-term friendship might actually be a possibility, if we put our cringe-worthy moments behind us—but I definitely am *not* smiling.

I clear my throat and force a no-nonsense expression on my face. "Now, tell me again what the doctor said?"

Dad gives his feel-good version of the doctor's visit ("excellent vitals," "since I started out so healthy," "positive attitude," yada, yada, yada.)

"Hey, Dad?" I ask when he wraps up his I'm-in-perfect-health-other-than-this-pesky-brain-cancer synopsis.

"Yeah, honey?"

"What made you fall in love with Lena?"

He gives me a double-take from the passenger seat. "What makes you ask that?"

"Just wondering."

"O-*kay*," he says. "Hmm. Well, you may have noticed she's drop-dead beautiful."

"Whatever," I say playfully.

"You asked."

I smile and merge onto the interstate. "I was expecting a deeper answer than that."

"Okay, deep, huh? Well, your mother is kind and caring and hardworking and responsible."

Your mother. He's still trying to make that happen.

I set the cruise control after easing into the traffic, considering whether to say what's in my head. Finally, I do: "Dad, does it bother you that I don't call Lena mom?" I ask, casting him a wary glance.

"No," he says genially. "It's just . . . I want to make sure you know she'll always be here for you."

My stomach tenses. *She'll always be here for you.* Whoa. I've been concentrating so much on Dad's cancer that I haven't given much thought to what comes next. And we both know what comes next. Dad will be gone, and I'll be . . . orphaned.

The thought catches in my throat.

I know it sounds overly dramatic. I'll still have Grandma, and I'll still technically be a part of a family. Plus, hey, I'm already an adult, right? But with Dad gone, what role will Lena have in my life?

My mother.

That's what Dad is trying to lay the groundwork for, just like he laid the groundwork for his career with all those years of training.

My brain turns blurry as I ponder the implications. Lena minus Dad. Why would she still want me around? Yes, she loves me, but she knows I've always held her at arm's length. Who would want to deal with that unless they had to?

I mean, sure, I'll be at community college next fall, but even if I end up going away eventually, there are holidays, and spring breaks, and summer vacations, and . . .

I swallow hard to dislodge the lump in my throat.

"Jade," Dad says gently, seeming to read my mind, "Lena

is your mother, in every sense of the word except biologically. She's done everything for you. Everything."

I bite my lip hard to keep my eyes from misting. Is he insinuating that I've been a brat all these years, insufficiently grateful for all of her sacrifices? Well, of course I have been. I never thought of it that way. I was always too busy viewing our relationship from my perspective: Behold this non-related woman who isn't my mom and who has killed all chances of my real mom coming back into the picture. A non-related woman who is my baby sister's mom and therefore even less connected to me in comparison. A non-related woman who will be less related than ever before once my dad is gone.

My mind drifts to the unanswered texts on my phone. My mom—my *real* mom—has contacted me a dozen or so times since she blew off our lunch date, and I've taken great pleasure in blowing her off. Now, I'm wondering if I should give her one more chance. One more chance to . . . what? I don't even know what she wants. Her breezy, just-saying-hi texts offer no clues whatsoever to her agenda. Does she truly want to reconnect with me? Maybe our broken lunch date really was unavoidable—you know, a once-off. I mean, things do come up. Or maybe she knows Dad has cancer; that could explain the timing of this blast from the past. That article about Dad selling his practice was in the newspaper. But Mom doesn't live in the area . . . I don't think. When we were going to meet, she picked Columbia, ninety miles from here, but I have no idea if she lives there or not. Or maybe Grandma Stella told her about Dad? I don't know if they stay in touch; I hardly ever see Mom's relatives, and they have enough of their own brand of crazy going on to drown out any conversation about Mom. And if Mom does know about Dad's cancer, well, what does that mean? Maybe she wants me back in her life. Maybe I'll have a home after all.

"Hey, Jade," Dad says, and I jump a little, startled. "I've been meaning to ask you: Have you started your college application essay yet? Those are really important, you know, especially for the colleges you're interested in."

"Right," I say absently, then murmur something noncommittal.

I can put off this conversation for a few more weeks. I don't want Dad trying to talk me out of my new plan.

No need for that discussion now.

● ● ● ● ●

ETHAN

I lean forward from the passenger seat and turn the radio volume higher as Mom starts the car. No offense to her, but concussions and chatty conversation aren't the best combination.

"Well," Mom says, turning the volume back down as she exits the neurologist's parking lot (sigh), "I for one am glad the doctor won't let you play tomorrow night."

I resist the urge to roll my eyes.

In the first place (yeah, here I go with Jade's places again) I guess a chatty conversation is in the cards after all. And in the second place, why does Mom assume she's the "one" who won't mind that I'll be benched tomorrow night?

Because she is the one, that's why. The one and only. Everybody else in my life will go ballistic. Coach Davis said he understood when I called him a few minutes earlier, but he'll no doubt make a big show of kicking chairs around in the locker room before the game tomorrow night. My teammates will be grumbling, too, pounding me for not being able to handle a little whack to the head, and during a practice, no less. And my dad? I can only imagine how understated his reaction will be.

Whatever. Coach Davis can kick all the chairs he wants; I'm no longer particularly inclined to risk my health for a game.

"That Jade girl seems real sweet," Mom says as she drives. It strikes me as odd that today in the waiting room was the first time Mom met her. We've been in school together for years, and Jade's in all the Honors Day ceremonies. It's crazy how long we've been living in parallel universes.

"Yeah, she's great," I say.

"Now, what is she again?"

I narrow my eyes and study Mom's profile as she tools down the street. I'm ashamed to say I already know what she means, but I can't help wanting to make her squirm.

Mom's a good person—truly, she is—and I've never heard her utter a racist remark, at least not a blatant one. But she was raised in Tolliver and, well, sometimes it shows.

"She's a human being," I respond.

Mom tosses me a baffled glance. "I know that. I was just wondering where her people are from."

I'm silent long enough for Mom to contemplate what she's said.

"Ethan!" Mom scolds, taking her eyes off the road long enough to glare at me. "I have never, ever judged a person based on skin color!"

"Then why are you asking me about Jade's?" I mutter, sinking deeper into my seat and closing my eyes.

"I wasn't asking about her skin color! I was asking about her, you know, her background. Just out of curiosity."

"You've never asked where Brianne's 'people' are from," I mutter, squeezing my eyes tighter as a fresh wave of pain sloshes against my eyeballs.

"Well, I know where her people are from. And speaking of Brianne, Ethan, what's going on with you two?"

I open my eyes to slits and peek at Mom suspiciously. She and my girlfriend talk way too much for my taste.

"What do you mean?" I ask.

"Well," Mom's fingers flutter against the steering wheel. "She says you may have heard some rumors that upset you."

Okay, this time I'm not bothering with subtlety as I roll my eyes. "She planted those rumors to make me jealous," I clarify, surprising even myself with my candor. I've been defending Brianne for so long—Jade's not the first person to throw shade on her—that up until now, it's just been a reflex to give her the benefit of the doubt. And it seemed like a good idea at the time. I mean, isn't that what loving people do? Defend each other? Overlook each other's flaws? I have no role models for healthy relationships, so my strategy the past couple of years has been to zig if I thought my dad would zag, and vice versa. Being loyal to Brianne is the opposite of what my dad would do, right? I don't know. Maybe the only person I've been fooling is myself.

"Brianne would never try to make you jealous!" Mom says, and I stifle my chortle because, truly, I don't think even she believes that. This isn't the first time, not by a long shot, that Brianne has pulled this trick out of her bag.

"I told Brianne I thought we should take a break," I tell Mom, again, surprising myself with my honesty. Maybe the concussion has made me loopy.

Mom gasps. "Ethan! You love Brianne! And she loves you! You can't let some silly high school gossip come between you!"

I'm gazing at Mom's profile again, not really staring at her so much as resting my eyes on her. It's kind of crazy that Mom is Brianne's biggest cheerleader. How insecure does she have to be to prefer a crappy relationship to no relationship? How insecure does she think I am? I know, I know. She just wants me to be happy. And she thinks Brianne makes me happy. I used to think that, too.

"It's not good for Brianne and me to be so serious so

young," I say sensibly. "Especially with college starting soon. No telling where we'll both end up."

Mom casts me a frantic glance. "You'll end up together! That's what you've always said."

"That's what Brianne's always said. But it's fine, Mom. We're still together. Whatever. She wore me down."

I sound more bitter than I intended.

"Wore you down?" Mom repeats, more fretful than ever. Wow. Mom's more invested in this relationship than I am.

"Ethan," she asks me warily, taking a right into our neighborhood, "does this have anything to do with that girl I just met? Is that what this is about?"

I sigh heavily. Yeah, Mom and Brianne talk way too much. And now I'm starting to get the whole picture. Not only is Mom pro-Brianne—the blonde cheerleader whose "people" come from all the right places—but she's anti-Jade, the girl she's definitely not judging based on the color of her skin. Right.

"Because, honey," Mom continues, "I don't know what happened that night in the gym, but you've been acting so—"

"Jade's a friend," I snap. "Actually, I invited her to come to church with me some time. I hope she takes me up on it."

Long pause.

"Well," Mom says, working her lip, "that was real nice. And she'd feel right at home. I've heard a lot of black people go to your church."

I toss my head back, exasperated. "Why not say a lot of white people go to my church?"

Mom casts me a confused glance. "Why would I say that?"

"Jade's half-white. If she's gonna get a default label, why not white? Would that make you feel better?"

"See?" Mom says. "That's what I was talking about when I asked where her people are from. You bit my head off, and now you're the one bringing it up!"

Wow. This conversation is seriously warped. But the fascinating topic of Jade's gene pool will have to wait, because Mom is nearing our driveway.

"Great," I mutter under my breath as I catch sight of Dad and Grandma Garrett on the front porch. Just what I need.

"What?" Mom asks.

"Why is Dad here?" I ask, jerking my head in his direction. Ow. No more head jerks for a while.

"Well, honey, naturally, he was concerned about you—"

"Mom, all I want to do is crash," I say as she eases into the driveway.

"Of course! We'll just have some supper, and then—"

"I don't want supper! And why do you still cook for Dad? Don't you get tired of being a doormat?"

Stone silence. I rub my eyes as my head throbs.

"I'm sorry, Mom," I say.

She turns off the engine but continues staring straight ahead, her expression hurt, yet steely. "A boy needs his father, Ethan," she finally says in a whisper. "Everything I do, I do for you."

Sigh.

I reach out to touch her, but she jerks away.

"Mom . . ."

She holds up a palm to cut me off, still refusing to look at me.

"Mom," I say again.

Another long moment passes.

"Let's just have a nice supper," she says crisply.

Mom gets out of the car and I follow, hating myself for hurting her.

"There's our hee-ro!" Dad hollers from the porch swing.

"Hi, Grandma," I say as I walk up the steps and approach them, ignoring my bleary-eyed father.

"Hey, baby," Grandma Garrett coos, rising unsteadily from the swing to embrace me. She presses her cool palms against my cheeks and kisses me. "Heard you got a concussion."

I nod.

"If he can't take down a hundred-pound thief, you honestly think he's gonna shake off a little bump on the head?" Dad says, staring at me from the swing. "I think his mama better put him to bed and bring him some soup while his teammates work their asses off at the game tomorrow."

"Oh, hush!" Grandma scolds him, still pressing her palms against my face. "Don't you listen to him, baby."

"Come inside," Mom hisses at Dad, and he follows her through the door, swaying precariously with each step.

"Sit, baby, sit," Grandma says, getting back in the swing

and patting the seat beside her. "Is your head hurtin'? You need some aspirin?"

"I'm fine," I say, joining her on the swing.

"Don't you listen to your daddy," she says. "You know he just likes to tease."

I turn toward Grandma, her hair a stiff, silver helmet. "Has he always been like this?" I ask her, genuinely curious. I mean, I know Dad's been a jerk my whole life, but at some point, he was just an innocent kid, right?

"Ethan, your daddy's a good man," Grandma Garrett says, her eyes oversized behind glasses with thick lenses. "But he's had it rough. Your granddaddy—God rest his soul—he was real hard on him. Your daddy and your Uncle Byron, too."

"I know," I say. "And I hate that. But he makes his own choices now. Do you ever talk to Dad about his drinking?"

"All the time!" she responds, pumping a frail fist with each word. "Your mama does, too. We both keep after him. Maybe one of these days, it'll take."

The swing creaks lazily.

"In the meantime, baby," Grandma tells me, patting my leg, "all we can do is pray."

Right.

I guess I'll just keep praying.

EIGHTEEN

JADE

"You're serious."

I sigh heavily as I take a book from my locker. "Please don't make a big deal of this, Gia. It's just a stupid football game. If you don't want to come with me, don't come."

Gia gazes at me evenly. "Will a bottle of rum be involved?"

I wrinkle my nose at her, then slam my locker door shut as we walk toward our second-period class.

"Jade, I'm trying to follow you," Gia says, and it takes a microsecond for me to realize she's speaking figuratively, even though she is literally following me. "You want to go to the game tonight because you had so much fun last week?"

After we enter our classroom and settle into our seats, I lean forward and speak into her ear. "Look, I know I made a fool out of myself last week. Maybe that's why I want to go: to prove to people I can sit through a football game without going ape-shit. I just thought it would be something to do. But if you can't make it, that's cool."

Our classmate, Victor, walks by casually and gives Gia a fist bump.

Gia turns around and gives me an apologetic smile. "The thing is, I kinda have other plans tonight."

Oh. Wait, what?

"You've got plans?"

Gia stiffens. "Imagine that."

"No, no, I didn't mean it like that. I just meant . . . you have plans?"

It's ridiculous how deflated I suddenly feel. Aren't I the one who decided Gia and I should snap the BFF tether, particularly since we'll be going in different directions in the fall? (No application essays needed for Tolliver Community College.)

"I'm going to a party," Gia says.

Something about my expression makes her turn over-conciliatory: "Look, it's no big deal," she says. I cringe, wondering how pathetic I must look right now.

"It's not even a party, really," Gia continues. "More like a get-together. You know what? You should come."

I feel my face grow hot.

"You should," Gia said. "Come. I'll pick you up at, like, nine? Totally casual, totally cool. Just some people getting together at Rachel's."

So Gia rated an invite, but not me?

"It's not like anybody's invited or anything," Gia says, apparently reading my pathetic mind. "It's just a pass-the-word kind of deal. So I'm passing the word. I was going to anyway. And I'm sure Rachel will mention it in calculus."

Mr. Finch claps his hands at the front of the room and says, "Okay, let's turn to page forty-seven in *Beowulf*."

Gia turns toward me one last time. "Tonight at nine," she whispers. "I'll pick you up."

God.

Now Gia's tossing me crumbs, too.

● ● ● ● ●

ETHAN

"So you're coming tonight?"

Okay, that sounded desperate.

But no big deal, right? I'm passing Jade in the hall as I head for my sixth-period class, and it's just natural to make conversation. All I did was ask her one more time if she's coming to tonight's game.

"One more time" being the definitive words. I already asked her in the doctor's office yesterday. But who's counting.

"You're okay to play?" she asks me, shifting the weight of her backpack as our classmates stream by.

"I'll actually be benched," I say. "Doctor's orders. But you can come watch me sit on a bench."

My smile's too big. I probably look like a hyena.

But Jade smiles back.

"I actually just got invited to a party," she says. "Well, not really a party, just some people getting together at

Rachel Cameron's house. But maybe I can make it to next week's game?"

I stuff my hands in the pockets of my jeans. "Sure, sure. Oh, darn. Next week's an away game. Of course, you're still welcome."

Geez! What am I, the chairman of the hospitality committee?

"Yeah, maybe," Jade says, glancing anxiously down the hall.

I wince. "I'm making you late for your class."

"No, no . . ."

"I'll let you go," I say, then feel ridiculous all over again. I'm sure Jade appreciates my permission.

"Hey, are you feeling better?" she asks me. "I mean, your head?"

"Yeah, yeah. It's nothing."

She holds my gaze. "It's not nothing."

My neck grows warm.

"Want me to rough up the guy who gave you a concussion?" Jade asks.

We grin.

"That would be epic," I say.

She pushes a curly lock behind her ear, then glances down the hall again. "I've really gotta go."

"Sure, sure. Me too. I just . . . I hope you have fun at Rachel's tonight."

"Thanks. I hope you have fun warming the bench." She

wrinkles her nose, then flutters her fingertips and folds into the hall traffic.

I'm still watching her as she makes her way down the hall.

Get a grip, Ethan. Quit staring.

I hoist my backpack higher and rush off to class.

NINETEEN

JADE

I'm sitting in front of my mirror brushing on mascara as I
wait for Gia to pick me up. I guess if I'm gonna be her pity
date, I can at least look halfway presentable.

Someone knocks on my door.

"Syd?" I ask.

"It's Lena," a voice calls back. I guess she hasn't gotten
the "call me Mom" memo.

"Come on in," I say.

Lena walks in, squeezing her arms together in an oversized sweatshirt, and closes the door behind her.

"Dress warm tonight," she says, sitting on the edge of
my bed. "Cold snap."

"Mmm."

"So, you're going out with Gia?"

"Mmm-hmm." I continue stroking on my mascara.

"Well, be careful."

I peer at her cryptically through my mirror.

"O-kay."

"I mean . . . really careful, Jade."

Uh-oh. Surely Pierce didn't mention my drunkfest?

"I'll be careful," I murmur, avoiding eye contact.

"No drinking, please?"

My heart sinks. I turn to face her. "Pierce told you?"

She surprises me by laughing. "Well, if he hadn't, you'd have just done an excellent job of busting yourself."

My head swirls with emotion. I'm furious at Pierce for ratting me out, irritated with Lena for initiating a Very Important Conversation, and ashamed of myself for setting all this in motion.

"Lena, please tell me Dad doesn't know."

She considers my words, then arches a brow. "I know."

She holds my gaze long enough to convey her message: She matters, too.

I lay down my mascara wand and fumble with my fingers. "I just meant . . . I'd hate for Dad to have one more thing to worry about."

Lena pauses, then folds her hands in her lap. "I don't keep secrets from your dad," she says. "But I'll let this one slide if you promise me it won't happen again."

"It totally won't," I assure her. "And I'm really sorry, Lena. I think I still had a little post-traumatic insanity going on." I'm betting I can milk a bit more sympathy from the robbery.

The ceiling fan whirs overhead as I wait to determine whether this was a safe bet.

"I know you've got a lot going on," Lena finally says, and another alarm bell flashes in my mind. She doesn't know about Mom, does she? I haven't breathed a word to anyone except Ethan. But now that Pierce has declared himself the town crier . . .

Lena continues, "We've all got a lot going on."

"Mmm," I say noncommittally, not wanting to make another unforced error.

"Sydney's taking Dad's diagnosis harder than she's letting on," Lena says, and my muscles relax a tad. At least the conversation about Mom isn't on the table. For now, anyway.

"Jade, Sydney looks up to you so much," Lena continues. "It means a lot that I can count on you to be a good role model."

Okay, this is the point in conversations with Lena when my attitude generally turns pissy. (Well, pissier, I guess.) Here we were talking about me (not that I was really loving that whole vibe) when she makes it clear that it's Sydney, not me, she's really concerned about. Or at least that's how it comes across.

"Sydney might not be 'letting on' to *you* about how she feels," I say frostily with air quotes, "but she 'lets on' to me all the time. You don't have to tell me to be a good big sister. That's covered."

Lena's back stiffens. "You don't get to tell me what I get to tell you, young lady. Particularly considering the reason for this conversation."

Tension hangs in the air.

I glance away. "Fine," I murmur.

I'm not used to Lena calling me out. She's generally the

one to make nice, even when I'm acting pretty impossible. But isn't it a step-kid's prerogative to act impossible? Isn't that the one advantage in that relationship?

But Lena's clearly not having it now. She's right, everyone's been through a lot lately, including her. I feel guilty that I never give that much thought.

"I'm sorry," I tell her in a small voice. "I didn't mean to sound bratty. I just wanted you to know that . . . that I agree with you. I want to be a good role model for Sydney. That's really important to me. I feel terrible about how I acted the other night."

Lena's face softens, and she smiles. "That's my girl," she whispers.

I smile, too. "I'll stop by Syd's bedroom and say goodnight before I leave."

"Can't," Lena says. "I just dropped her off at Alicia's."

My eyes widen. "Alicia's?"

Lena nods. "Yeah. For a sleepover."

My stomach clenches. "Lena, that's not a good idea. Alicia and her friends have been bullying Sydney."

Lena leans closer. "Bullying her?"

I nod. "She was in tears after last weekend's sleepover. They were going around in a circle naming their best friends, and nobody named Sydney. That kind of stuff. She shouldn't be there. I told her she needed to blow those girls off. I thought she'd listened."

"Maybe you're just being overly sensitive."

"Lena, they were even making remarks about her appearance. Racist stuff."

"Racist?" Lena says. "Those girls have never cared about her race."

"Lena, you don't get it," I say, rising from my chair. "You don't get the kind of stuff we have to deal with."

"I don't get it?" she challenges, pointing at her chest.

I open my mouth to respond but hear a horn honk from the driveway.

I sigh. "Gia's here. But Lena, seriously, I don't think Sydney should—"

Lena rises from my bed, waving her arm to silence me. "Go have fun with Gia," she tells me. "*Safe* fun. And don't worry about Sydney. She knows she can call me any time."

"I know, but she won't want you to—"

Lena puts her hands gently on my shoulders. "Jade: There's some stuff Sydney's gonna have to deal with on her own, just like you and I have had to."

She searches my eyes and repeats the last part of her sentence: "You *and* I."

My eyebrows weave together. "I don't want her to be hurt."

Lena nods. "I don't either. But she's the one who had to deal with how they acted last weekend, and she's the one who chose to go back."

Again, she pauses to make sure her words sink in, and I finally nod.

"She'll call if she needs me," Lena says. "Now, go have fun."

I hesitate a moment longer, then grab my purse. Lena waves as I rush out the door. I fold my bare arms once I'm outside. It's cooler than I anticipated. Shoulda listened to Lena. I contemplate going back in for a jacket, then . . .

Who's in my driveway? I peer to get a better look at the unfamiliar car and see Gia waving me over from the passenger seat.

I approach the car, still trying to make out the driver.

"Hop in," Gia says.

As I climb in the back seat, she says, "You know Victor, right?"

He nods in my direction, then begins backing out.

I'm still trying to orient myself: Why am I in Victor's car? Why is Gia in Victor's car?

Oh no.

This is a *date*. Victor and Gia's date. Why haven't I noticed all their flirting in the last few days? As I squeeze my eyes together, I almost choke on the irony. I've been trying to gently cut Gia loose for the past two weeks, and darned if she's not one step ahead of me. What an idiot I am. Here I was, worrying if she could somehow, some way, make her way alone in the world without being glued to my hip. How would I break it to her that we're not going to college together? How could I branch out and shed my reputation as part of a unit without crushing her spirit?

No worries. I've been the one holding her back. She's

been busying herself forging a relationship with the cute, skinny, Goth-lite musician in our English Lit class, and damned if she doesn't have some pathetic best friend cramping her style by nagging her to tag along to football games.

And why? Because for all my stupid protestations, I can't stop thinking about a guy with whom I have nothing in common.

What a loser I am.

Nothing like being a third wheel to put your ego in check.

"How's it going, Jade," Victor says gamely.

"Good," I say, digging my nails into my palms. "How've you been doing?"

Christ. I sound like a church usher.

"Good, good," Victor says. "Sorry to hear about your dad."

Well, at least we got that out of the way.

I unsnap my seat belt and lean up. "Look," I say, "I am clearly horning in on your plans. Sorry for the inconvenience, but if you could just turn around and take me back home?"

Victor and Gia start a chorus of cooing protests: "No, no."

"Please," I say, trying to sound firm and non-pathetic. "I'd really rather go home."

"Zip it, Jade," Gia says without turning around. "You're coming."

I can't tell if she sounds protective or annoyed. I loathe both alternatives.

I reconnect my seat belt and slouch in my seat, resigned to being stuck. Victor is playing Elliott Smith on his iPod, his gloomy, brooding poetry and squeaky acoustic guitar filling the car. At one point, Gia's fingers dangle close to Victor's, and Victor's hand gently entwines them. They share glances occasionally—Victor's watery, blue eyes locking with Gia's smoky, dark ones—and I feel like I'm watching one of those mating episodes on *National Geographic*. Maybe their turbo-charged chemistry will make the car spontaneously combust, at which point I will dissolve into ashes and spare the world my loserdom once and for all.

I'm still dwelling on how I missed the signals that these two were seriously hot for each other. It seems so obvious, now that sparks are practically flying from their fingertips. I just figured that both Gia and I were too cool and mature for any of the morons in school ('What's that word? Superior?') and that we'd find our soul mates in college, or maybe even afterward, when we were busy making our oversized marks on the world.

And if either of us diverged from the path, I figured it would definitely be me. As childish as it makes me feel, it definitely rankles that Gia has veered off-message. We're supposed to be above it all: above holding hands and sharing private glances with a Goth-lite musician in the front seat of a cluttered, musty-smelling, Elliott Smith-infused car on the way to a lame high-school party.

With a pathetic friend sitting in the cluttered, musty-smelling back seat. Can the earth just swallow me whole already?

Victor drives a few more blocks, then pulls into a driveway scattered with half-a-dozen or so cars. I try to calculate how far I am from home: Three miles? Four? I'm wearing heels (stupid heels!) so walking home isn't practical. God. I'm really stuck.

"C'mon," Gia prods as she opens her car door, seeming to read my mind.

"I really wish you'd let Victor just run me home."

"Come *on*." Again with the annoyed/protective tone. I sullenly follow her and Victor to the door, where the sound of rap music spills onto the front porch.

Gia opens the door and Rachel answers with a broad smile. "GI-Joe!" she squeals, hugging Gia around the neck, and I feel yet another pang of ridiculous jealousy. Other people don't give Gia nicknames! Have I really been so distracted by my dad's health the past few weeks that I haven't noticed my BFF actually having a life?

"Hey, Victor," Rachel says as her arms fall back to her side. "Oh, and Jade!"

Yes, I'm the afterthought, the tagalong, the nobody-invited-you-but-what-the-hell-come-on-in guest. I offer the subtlest of waves, the kind you give when somebody waves in your direction from across a room and you're not sure if he's waving at you, but you figure you better wave back just in case.

"Victor, did you bring your guitar?" Rachel asks.

"It's in the trunk," he says.

"Well, get it!"

Victor nods and heads back for the car.

This is my chance.

"Gia, I want to go home," I hiss into her ear.

"Yeah, well, in the immortal words of Mick Jagger, you can't always get what you want," she says, peering deeper into Rachel's greatroom.

"I didn't know you were on a date!"

"Would you chill already?"

"Gia, I'm serious! How long have you and Victor been seeing each other? And why am I the last to know? Not that finding out in the back seat of his car isn't totally un-awkward."

"Un-awkward isn't a word," she murmurs, still checking out the crowd.

"Jade!"

I glance at the guy who's just grabbed my arm from the side.

"Hi, Rob," I say, and I say it much less enthusiastically than it merits, considering I'm ridiculously relieved that somebody seems glad to see me.

"How's it goin'?" he asks me. "Can I get you a drink?"

"Um, sure, thanks. Diet Coke?"

He nods and heads toward the kitchen. Victor walks in with his guitar. As he leads Gia by the fingertips toward the greatroom, Gia turns around and gives me a thumbs-up with her free hand. As in, 'Good job, Jade! Good job being non-pathetic enough to attract someone else's attention long enough to finally give me a free moment with my new boyfriend.'

At least that's how I interpret it.

Rob comes back from the kitchen and hands me a Diet Coke. "Sure you don't want a beer?" he asks. "We have to have it cleared out by the time Rachel's parents get back at midnight, so, you know, you'd really be doing her a favor by drinking it."

"I'm good," I say. Rob puts his arm around my shoulder and leads me into the greatroom. Someone hands him a beer en route, and he takes a swig.

"I am seriously stoked you came tonight," he says. "Who would guess it: a Jade sighting at a party!"

I smile weakly as he sits on a sofa, patting the space beside him. I consider my options, then grudgingly take the seat. Rob's a nice-enough guy—a little buttoned-up for my taste, but definitely smarter than most of my classmates. Is it really that beneath me to share a conversation with a nice-enough guy from school? At this point, I don't have much of a choice.

"So," Rob says, acting like he's stretching his arm so he'll have an oh-by-the-way opportunity to drape it around my shoulder. The stiff sleeve of his Oxford shirt brushes the back of my neck. "What brings you out tonight?"

God, I hate small talk.

"Just hanging out," I say.

"What colleges are you applying to?" he asks, every strand of his tidy haircut in place. "I'm sure you can pick and choose wherever you want to go."

I drop my chin and smile. "Not really. My SATs are pretty good, but I've made a couple of B's in my math classes."

"Aww, a couple of B's," Rob says, making an exaggerated pouty face. Okay, that's annoying.

I clear my throat. "Anyway, I've decided to stay home next year, so I'll either go to Tolliver Community College or just work."

"Tolliver Community College!" Rob says, his mouth gaping. "I figured you'd be an Ivy Leaguer."

I stare at my Diet Coke. "Nah."

"Don't you want to go to medical school?" he asks.

"I dunno."

Rob's eyes suddenly widen. "Oh, your dad," he says. "I'd forgotten about that. Is that why you're staying home?"

My stomach clutches. What do I say? Oh, what the hell, why not the truth? I clamp my can tighter and say, "Yeah."

Rob's eyes fall and he gives a low whistle. "That's intense," he says, his voice kind. "Is your dad making you stay?"

My jaw tightens. "Of course not. He doesn't have a selfish bone in his body. Actually, he doesn't even know I'm staying. I'm waiting as long as possible to tell him so he won't have the option of trying to change my mind."

Rob's eyes flicker toward mine. "That's really something. Really admirable."

I squeeze my lips together and shake my head. "No, it's not. I just don't want to miss any time with him, you know?"

He nods solemnly. "Yeah. I do know. My grandma died recently. Alzheimer's. As awful as it was to see what she was going through, I'm so glad I had that time with her."

I smile, genuinely touched.

We sit there a couple of moments, his fingers still dangling over my shoulder.

Rob takes another drink of his beer with his free hand and asks, "Hey, did you hear about Mrs. Berry's meltdown earlier this week?"

I smile. "'A pen is not a toy!'" I quip in the ancient physics teacher's tremulous old-South accent.

"She made us come up with calculations to determine the amount of damage a pen can do when used as a missile," Rob says, an easy smile spreading across a face that, I'm slowly realizing, is somewhat cuter than I've ever given it credit for.

"Well, you don't need a physics degree to know it can put out an eye!" I say in Mrs. Berry's accent.

We laugh lightly.

"How old do you figure she is? A hundred?" Rob asks.

"I think her *shoes* are a hundred," I reply, and we laugh some more.

"So how did I get lucky enough to be in the same place

with you tonight?" Rob asks, polishing off his beer while subtly scooting closer to me.

I wrinkle my nose. "Truthfully?"

His eyes twinkle, and Rachel takes his empty can and hands him another beer. "Truthfully."

"I asked Gia if she wanted to go to the football game with me, and rather than let me down easy by telling me she had a date, she invited me along."

"Ahh," Rob says. "The ol' third wheel."

"Except that I didn't know it was a date until she showed up in my driveway with, well, you know . . . the aforementioned date. Which makes me somewhat less pathetic. Right?"

Rob squeezes me closer and says, "I'm just glad you're here."

And you know what? Suddenly, damned if I don't feel the same way.

● ● ● ● ●

". . . and then Jade bolted out of the room while I stood there holding the lizard by the tail!"

Everybody laughs at Gia's story, including me. As the evening has progressed, the scattered clumps of people at Rachel's party have morphed into a single group, Victor strumming his guitar softly on the floor while everyone else sits around, singing along to his tunes or sharing a story. A couple of hours have passed, and although several people seem pretty buzzed, nobody's acting rowdy or obnoxious. This is—dare I say—a sort of pleasant evening. Why have I never grasped that a get-together (or even, gasp, a party!) could be fun?

Could a non-gay boyfriend even be in my future? Yes, Rob's a little preppy, but I haven't totally hated hanging out with him. And he's clearly interested in me. Right? My instincts are failing me about virtually everything these days, so I can't be sure, but he's been glued to my side practically the whole evening. Do I feel much chemistry? Nah, but maybe chemistry builds over time. Of course, that's not how it happened with Ethan, but . . .

Forget Ethan, idiot!

Geez! Why can't I shake him out of my head?

And why am I thinking about guys, period? All these guys—Ethan, Rob, all of them—are moving on with their lives after graduation this spring. I'm the one staying home to take care of my dad. This is a hell of a time to consider unleashing my inner social butterfly.

But this moment, this evening: This is okay. This is actually kinda nice.

● ● ● ● ●

ETHAN

"Why Rachel's?"

I glance at Brianne from the driver's seat and shrug. "She just mentioned she was having a few people over and asked if we wanted to drop by after the game."

Which is basically true. Okay, maybe the invite didn't come directly from Rachel, but my version is close enough.

"Her friends are a bunch of Goths," Brianne says acidly.

"They're my friends, too," I say in a tight voice.

Her eyes stay glued on me, but I'm staring straight ahead as I drive.

"You're sure you're up to it?" she asks, her voice dripping with sarcasm. "I mean, you just spent two hours warming the bench. Aren't you exhausted?"

I press in my lips.

A tense moment passes, then Brianne leans over and kisses my cheek. I resist the urge to jerk my head away. "Aw, baby," she coos, "you know I'm teasing."

Yeah. I can't get enough of her teasing.

"I really am worried about you," she continues. "The doctor said you should be taking it easy."

"Look, if you don't want to go, I can drop you off."

Again, I feel her eyes boring into my face. "Of course I want to go," she says, her tone chilly again. "I want to be with you. Is the feeling mutual?" It's a challenge, not a question. But surely she knows she's pressing her luck. Her manipulations don't pack a punch anymore.

"Well?" she demands.

I glance at her testily. "Let's just go have a good time," I finally say. "We don't have to stay long."

She hesitates, then leans over the gear-shift console and burrows her face into my neck. "I always have a good time when I'm with you, baby."

I cringe as I recall how easily these techniques of hers used to work. Cold to hot, demanding to demure, bossy to flirty; whatever was needed to make sure she kept the upper hand. She said she was up for a new set of ground rules—no more games—but I guess old habits die hard. On the other hand, I don't even know how I feel anymore, so I can't blame her for being confused. Still, I wish Brianne had let me drop her off at home.

No such luck.

I pull into Rachel's leafy, well-manicured neighborhood and see cars lined along the curbs of her street. As I park behind one of them, I hear faint guitar strumming coming from inside and see a handful of people on the porch. I scan their faces, squinting to make out their features in the dark, then frown. No Jade. Maybe that's for the best. I'm accusing Brianne of playing games when I can't stop thinking about another girl? This is ridiculous. We'll just stop by, say hi, and call it a night.

We get out of the car, Brianne slipping my letter jacket over her cheerleading uniform, and walk up the driveway.

"Hi, guys," I call to the people on the porch. They glance up, look vaguely surprised, then wave.

"Ethan?" a girl in my anthropology class calls. "Is that you?"

"Yeah. Hey."

Brianne and I walk up the steps and join them, her hand squeezing mine. I'm still sensing a weird vibe in the air—okay, fine, this isn't my regular crowd—but I push past it. "You guys having a good time?" I ask, Brianne glued to my side.

"Uh, yeah," my classmate responds. "How about you? Did you guys win tonight?"

"Nah, not tonight."

"It doesn't help when a little bump on the head keeps the starting quarterback out of the game," Brianne says, wrinkling her nose at me. Ha ha.

The others chuckle.

"You'll get 'em next time," says my classmate, who clearly couldn't care less whether we "get 'em" or not. So football's not the be-all and end-all for some people, huh? Imagine that.

"Hey, there's a cooler in the garage if you two want something to drink," a skinny guy with shoulder-length hair tells us. Philip. I think his name is Philip. Or maybe Peter. *Yeah, these are my friends, too.*

"Perfect," Brianne says, pulling me back toward the steps.

As we head for the garage, she leans in and whispers through gritted teeth, "What are we doing here?"

I ignore the question and keep walking. "Want something to drink?" I ask, heading for the cooler.

"No," she hisses.

I reach into the cooler and pull out a Sprite, then head for the kitchen door. Brianne's still standing in the garage, hugging my letter jacket tighter against her arms.

"Coming?" I ask her.

She huffs dramatically and stays planted in her spot. Suit yourself.

It's as I walk through the door that I see Jade pulling a Diet Coke out of the refrigerator.

Our eyes lock.

"Hey, Jade," I say, my heart skipping a beat. "What's up?"

She looks startled for a second, then smiles. "Just hanging out," she responds, her caramel-colored shoulders smooth and silky under a green sundress. The sundress matches her eyes. "So the game's over?"

"Yep," I say. "We lost."

"Ah. Sorry. Well . . . see ya."

She starts walking toward the greatroom, where most of the crowd is gathered. Guitar music is still filtering through the air.

"Jade?"

She turns around to face me. "Yeah?"

"Um, are you working tomorrow?"

She nods. "One to six. Are you coming?"

"Yeah!"

I clear my throat and rub the back of my neck, embarrassed by my weirdly fast and eager reply.

"See you there," she says, then starts to leave again.

"Jade?"

She turns around to face me yet again.

"I'm just really glad to see you."

She gazes at me with an expression I can't read. Am I annoying her, crashing a party where I clearly don't belong?

Does she think I just show up anywhere I want and act like I own the place? Ironic, since I don't feel like I belong anywhere these days.

But whatever she's thinking, her eyes soften and she seems to hit a reset button. "How's your concussion?" she asks me.

"Oh, that was nothing. I'm—"

The door swings open, jolting me from my spot.

"Hi, Brianne," Jade says.

Brianne's eyes bore into Jade's. She says nothing.

"Brianne?" I prompt.

"I don't need another lesson in manners from you," she tells me, still glaring.

"Seems like you do."

She tosses me a venomous glance, then looks back at Jade. "You're right," she says. "Where are my manners? Hi, Jade."

Jade offers a tepid wave.

"Hey, Jade," Brianne continues, "there's something in Ethan's car I want to show you. Mind if we step outside a minute?"

What the hell?

"Brianne," I say, but she dangles her fingers at me dismissively.

"It's girl stuff," she tells me. "Please, Jade? Just for a minute?"

"Sure," Jade responds warily.

As she and Brianne walk toward the door, I try to follow

them, but Brianne puts her palm on my chest and pushes me back the length of her arm. "We don't need a babysitter."

I catch Jade's anxious eyes as she closes the door behind me.

What in the world?

TWENTY

JADE

As I follow Brianne to the driveway out front, I feel vaguely nervous, but mostly curious as hell. Is she gonna go all *Sopranos* on me and claw my eyes out? I have no idea what to—

"Here's the deal," Brianne says coolly, spinning on the toe of a white sneaker to face me with a single arched eyebrow. "Stay away from my boyfriend."

I'm stunned, yet slightly amused. "Um, you're the one who came to a party I've been at for the last two hours."

"Cut the shit," she snaps. "You're practically stalking us."

My jaw drops. "You mean by going to my school? Or the place where I work? Or a party I didn't know you were coming to?"

"Like hell you didn't know," she says icily.

"Brianne!"

We look toward Ethan's voice. He's followed us outside.

"Worried about your girl?" Brianne asks him in a shrill tone.

I shake my head slowly. "You have *got* to be kidding."

Ethan holds up his hands. "Everybody just chill," he

says, his voice deep and steady. "Brianne, you are way out of line. I've got something to say to both of—"

I hold up a palm. "I am *so* out of here."

I walk back into the kitchen and take a deep breath, exhaling slowly through puffed-out cheeks. Adrenaline is shooting through my ears, but I'll be damned if I give Brianne the satisfaction of knowing it.

I've actually had lots of practice at this. Those times I'd convince myself as a kid that my mom would show up at my birthday party, or my First Communion, or my Honors Day ceremony, or my Brownie troop's mother-daughter tea? I'd have the world's most chill poker face as I surreptitiously scanned every face walking through the door of whatever event I'd gotten all dressed up for. No one had a clue my heart was pounding wildly beneath my dress as I secretly wondered if I'd even be able to recognize my mom if she walked in the room. And if so, would I able to bring to life my fantasy of giving her the coolest of fist bumps upon her arrival, like, "duh, of course my mom's here, why wouldn't she be?" And when reality set in and it was clear she'd be a no-show, as always? I was all smiles as I choked down my cupcake or crust-free cucumber sandwich, the other girls chatting casually with their moms while Lena and I sat stiffly beside each other. It was my little secret that I'd cry myself to sleep that night.

Think you can knock me off my game, Brianne? Pffft. Amateur.

I take a couple more deep breaths, then rejoin the party and walk over to Rob. His face brightens when he sees me.

"Hey," I tell him conspiratorially, leaning close. "Remember what I told you about being a third wheel tonight?"

"Yeah?"

"Well . . . think you could give me a ride home?" I twirl a ringlet in my index finger.

That's right: I'm actually being bold. This is definitely a night of firsts.

"Sure," Rob says. "Now?"

I tilt my head to one side. "Just whenever you're ready."

He grins. "I'm ready now."

I smile, then call to Gia across the room that Rob is taking me home. She pushes past a look of confusion and gives me a weak little wave.

I lead Rob through the kitchen and out the door. As we walk past Ethan and Brianne, still seething on the driveway, I slip one hand into Rob's and squeeze his arm with the other.

Rob tosses Ethan and Brianne a friendly wave, blissfully ignorant of the drama that just unfolded.

He opens the passenger door for me, and as I settle into his car, I catch Ethan's eyes for just a nanosecond, his hands clasped together.

Yeah, sorry I didn't hang around for more of Brianne's badass routine, or for your self-righteous lecture. Later.

That's what I'm trying to convey.

But Ethan looks so sad that I wonder if my heart will crumble.

● ● ● ● ●

ETHAN

"Let's go."

Brianne plants a hand on her hip and glares at me as Rob and Jade peel out of Rachel's neighborhood. Rob and Jade! What in the world is up with that? Are any two people on earth less compatible than Rob and Jade?

"Go? I thought you wanted to come party with your 'friends,'" Brianne says, her words dripping with contempt.

"Yeah, that's before you turned into a stark-raving lunatic."

"Just so I'm clear," Brianne says through short, jagged breaths, "the reason we're leaving is because your gym buddy took off. I mean, the only reason we came was so you could see her, right?"

I frown. "Look, I'm leaving. Are you coming or not?"

Our tense standoff continues as several party-goers hover around, waiting for our next move. Great. I should get some kind of retainer for being the school's one-man entertainment act.

Brianne is still glowering at me, her chin jutting out and her cheerleader ponytail frizzing in the cool night air.

"I'm going whether you want to or not. Should I give you

money for an Uber?" I ask, at which point she shoots one last set of daggers from her eyes, then stomps to my car.

I follow her, retrieving my keys from my jeans pocket and trying to ignore the sea of eyes on my back.

Brianne gets in the passenger seat and slams the door shut. I pause and take a deep breath. This is it. I'm telling her we need to go our separate ways. The jealousy and snottiness was bad enough, but now an actual throw-down in some poor girl's front yard? I'm done.

I get in the driver's seat, muster enough restraint to avoid slamming the door myself, then put the key in the ignition and turn to Brianne.

"Look," I say.

But she turns away, raising her hand as a stop sign.

"Brianne, we need to talk."

She shakes her head, the ribbon in her ponytail bobbing.

My heart races as I steel myself for one final and definitive break-up conversation. No more gray area. No more ground rules that she has no intention of following. No more games. I'm prepared for her bag of tricks: her fury, or her indignation, or her baby talk, or her neck nuzzling, or whatever she thinks might keep her in control. I'm not falling for it this time.

"This clearly isn't working," I say.

She says nothing. She's not screaming, or arguing, or cajoling, or . . . anything. She's just sitting there, still turned toward the window with her pinkie dangling by her bottom lip.

"You know it as well as I do," I continue, at which point I see her shoulders shake. It's subtle at first, but then they shake so hard, they're practically heaving. Then I realize she's crying.

"C'mon, Bree," I say, running my fingers through my hair.

She's still sniffling, so I reach for my glove compartment and retrieve a packet of tissues.

"Here."

She takes the packet without looking at me, still sniffling.

"Please don't cry," I say quietly.

But she's still crying. So I keep sitting there, with multiple sets of eyes still glued to us. Geez.

She cries some more, then turns to me, her cheeks blotchy and her eyes red. "Will you please take me home?"

I sigh. "Brianne, I—"

"Please. Please just take me home?"

My eyebrows weave together and I run my fingers through my hair again. "Of course."

I start the ignition and ease down the street, glancing at the crowd in the front yard from my rear-view mirror. Show's over, folks.

"I get that you don't love me anymore," Brianne finally says, her voice barely audible. "What I don't get is why you wanted to humiliate me."

I glance at her, then turn my attention back to the road. "Humiliate you?"

"It's obvious the only reason we came was because Jade was there," she says.

"That is not true," I lie.

"So you not only wanted to break up with me, but you wanted to rub it in my face?"

No! She is not pinning this on me! I didn't ask her to go ballistic. She's the one who decided to make a fool of herself and insult Jade in the process. She's the one who humiliated us, not me.

"This is on you, Brianne," I say simply, staring straight ahead. "The way you acted? That was horrible. Horrible and embarrassing and—"

"I get that now," she says, dabbing her nose with a tissue. "I get that I'm an embarrassment to you. It took a while, but—"

"I wasn't embarrassed until you jumped on Jade like some kind of a redneck thug," I say, my voice louder than I intended. "Didn't see that one coming."

She laughs ruefully, roughly wiping tears from her cheeks. "Yeah. I couldn't quite put my finger on it, but that's what I am to you: a redneck. I wasn't until Jade came along, but once you compared and contrasted, you—"

"That is *so* not fair," I say, my heart racing harder than ever. "I've never called you names. At least not until you practically threatened to beat some girl's ass at a party.

Classy." Now, my voice is the one dripping with contempt. I don't like the way this is going.

"'Some girl,'" Brianne repeats, her voice now a dull monotone. "Some classy girl. Can't compete with that."

"You are totally putting words in my mouth!"

"Except that I'm not." She's looking at me now. "I couldn't figure out what was up until you spelled it out for me. I'm a trashy redneck. Jade's classy. I finally get it."

I stop at a red light and look at her. "Brianne, you cannot pin this on me," I repeat. "The least you can do is own the way you acted."

She nods, her expression somber. "I was thinking the same thing about you."

I swallow hard and grip the steering wheel tighter.

"Bet Jade's mom has never shown up at a beauty pageant drunk," Brianne says, her voice eerily flat. "Bet Jade's family has never had their utilities cut off."

I shake my head in astonishment, then fling an arm in the air. "What are you talking about? You know I've never judged you! How could I? My family's just like yours!"

She nods, her chin quivering, then starts weeping again. "I think that's the problem," she says through her tears, burying her face in a tissue. "Sorry I'm a redneck, Ethan. But maybe it takes one to know one. Oh, but Jesus is your BFF, so it's all good, right?"

A tornado of emotion swirls through my brain as I continue driving.

Why do Brianne's accusations suddenly sound a lot

like Jade's? *Superior. Self-righteous. Holier than thou.* It makes no sense. Brianne feels just as strongly about her Christianity as I do. We go to church together all the time! And she actually manages to act halfway Christian when she's not throwing down on some girl she hardly even knows.

The truth, of course, is that I hardly know Jade either. Sure, we kind of bared our souls that night in the gym (near-death experiences tend to have that effect), but Brianne's right: Jade and I really don't have anything in common. She's way out of my league—deep, ambitious, and naturally smart, unlike me, who has to cram for hours before every test. Jade can jump into a conversation with a teacher about almost any subject at all, peeling off onto a thousand different tangents and sounding like she's been studying the topic all her life. Me? I can regurgitate the facts I memorize in books.

So, yeah. Jade's out of my league. But that doesn't mean I look down on Brianne . . . does it?

I don't know. All I know, as I pull into her driveway, is that I really hate to see her cry.

I turn off the ignition and tap my fingers together.

"I'm really sorry," I say.

I say it because I am. I hate that what happened tonight somehow got turned around on me, but as I see Brianne pressing her face into a tissue, all I want to do is comfort her.

Which is why I lean over and fold her into my arms.

Yes, I'm still conflicted, but it feels good to reconnect with her. It feels good to make her happy again.

"It'll be okay," I murmur into her ear. "We'll be okay."

• • • • •

JADE

"Oh, sorry. What?"

Rob turns down the radio. "I asked if it's too chilly for you."

"No, no. I'm fine, thanks."

I bite a nail, tossing out an occasional direction, as Rob drives.

Rob taps his steering wheel idly, then says, "So, Victor and Gia, huh? They seem like a real couple all of a sudden."

"Yeah. They're cute together."

Rob shrugs. "Gia's a little ditzy. But if Victor's into that sort of thing . . ."

I bristle. "Ditzy?"

"Yeah, just kind of in her own little la-la land." Pause. "But, hey, Victor's kind of the same way, right?"

"Whose little land should she be in?" I ask, genuinely curious.

"Whoa! Don't go all snark on me!"

I roll my eyes and turn toward the window.

Rob reaches over and touches my arm awkwardly.

"Really, no offense. Sorry, okay? I know you're best friends. I respect that. I wouldn't want anyone dissing my best friend."

I nod, still gazing out the window. Rob keeps talking, segueing into a story about a recent beach trip with his best friend, or whatever, but I still can't shake Ethan's expression. That sadness in his eyes: What did it mean? Sure, he was upset about his psycho girlfriend, but was there something more? Was he jealous to see me walking hand in hand with Rob? Was I trying to make him jealous?

Okay, sure, it felt good to finally feel like I had the upper hand. Brianne thinks I'm sitting around waiting for her boyfriend to toss me a crumb? Yeah, right. I've got my own life, thank you very much. And my own friends. And no, for Ethan's information, Gia and I are not joined at the hip. Did we make that clear tonight? Good. It's so insulting, really, when you think about it. I don't go around making judgments about his friendships. And why is he noticing, anyhow? He thinks he's got me all figured out, huh? Well, figure out Rob and me leaving a party hand in hand.

I swallow hard, murmuring an occasional "mmm" to Rob's story. Why am I mad at Ethan? He didn't do anything. He's never been anything but sweet and strong and supportive and—

Stop it! Ethan is not in my life! He's a nice guy that I had an involuntary over-nighter with, and we've bumped into each other a couple of times since. That's it! Nothing to figure out! No reason to try to psychoanalyze what he could possibly see in Brianne. No reason to tease out our zillion differences and our scant commonalities. No reason to care about his religious beliefs, or his girlfriend, or his concussion, or his alcoholic dad, or whether I'll see him in the gym tomorrow, or . . .

"Take this right," I say to Rob. "My house is the one with the green Jeep out front."

He follows my directions and pulls into the driveway, tapping his fingers a little faster now.

"Thanks for the ride," I say, reaching for the door handle.

"Hey, Jade?" He turns off the engine.

"Yeah?"

Rob turns toward me, leans over, puts a hand behind my neck, and kisses me.

Whoa. I know it's crazy to say I didn't see that coming, but . . .

His lips press harder against mine, and his tongue is on some kind of exploring expedition.

So I guess I should kiss him back.

Rob is breathing heavily and tilting his head from side to side, stroking my hair with one hand and pressing my face closer to his with the other.

I try to synchronize my movements. Yeah, I guess this is going okay, but I'm too excruciatingly self-conscious to contemplate anything but technique. I mean, we barely know each other! Maybe I should play with his hair. But it's so short, too short to grab ahold of. And is hair-grabbing sexy in the first place? What if I rub his head? That's just weird, right?

If this is supposed to be fun, someone forgot to send me the memo. Enjoyment is not on my radar right now.

But why not? Rob's cute, he's nice, he's interested.

Well, his Oxford shirt is a little scratchy, and he tastes like stale beer, but other than that.

Stop thinking, Jade. Just keep kissing him.

So I kiss him some more, trying to push past the scratchy sleeves and the beer breath. Trying to push past my own head. Trying to stop thinking.

But who am I kidding? I can't stop thinking.

I can't stop thinking about Ethan.

TWENTY-ONE

JADE

"Why haven't you returned my texts?"

"I did," I respond to Gia, swiping her card at the front desk of the gym as blanched afternoon sunlight pours through the windows.

"One measly smiley face," she protests.

"You asked if I was okay; a smiley face means I'm okay."

"A smiley face means bite me," Gia says, looking extra willowy in her workout clothes.

"No, I think there's a bite-me emoji now."

Gia laughs. Good. I laugh, too. But I still feel terrible. I don't want her to feel blown off. But what could I say last night? I wasn't ready to talk about Rob. I'm still not ready. I don't know what to say, because I don't know how I feel. Rob asked me when he walked me to the door if he could call me, and I said sure, then he kissed me again, so it's all good, right? If my heart's not in it, well, maybe it'll catch up.

That's a lot of ground to cover in a text.

"So Rob took you home last night," Gia prods, rolling a hand.

"Yeah. I was trying to relieve you and Victor of

babysitting duty. You could have told me I was crashing your date, by the way."

She gives me a pleading look. "We totally wanted you to come with us. It wasn't a date. We're just friends."

I look at her evenly. "I saw you together. Pret-ty friendly."

Gia laughs. "Look who's talking! You and Preppy Rob, huh? Who'd have thunk it?" She props her elbows on the counter and her gray eyes sparkle. "Tell me what happened when he drove you home."

I shrug. "We kissed. He texted me when he got home. He got a smiley face, too."

Gia shakes her head slowly. "Whoa. Still trying to wrap my head around you and Rob. This is too weird."

"I guess stranger things have happened. Hey, by the way, you and Victor are totally cute together."

She wrinkles her nose. "Ya think?"

The door creaks open and I see Ethan walking in. I force myself to look away.

"Hi," he says in a clipped voice, without making eye contact, as he hands me his card.

"Hi," Gia says.

I swipe the card and hand it back to him.

"Thanks," he says, still looking down, then heads for the locker room.

Gia's brow furrows. "What was that about?"

My eyes are still following him. "What do you mean?" I say.

"Why is he acting so weird?" Gia asks. "I've never seen him be rude before."

But then her eyes widen. "Oh, the throw-down! I heard he and Brianne had a fight at Rachel's last night."

I play dumb, but the wheels in Gia's head are clearly still turning. "And somehow you were involved," she continues, speaking v-e-r-y slowly. "And now he's acting weird."

I clamp my lips shut and shrug.

Gia looks more suspicious than ever. "And now *you're* acting weird."

I *tsk* impatiently. "What are you talking about? Nobody's acting weird."

Gia stares at me a second, then nods. "It's true. You are hung up on Ethan."

I ball my fists together. "Would you stop with that already?"

"So hooking up with Rob, that was to make Ethan jealous?"

My jaw drops. "Would you stop!"

Gia lowers her voice conspiratorially: "You can't fool me, girlfriend."

"Drop it, Gia."

Her hands fly up. "Consider it dropped."

I cross my arms and stand there glaring into space.

Gia leans closer and tugs on the braid I have pulled to one side. "Just be careful," she says. "I don't want you getting hurt."

"Pretty busy today, huh?"

I avert my gaze from Ethan, who is jogging on a treadmill, and smile at Stan. "Yeah," I say. "I've had to refill the towels three times already. And four—no, five—people have filled out membership forms."

Stan nods. "Good, good. You mind wiping down some equipment while there's a lull?"

"Sure," I say.

I open a nearby cabinet, grab my cleaning supplies, step out from behind the counter and survey the gym. About half of the ellipticals are being used, and the free-weight section is buzzing with diehard jocks, so no use cleaning those sections just now. Let's see: The body weight section is pretty busy, too, and the mats are all being used in a cardio class, so there's really nothing to wipe down right now except the unused treadmills. Yeah, I have no choice but to head for the treadmills.

I walk over to them, staring straight ahead with a no-nonsense expression.

I start at the far end of the line of treadmills, about six away from Ethan. He's pumping his arms as he runs, perspiration dotting his shirt. He occasionally swipes his forehead with the back of his arm.

Not that I'm noticing. I'm working, wiping down the machines. It's my job. I can't help it if my presence is making him feel awkward.

And why the hell should he feel awkward, anyway? I managed to deflect Gia's questions a few minutes ago, but what *was* up with his cold shoulder? He should have been falling all over himself apologizing, explaining earnestly that he's sorry he has the most clingy, snotty, idiotic girlfriend on the face of the earth, and he feels terrible about Brianne ripping me a new asshole for no earthly reason other than to prop up her massive ego.

But instead, he acts mad at me?

So mature. So Christian.

Yeah, I said it. He seems more like a hypocrite every day. Sure, he puts on his game face when needed, but how could a truly good person be interested in Brianne?

I'm working my way in, wiping down one treadmill after another as I inch ever closer to Ethan. He's still staring straight ahead as he runs, still pumping his arms. A couple of times, our eyes lock, but we both look away quickly.

When I reach the treadmill next to his, I'm extra-vigilant wiping it down, taking time to reach every nook and cranny with my paper towels. Then I do it all over again. Just trying to be thorough, that's all.

As I'm finishing, Ethan lowers the speed of his treadmill and looks at me.

"Need me to get off?" he asks, his tone grudging.

I crinkle my brow. "What?"

"Need me to get off this treadmill so you can wipe it down?"

I curl a lip. "Of course not. The gym is for our customers."

"I was just asking," he snaps.

"I was just answering."

"Okay, then."

"Okay, then."

He turns the speed back up and resumes running. I walk past him with narrowed eyes, then wipe down a couple of unused ellipticals, putting extra muscle into my motions. The nerve of that guy! He's not even going to acknowledge his psycho girlfriend's temper tantrum? And since when did employees chase customers off treadmills to wipe them down? Was that part of his holier-than-thou selflessness? How desperate is he to win the Good Guy of the Year Award? Maybe it's time for another PowerPoint presentation to remind everybody how gosh-darn fabulous he is.

I walk back toward the counter, pausing to drink from the water fountain.

"Hey, Jade," I hear somebody say as I take a sip.

I look up and see Rachel.

"Hi," I say.

"I'm so glad you dropped by last night," she said. "Everyone was talking about how cute you looked."

I smile. "Thanks."

"And Rob texted me this morning asking what time you were working today. Like I'd know! I think he wanted to 'just happen' to work out while you were here."

I smile again, but my shoulders stiffen.

"So should I text him now and let him know you're here?" Rachel asks.

Umm . . .

"Whatever," I say, aiming for friendly and blasé simultaneously.

Yeah, this is why I hate high-school relationships: person A checking with person B to find out about person C. And do I want Rob to drop by or not? I kinda like the thought that he wants to, but I feel a little sick to my stomach. I don't know what I want.

"Hey, your party was really fun last night," I tell Rachel. "Thanks for inviting me."

Okay, that was awkward, considering she didn't invite me.

But she gives me a big smile. "I'm really glad you could come," she says.

I smile back at her, then return to the desk. Whew. Stan has some forms for me to complete. Mindless paperwork has never sounded so good. I spend the next half hour filling out the forms on the counter, swiping an occasional card as customers dribble in and trying to shake nausea-inducing thoughts from my head. It seems like expanding my horizons isn't doing anything but expanding my stress level.

I check a few more boxes on a form, then realize a customer is hovering at the counter. I glance up and see Ethan.

$$\bullet \quad \bullet \quad \bullet \quad \bullet$$

ETHAN

"I don't get you," I say, clenching my sweaty fists.

"Me?" Jade asks, looking from left to right and then

pointing to her chest. "Let's see, according to your girl-friend, I'm a desperate, pathetic stalker. Does that answer your question?"

"I don't get why you just took off last night," I respond, my jaw tight.

"Uh, because I wasn't in the mood for a catfight?" Jade *hmph*s indignantly. "Please! I was minding my own business when your precious girlfriend decided to go all gangster on me. I don't get why you're not falling all over yourself apologizing to me!"

My eyes narrow. "If you had stood still long enough to let me explain—"

"Explain what? What exactly is it that I need to understand?"

"—explain to Brianne," I say through gritted teeth. "If you hadn't gone running off, I was just about to tell her, in front of you so everybody would be clear, that I'm perfectly entitled to my friendships. I was going to tell her that there's enough room in my life for both of you."

Jade considers my words, then softly says, "Wow. Aren't we the lucky ones."

My fists tighten. "I didn't mean it that way!"

Jade holds my gaze, I guess giving me time to tell her how I did mean it. But I can't think straight. My head's pounding.

"I've been nothing but nice to you!" I finally sputter. "I send texts and emails to check on you, most of which you ignore, by the way. I track you down in school so I can make sure you're okay, I invite you to my church and my football games, I sit with you during—"

"Gee," Jade says, looking at me evenly. "Here I was, going about my own business, thinking I was getting along just fine. But then you swoop in and toss me a few crumbs. Wow, my luck's really turning around."

Our narrowed eyes stay locked as she gets her second wind. "Oh, and you have room in your life for both your girlfriend *and* me!" she continues. "What a stand-up guy! I guess I should feel flattered to get pulled into some tacky high-school drama. If only I was pure and righteous enough to be grateful for your pats on the head."

My heart pounds beneath my sweaty shirt. "That's right," I say. "Make fun of me. Make me out to be some kind of jackass. That's what you always believed, and that's what you have to keep believing to make yourself feel superior. You're so above it all, aren't you, Jade? Too good for any stupid high-school stuff. Too good for a hayseed like me. Too good for religion. That's just feel-good crap for people too stupid to know better, right?"

A woman in workout clothes walks in the gym. Jade forces a smile and swipes her card. As the customer walks away, she resets her scowl, leans into the counter and says, "I'm working."

I rest a hand on my hip. "You and Rob," I say. "You're together now?"

Jade shrugs.

"Maybe we are."

TWENTY-TWO

JADE

It's about time you texted me back!

My muscles tense as I peer at the screen on my phone after tossing my purse on the bed.

Sigh. I finally responded to Mom for the first time since she blew off our lunch date. She got a smiley face, too.

I don't know why I sent it. It was last night—I guess I was temporarily insane after the whole scene at Rachel's party—and Mom's just now responding. Regret is surging through my veins. I'm too tired for this. I've just finished an exhausting shift at the gym. First, I had to deal with Gia, then Ethan, then Rob, who stopped by near closing time and invited me out for pizza tomorrow night—fine, whatever—but all I want to do now is hibernate. I don't want to deal with psycho girlfriends, or nosy BFFs, or a birth mother who's suddenly decided to make a cameo appearance in my life.

The phone rings as I settle into my chair and I glance at the screen. Mom. I silence the ringer.

A moment passes and my text notification dings.

Jade, please pick up!

Nah. Think I'll pass. I pull the elastic out of my braid and shake my curls free, glancing in the mirror at the green eyes that look so much like hers.

Another moment passes, then another text: **Just know how much I love you, baby girl. xoxoxoxo**

I stare at the screen, squeeze the phone tighter and swallow a lump in my throat.

Why am I doing this to myself? Mom loves me. So what? A lot of good that's done me. I wish I could follow Pierce's lead and block her number. But I can't seem to resist the urge to occasionally dip my toe in the water, which just keeps her coming back.

Coming back.

That's all I wanted when I was a kid: for my mom to come back.

My memories are so spotty. Sure, there are some happy ones: Mom drumming on the kitchen table with celery sticks while I danced in the kitchen, or threading together daisy bracelets at the park, or making up silly songs about whatever mess I was making at the time. But most of my memories are nausea-inducing: Mom smelling of beer and yanking my arm way too hard when Grandma was trying to talk her into letting me stay at her house overnight; Mom screaming an obscenity at a stranger asking if I was adopted; Mom chasing an obnoxious driver at lightning speed for miles with her horn blaring while I shuddered in my car seat; Mom showing up at my Hello Kitty birthday party an hour late, then storming out while I opened the My Twin doll Lena bought me.

That's the last time I saw her. Mom called a handful of times after that, always promising that a Funsville visit or beach trip was right around the corner. But by the time I stopped believing her, she'd done me one better by blowing me off entirely. No more calls. No more cards. No more anything.

Until a few weeks ago.

I'm furious that I let myself get excited when I read that first text, just like I used to let myself get excited about theoretical Funsville visits.

So why am I wavering now, particularly after our broken lunch date? Yes, my life is currently a shit storm, but do I truly think this flake is gonna make it better?

But the flake is my mom. And I'm about to lose my dad. And I can't help wondering if I'll still have a place in Lena's life after he's gone. My sadness feels like it will swallow me whole.

So what the hell. I'll text her back. No phone calls, of course (I seriously think the sound of her voice would make me break out in hives) but what's the harm in a heart emoji? I tap it onto my screen, stare at if for a few seconds . . .

. . . then press send.

"We're home!"

I jump at the sound of Lena's voice downstairs. Oh,

that's right: she was picking up Sydney from her sleepover at Alicia's. Speaking of a shit storm.

I rush out of my room, lean over the bannister and call, "Syd!"

She looks up from the foyer and smiles sweetly, looking tired.

"Come tell me about your sleepover," I call.

"One sec," she tells me, holding up an index finger and sounding unperky. Uh-oh. This isn't good. I'm tempted to bound down the stairs and scoop her into my arms, but I've got to give her some space. I guess Lena's right. I can't protect her from everything.

I slip back into my room, sit at my desk and see that Mom's texted me back.

YAY!!!!!!!! You haven't fallen off the face of the earth! Call me. We need to reschedule our taco date.

I bite my lip. Why did I text her back? Do I really need one more complication in my life? Whatever. Too late now. I sigh, then tap out a text before I can give myself a chance to rethink it: **Just let me know when and where.**

I hit send and shrug. That's noncommittal enough, right? God knows I'm not calling her, but a friendly text along the lines of how you'd respond to, say, a girl in your art class arranging to work together on a class project? Yeah, I can do that. Who knows: Maybe I'll even give myself the satisfaction of standing Mom up.

I peer at the screen awaiting a reply, then curse myself for doing it. I slap the phone on my desk, grab my remote control and flick on my TV set, hugging my legs against my chest.

It's just as I'm rolling my eyes at *Catfish* that Sydney slips in. She closes the door and sits on the foot of my bed as I mute the TV.

"You went back to Alicia's?" I groan.

She looks at me sheepishly. "It's not what you think," she says, her onyx eyes looking sad. "See, I agreed with everything you said after the last sleepover. She was *so* snotty. Like, duh. But then . . ."

"Yes?" I ask warily.

"Well, I'd decided not to sit with her and the others at the lunch table Monday."

"Good call."

"But then I couldn't decide where I should sit—I mean, it would look so weird to just go up and randomly sit at somebody else's table."

Grrr. Not a fan of where this is going.

"So I thought, whatever, I'll just go sit with them, and if they start being mean, I'll take out my biology notes and start studying."

"O-*kay* . . ."

"And everybody was acting normal—like, really cool," she explains. "Then Alicia started talking about this video that went viral of a really sweet father-daughter dance at a wedding, and she started talking about what kind of father-daughter dance she wants at her wedding."

Oh god.

"And I started crying," Sydney says, her eyes misting at the memory. "I felt so stupid, but all I could think about was Dad, and—"

"Oh, Syd," I murmur, reaching over to dangle a lock of her shiny hair in my fingers.

"I felt so lame, but then, Jade, everybody was sooo sweet. They were, like, hugging me and telling me how sad they were about Dad, and—"

And I'd love to give Syd a reality check about why that particular topic might have come up in the first place (Alicia, I've decided, is pure evil), but my heart is aching too much to dump more pain on her.

"And they've been really sweet ever since," Sydney says. "So when Alicia invited me to another sleepover, I thought it would be a lot of fun."

I walk over to join her on the foot of the bed. "And?"

Sydney shrugs. "It was okay. Alicia and Rhee are definitely best friends now, so I felt pretty left out. But I just told myself I needed to have fun and make the best of it."

Either that or get the hell out.

"You can always call me," I tell her softly, putting my arm around me and squeezing her close. "No matter where I am, no matter what I'm doing, I'll drop anything for you."

She smiles. "It really was okay," she assures me unconvincingly. "Nobody said mean stuff about me. But . . ."

I swallow hard. "Yeah?"

"Alicia and Rhee decided to come up with a diet plan for Charlotte."

Well, of course they did.

"At first, it was kinda fun, because we were talking about healthy foods and smoothie recipes and stuff like that."

God, how I'd love to hit a fast-forward button on Sydney's life. Say, ten years or so.

"But then it was, like, so obvious, that Charlotte's feeling were getting hurt."

Ya think?

"I tried to change the subject, and Rhee was, like, 'Sydney, we're just trying to help her!'"

I lean down and peer into my little sister's eyes. "Sydney, people who get a kick out of making other people feel bad are *not* good friends."

Her face crinkles as more tears fill her eyes. "I don't want to be the girl with no friends."

I take a deep breath.

"Sydney," I say, "when I was your age, I never felt like I fit in anywhere. Dad's always told us not to think about stereotypes, and I really tried but . . . well, I never felt like I was black enough for the black kids, or white enough for the white kids, or cool enough for the artsy kids, or popular enough for the cheerleaders, or whatever. But I finally decided that all I needed to concentrate on was how I felt about me. If I was okay with myself, maybe other people would be, too. And if they weren't, then maybe they weren't the kind of people I'd want to hang around with anyway."

"But Alicia and I have been best friends since second

grade," Sydney says pleadingly, her tear-stained eyes sparkling.

"But if she's not nice anymore, then . . ."

"She's *usually* nice."

"Nothing you've told me about her lately sounds nice," I say with a raised eyebrow. "And fine. Whatever. She can act any way she likes. But do you know how I want you to act to her?"

Sydney's eyebrows weave together. "How?"

"Like you act when you're with Petra."

She considers my words, then sputters with laughter. "What?"

I smile. "You know how annoying Petra is?" I say, referencing our least-tolerable cousin.

"Yeah?"

"Well, you're always polite to her, but you kind of avoid her when she's being really obnoxious. Just like I do."

Syd's smile is broader now.

"And right now, Alicia is acting really obnoxious. So avoid her. Act like you're over it."

"What if she doesn't mean to be obnoxious?" Syd asks, warming to the subject.

"Well, Petra doesn't mean to be obnoxious," I point out.

"But Petra's only nine!" Syd says, laughing.

"So Alicia has even less of an excuse than Petra does. Hey," I add, wrinkling my nose, "does Alicia ever ask everyone to pleeeze be quiet while they're eating pumpkin pie so she can use a bottle of Reddi-wip as a microphone and pretend she's on *America's Got Talent*?"

Sydney doubles over chortling, thinking back to last year's Thanksgiving dinner at Aunt LaShea's house.

"Petra for sure was the wind beneath my wings," I deadpan, holding both hands over my heart.

"Remember how hard we tried not to laugh?" Sydney says, and I recreate our deer-in-the-headlights expressions, making her laugh even harder.

But after a moment, I turn semi-serious again. "I can't be with you all the time, you know," I say wistfully. "You gotta watch out for yourself. Remember, when the mean-girl stuff starts, just picture Petra's Reddi-wip microphone in Alicia's hands and make a beeline for the exit.'"

Syd looks up at me, her eyes glistening. "So that's what you used to do?"

I shrug. "When I had the guts. I didn't always have the guts, but I got better with practice. And you're way cooler than me, so you can be fabulous in, like, no time at all."

"I am sooo ready to be fabulous," Syd says.

"Trust me," I say, hugging her, "you already are."

● ● ● ● ●

ETHAN

"Hey, got a minute?"

Pastor Rick glances up from his desk and waves me inside.

I took a chance that he'd be in his office when I left

the gym. I volunteer as often as possible for the church's Saturday-evening *Psyched!* program for tweens, and the timing right now is perfect. My body isn't quite as battered as usual since I sat out last night's game, and Brianne will be at her aunt's house tonight. I'm happy to have a breather.

"Come on in, Ethan," Pastor Rick says in his Southern drawl, smiling and leaning into his desk. He's wearing jeans and a University of Georgia T-shirt, the stubble of a new beard getting thicker.

"I'm a few minutes early for *Psyched!* and got here a little early," I tell him, smelling of the soap I used in the Regal Gym shower after my workout.

"Glad you stopped by," he says earnestly. "Still grappling with those doubts we were talking about the other day?"

I tighten my grip on the arms of my chair. "I actually have some *other* doubts I wanted to discuss."

He spreads his arms. "Fire away."

The skeptics of the world (okay, so I have one particular skeptic in mind) would no doubt call me out for coming back to Pastor Rick for advice after I didn't get much more than platitudes a couple of weeks earlier. But I know he means well and cares about me. And who else do I have to talk to?

I fold my hands in my lap and stare at them. "I'm really struggling with my relationship with Brianne," I say.

His jaw drops. "Really?"

Okay, that's annoying.

I guess my irritation shows on my face, because Pastor

Rick quickly recalibrates, touching his chin for a more somber look. "I can't say I'm not surprised. I guess you just seem so perfect for each other."

I chew my bottom lip for a few seconds. Then Pastor Rick nods knowingly. "And maybe that's the problem," he surmises, talking slowly. "If everybody thinks you're perfect, it might be hard to admit you're not."

I squeeze my hands together. "I just think we're too young to be this serious," I say, still staring at my lap.

Pastor Rick nods, gazes past me momentarily, then says, "You know, Stacey and I were childhood sweethearts."

"Yeah?"

He nods. "Started dating in ninth grade. I invited her to the Spring Fling."

His eyes sparkle, which I guess is my cue to smile. But I'm not sure where he's going with this.

"Oh, she looked so pretty in her ruffly blue dress," he says in his folksiest voice. "Matched her eyes."

My heart sinks as I sense a teachable moment.

"From that moment on," Pastor Rick says, fingering the glasses on his desk, "she was my girl."

I shift in my seat.

"Clearly, that turned out great," I say after an awkward pause, trying to anticipate what he wants to hear and anxious to cut to the chase.

He shrugs sheepishly, then flicks on his glasses. "I guess she's stuck with me. We exchanged our vows and became one flesh. Then, little Ty came along, and next thing you know, he had a precious baby sister."

I smile, but my stomach muscles tighten. This conversation isn't exactly what I signed up for. I don't even want to keep *dating* Brianne, and Pastor Rick seems to be envisioning my future children. But truth be told, this is exactly the trajectory I'd always assumed was in the cards. Clearly, everybody around me assumes it, too.

"So you think I should stay loyal to Brianne," I say, more impatient than ever for the upshot.

He shrugs again, a bemused look on his face. "I'm just saying that there's a lot of fulfillment in making a commitment and sticking to it. But if you and Brianne want to break up . . ."

"Brianne doesn't want to," I qualify.

Pastor Rick adjusts his glasses. "But you do."

I squirm. "I dunno. I just want to do the right thing. And I don't want to hurt her."

He nods. "Yet it's hurtful for someone you love not to reciprocate your feelings."

I glance at him. "I used to reciprocate her feelings. I *want* to. I don't know how I feel right now."

Okay, the ball's back in Pastor Rick's court. But he's waiting me out. So finally, I say, "You're absolutely right. I'm not doing her any favors staying with her if my heart's not in it. But I've tried to break up with her, and she won't let me."

He gives a sharp laugh. "Won't let you?"

I squirm some more. "She just gets really upset. And that upsets me. We've been through a lot together. Like I said, I don't want to hurt her."

Pastor Rick fingers a pen on his desk. "Why do you think you've had a change of heart, Ethan?"

Because I can't stop thinking about someone else.

"Because we'll graduate in a few months, and I think both of us should be open to new experiences."

"So you're doing it for her."

Not crazy about his tone. "In a way, yes," I say testily. "I want the best for her. I don't want her looking back twenty years from now with regrets. I don't want to be a regret."

Pastor Rick *mmm*s. "And you don't want to have any, either, I'm assuming."

I shake my hair from my eyes. "Nobody gets through life without regret," I say. "I don't want to be the guy who bails at the first sign of trouble. Proverbs says, 'Never let go of loyalty and faithfulness.'"

The pastor cocks his head. "Ethan, you and Brianne have been together forever. Nobody would accuse you of bailing at the first sign of trouble."

Annoyed again. I know Pastor Rick is trying to be supportive, but "together forever?" I'm barely eighteen years old! Nothing I've done up to this point should qualify as a forever choice.

But then he says something that surprises me.

"Ethan," Pastor Rick says, once again leaning into his forearms, "I've heard a lot in the past few minutes about

Brianne: about how your relationship affects her, about her feelings and her future, about what's right for her. But at some point, you're gonna have to own a position."

My eyes flicker toward his. "Yeah?"

Pastor Rick nods. "You're gonna have to own what *you* want."

TWENTY-THREE

JADE

"The whole plot was just so contrived!"

I narrow my eyes and slurp noisily through a straw as Rob and I sit in the Burger Guy drive-in. It's one of those places where people order from their cars and have their food brought to them by roller-skaters. The place is always packed on Saturday nights, so I've scrunched down ever-so-slightly in the passenger seat of his car in case anybody's around that I know.

Why should I care? I dunno. Rob and I have been out a few times now, so our coupledom is starting to feel like an actual thing.

I'm not sure how I feel about that. My dates with him have been okay; he's smart enough, cute enough, nice enough. But as I get to know him better, I'm increasingly annoyed by his know-it-all vibe. Still, I'm pushing forward, determined to give him a chance and not sabotage a good-enough relationship by nitpicking him to death. So I've overlooked his condescending attitude with waiters, his fake-hearty laugh, his habit of pointing an index finger when he mansplains, his starchy shirts, his chronic throat-clearing, his conservative talk-radio presets.

Really. I've overlooked all these things and have even managed to feel slightly less self-conscious during our end-of-date make-out sessions. He's an okay kisser, and he never pushes me to take things farther than I want to go, so what's the harm? Are fireworks flying? No, but kissing him isn't entirely unpleasant, and I'm managing to be slightly less anthropological about the whole experience.

He's a perfectly acceptable boyfriend. I've even referred to him as my boyfriend a couple of times, though the word tends to stick in my throat.

But who cares. Our dates give me something to do, somewhere to be. On a couple of occasions, I've actually kind of reveled in my new role as half of a couple: "Sorry, can't tonight. Rob and I are going to the movies." Or: "Yeah, Rob warned me that test was a killer." Or: "Next Saturday night? Sure, we can make it."

And yes, I've halfway enjoyed Ethan's subtle peeks when he sees us walking hand in hand changing classes. Guess I wasn't that desperate for your "friendship" after all, huh?

Granted, as I found out with Calvin last year, the idea of being a girlfriend is proving to out-glamorize the reality, but isn't that what high school romances are all about? Maybe tolerable is the best you can hope for.

Still, my nerves are shot right now. Rob carried a running commentary throughout the entire movie we just saw, poking holes in the plot or guffawing indignantly at some inconsistency or sniffing at the "sub-par" acting or what-the-hell-*ever*. I just wanted to watch the movie, for chrissake. The evil glances and neck turns from the people around us were enough to make me consider taking a ninety-minute bathroom break.

"It's so great to have somebody I can really have a conversation with," Rob says, munching a fry.

"Thanks," I say, taking another slurpy sip, but I almost laugh at the irony. When Rob and I are together, the only one doing any talking is him.

"I thought I'd have to wait for college to get any intellectual stimulation," he continues.

"Mmm."

Is Rob's vibe the same one I give off, even unintentionally? I cringe at the thought. What's that word, Jade? Superior?

"You are so bright," Rob gushes, and I have to force myself to avoid rolling my eyes.

"Hey, speaking of which . . ."

"Yeah?" I ask absently.

"That night that you and Ethan were locked in the gym together: How in the world did you make it through?"

I look at him from the corner of my eye, straw still planted in my mouth. "What do you mean?"

"I mean, he's such a moron."

I bristle but keep quiet.

"Sure," Rob says, "he makes good enough grades in school, but he's one of those people who learn how to ace tests without ever bothering with things like critical thinking or original thoughts."

One of those people?

"So what did you two talk about all night?" he asks with a snort. "The finer points of throwing a ball in the air? Or Jesus?"

I dig my nails in my palm. "He's entitled to his beliefs," I say in a clipped voice.

"The opiate of the masses," Rob says, smiling at his own cleverness.

"What?"

"The opiate of the masses. That's what Karl Marx called religion. Marx is the—"

"I know who Karl Marx is."

"You know who Ethan should've been locked in that room with? Gia! It would have been classic. She'd rip him to intellectual shreds!"

So Rob has seriously used the word intellectual twice in the space of five minutes.

"Gia doesn't try to force her opinions on anybody," I say. "For that matter, neither does Ethan."

"So he didn't subject you to any prayer sessions that night?"

His voice drips with such contempt, such disdain, that I contemplate bolting from the car. I guess Rob sees it in my face, because he abruptly touches my arm.

"Crossed a line again, huh?" he says. "Sorry."

He says it with a faux-pouty face that makes me want to hurl. But at least he apologized, right?

"I just don't like slamming people," I say. "Especially when they're not around to defend themselves."

"And kudos to you for that," Rob says. He picks up his milk shake from his cup holder. "I'm a fan of integrity. So . . . cheers?"

I grudgingly tap my cup against his.

"Cheers," I say.

Whatever.

As I watch him sip his shake, a memory drifts into my head: I was toddler, sharing a shake with Mom in the car. Pierce was in a car seat behind me. I probably should have been in the back seat, too (I couldn't have been more than three), but I was sitting shotgun.

Mom and Dad must have already been separated, because I remember him calling her as we sat there and Mom screaming at him to leave us alone. I don't remember any specifics, just the tightness in my chest that always accompanied Mom's screech-fests. But it was nothing I hadn't heard before, so I tried to tune it out and enjoy my milkshake . . . until Pierce started crying in the back seat. I glanced back at him and saw his chin quivering as he frantically sucked his thumb, his enormous eyes filled with tears. Mom was oblivious, still screaming at Dad. Then Pierce lost it, sobbing full throttle and yanking helplessly at the straps of his car seat. I reached back to try to soothe him, but my arm was too short to touch him. I considered crying, too—it was the first time I realized I could make a conscious choice about the matter—but I got mad instead. Why was Mom upsetting my baby brother? Why wouldn't she shut up? Why were her needs more important than his?

So I grabbed the phone from her hand and dunked it in my shake.

Mom was too stunned to react right away, and I honestly had no idea what was coming. She was never mean to Pierce or me—she really seemed to get a kick out of us a lot of times—but I knew even then that trying to predict her behavior from one moment to the next was a total crapshoot. And fury definitely flashed in her green eyes for a second or two.

But then she laughed.

Like a cellphone dunked in a strawberry milkshake was the funniest thing she'd ever seen. I should've been relieved, but her laughter just made Pierce cry harder, and my sole mission at this point was to calm him down.

I spun around in my seat, peeked my face over the armrest and said, "It's okay, Pierce! *I'll* take care of you."

Yep. I was always on call when Mom was around.

Which makes me furious that my next reaction is to reach into my purse and pull out my cellphone. I turn the ringer back on that I'd silenced during the movie, then peer at the screen anxiously to see if I've missed any texts.

"Everything okay?" Rob asks.

"Yeah," I murmur, still staring at the screen. "I just

don't like to be disconnected for too long in case my dad might need me for anything."

"But everything's cool?" he asks, sipping his shake.

I nod but feel a thud in my stomach.

Why? Why should an empty inbox feel so . . . empty? It's Saturday night and I'm on a date, aren't I? And everything's okay with Dad, right? I should have no complaints at all. Still.

My mom hasn't responded since I told her to name a time and a place for a taco date. It's been three weeks. I'm so furious at myself for assuming she wouldn't once again fall off the face of the earth. Why did I have to creak that door open one more time? Why did I agree to another meeting, particularly after she blew me off for the first one? This should be good news, she's finally stopped texting. Woo-hoo! I stumbled onto the winning formula: Try to pin her down for an actual commitment and she scampers back down her black hole.

But god, what an asshole she is. She couldn't at least give me the satisfaction of standing her up?

And she's not the only one who's stopped texting. No more "just checking in" messages from Ethan. He's done his stint, right? Our overnighter in the gym is *so* last month. No need for him to push the good-guy routine too far. He's fine, I'm fine. Moving on. He's even stopped coming to the gym, at least during my shifts. Guess he finally got the message that I wasn't desperate for his friendship crumbs. Good.

Yeah. This is all good.

I push a curl behind my ear and squeeze my nails into my palm.

Buck up, Jade.

"Hey, you gonna finish those fries?"

"What?" I glance at Rob, disoriented, then process his question and try to hide my annoyance. "Oh . . . no. Help yourself."

As he grabs them and digs in, I can't help wondering: If I'm sitting three feet away from him, why do I feel so lonely?

• • • • •

ETHAN

Brianne glances at her phone as I exit the parking lot of the Italian restaurant.

"Hurry," she tells me as I pull into traffic. "Jocelyn said they're waiting on us to start Cranium."

"I thought we were watching the Bulldogs," I say.

Brianne leans over and pinches my arm lightly. "We can watch football and play a game at the same time, silly," she says.

Sigh.

Brianne and I have been holding steady the past few weeks. We've both made adjustments, which is good. She's less moody, and I've worked hard to give her less reason to be. For instance, I've opted for the school gym lately rather than Regal. Not the best timing, considering Regal gave me a free lifetime membership after the robbery. Still, it makes Brianne happy, and it's no big sacrifice, right? Yes, I'm entitled to have friends—and I made sure Brianne heard it loud and clear—but if I can avoid hurt feelings or misunderstandings, why not? Besides, Jade practically announced on a neon sign that she's not interested in my friendship. Looks like she and Rob are definitely a couple now. That makes no sense to me (what in the world do those two have in common?) but it's none of my business.

Brianne, on the other hand, *is* my business, and if things are feeling strained these days, well, I'm sure we'll make it over the hump. My mind has been a mass of confusion lately, but now that the fog has cleared, it feels good to recommit to my values. When I'm in, I'm all in.

"Let's not stay too long, okay?" I say, taking a left toward Jocelyn's neighborhood. "I'm kinda wiped out from the game."

Brianne leans over and nuzzles me. "Oh baby, you were on fire last night," she says.

Yep. The status quo has definitely made a comeback. I broke my passing record yesterday with 703 yards, so by the fourth quarter, the Jaguars were out for blood, pulverizing me every time they managed a sack. I feel like I've been leveled by a freight train, but we won, so all is right with the world. All it takes in my school—hell, in my town—is a win to go from zero to hero. I even rated a standing ovation in church last weekend after we beat the Stallions, our biggest rivals.

My phone rings and I answer it.

"Ethan, I hate to bother you," Mom says on the other end of the line, her voice a little shaky. "But your daddy . . . he's stirred up some kind of trouble at Squeaky's and they want him out of there."

Brianne, who can hear the conversation over the speakers, twirls a lock of hair, bored. We've been through this before.

"Your Uncle Byron's there but he won't take him home," Mom continues, sounding more tired with every word. "I think your daddy punched him in the nose. Honey, can you go take care of it?"

I roll my eyes. "Why are they calling *you*, Mom?" I ask. Uh-oh: Status-Quo Ethan knows the answer to that question. It's Agitator Ethan who demands reasonable explanations for ridiculous situations. I remind myself that I'm back to being Status-Quo Ethan. It's easier, even if it involves unscheduled trips to Squeaky's.

But Mom's trying to answer my question anyway: "They called Grandma, honey, but she's still worn out from dialysis, and—"

"It's fine, Mom, it's fine," I say. "I'll handle it."

I disconnect the call and I glance at Brianne. "Sorry." She shrugs. "No big deal."

I want to say, 'Isn't it sad that it's not?' But whatever. We're used to picking up my dad drunk from bars, and putting Brianne's mom to bed when she passes out on the couch, and making nice at dinner a day later like nothing ever happened.

That's our status quo.

"I'll drop you off at Jocelyn's," I say.

"You don't have to," Brianne says, still sounding bored. And truthfully, I know from experience that she'd be happy to give Dad a big smile and chat about last night's game while I load him in the back seat, ignoring the dried blood streaming from his nose. It's what we do.

But I don't want to do it again.

Is this why I feel so conflicted about Brianne? Does she know me too well? Is it too hard to pretend I'm somebody I'm not when I'm with her? Is it too hard to try for something better?

"We're almost at Jocelyn's," I say, taking a left at the stop sign. "It makes more sense to go ahead and drop you off."

Brianne inspects her nails lazily and says, "Well, okay, but hurry up."

My heart sinks. I don't want to hurry up. I don't want to deal with my dad only to rush back to Joceyln's and fake my way through a board game I don't want to play. I don't want to share another awkward goodnight kiss with Brianne when I drive her home, assuring her that yeah, yeah, everything's fine, I'm just really tired.

"Bree, do you mind if I pass tonight?" I say. "By the time I get Dad home, it'll be late, and I'm really wiped out."

I feel her eyes bore into me. "So it's back to this," she says icily.

My shoulders droop. "Back to what?"

"Back to you finding reasons to blow me off."

"Bree, please—"

"Just drop me off," she snaps as I approach Jocelyn's house. "And don't bother to pull in the driveway. I wouldn't want to put you out."

My grip on the steering wheel tightens. "Bree, please don't be this way."

"Bye," she says, flinging the door open before I've come to a complete stop, then slamming it shut. I'm still looking out the window at her as she offers a parting shot: "Oh, do me a favor? Kiss my ass," she says, slapping her jeans-clad rear end.

She spins around on a heel and stomps toward Jocelyn's front door.

● ● ● ● ●

"There's my boy!"

Dad's in hero mode in front of his bar friends as I walk in the door. The VIP from last night's game has arrived. Geezers with bloodshot eyes applaud lightly as I approach their stools, one even offering a wolf whistle. Drum roll, please.

Dad's teetering on a bar stool, clearly lit. Uncle Byron is swaying on his feet nearby and cupping both hands around a swollen nose, shooting homicidal glares at Dad.

"You better git that sumbitch outta here," he growls at me.

"Hello to you, too, Uncle Byron," I say amiably, making all the other drunks laugh.

"Boy, how many yards did you throw for last night?" asks a guy who clearly feels like Dad's version needs a reality check.

"I dunno," I murmur. "A few."

"A few hundred!" Dad exclaims, hoisting an empty beer mug skyward.

"We're proud of you, son, but it's time to take this fella home," Brownie, the owner, tells me with a wink. He tips an empty hand by his lips to simulate what Dad has spent the past few hours doing. Not that there was any question.

"Let's go, Dad," I say, standing close enough for him to lean on me as he inches off the bar stool.

"Damn right!" Uncle Byron calls. "Out! Out with yer sorry ass!"

"We'll pick up where we left off later," Dad slurs to him in an ominous tone, collapsing against my weight as he stumbles off the stool. I pull one of his arms around my shoulder and lead him toward the door.

"Good riddance, you goddamn maniac!" Uncle Byron calls.

"You have a great night, too, Uncle Byron," I respond, eliciting more laughter. How he's gonna get home, I don't know. But I don't trust these two in my car together. I'm hoping he's made fewer enemies tonight than Dad and that somebody will take pity on him by the time Brownie hollers, "Last call."

I drag Dad out the door, then through the parking lot in unseasonably muggy air. Getting him in the car is always tricky; his legs tend to turn to Jell-O at the least convenient times. But I manage to maneuver him in the passenger side, giving him a shove at the last minute that, oh darn, just happens to involve knocking his forehead against the door frame.

He's moaning lightly and rubbing his temple as I shut his door, then slip into the driver's seat and start the ignition.

"What's up with slugging Uncle Byron?" I ask him, though I really don't care. Trying to tease out details with those two is like refereeing a toddlers' free-for-all.

"Your Uncle Byron," Dad says, jabbing his index finger for emphasis, "is a hard-headed son of a bitch."

"Strange. He just called you the same thing," I say drolly, pulling into traffic, "which I guess makes sense seeing as you have the same mother."

Dad's wobbly head jerks to attention. "You callin' your grandma a bitch, boy?"

Oh geez.

"No, Dad."

"Better not be!"

"I'm not," I say, feeling repentant that I kinda did. As if Grandma doesn't have enough problems.

"You treat yer grandmother with respect!" Dad booms.

"Dad, fasten your seatbelt so the car will stop dinging," I say, knowing even as I utter the words that they're futile. If he manages to process the words, he'll lack the hand-eye coordination to complete the task.

"You hear me?" Dad rants. "You treat your grandma with respect! That there is a good, God-fearin' woman!"

I glance at him with a mixture of curiosity and contempt. "Why don't *you* treat her with respect?" I ask. "What are you doing getting drunk in public and belting your brother?"

Not that it hasn't happened dozens of times before.

I feel Dad glaring at me. "Don't you go gittin' too big for yer britches," he says, his tone now low and sinister. "You think you're Mr. Big Shot just for winning a football game? You got any idea how many football games I won?"

"I kinda do, Dad," I respond wearily.

"Ah, the big shot!" he says to no one. "The big shot that couldn't even take down a hundred-pound weasel in a gym!"

"A hundred-pound weasel with a gun," I clarify in a flat tone, though I don't know why I'm bothering.

"My son, the big shot!"

Dad closes his eyes, snores briefly, then pops his eyes back open. "You really think you can teach yer daddy anything I don't already know?"

"Not trying to teach you anything, Dad," I say, turning right on a green light. "Just wish I didn't have to keep bailing you out."

Dad gasps. "Bailing me out? Have I been arrested?"

I almost laugh. "Not this time."

He rests his eyes again, long enough this time for me to hope against hope I've heard the last of him for the night.

But as I pull onto his street, his bleary eyes pop open again. "Yer a good boy, you know that?"

"Better than you deserve," I mutter.

Then he starts crying. "You *are* better than I deserve, boy," he says. "And that is the God's-honest truth."

"I know, Dad," I say, pulling into the gravel driveway of his trailer. "I know."

● ● ● ● ●

On my way home, I text Mom. I dragged Dad to bed, dabbed the blood off his face with a washcloth and slipped his shoes off before I checked his pantry to make sure he's got enough food. It's as I'm slipping out the door that I let Mom know I'll be home soon.

So when my phone rings seconds later, before I reach my car, I assume that it's her.

But it isn't. I look at the screen and see that it's my friend, Brent.

"Hey," I say, answering the call.

"Hey, Ethan," he responds. "Everything okay with your dad?"

"Yeah. Same ol' same ol.'"

"Did you take him to the emergency room?"

"Nah. He's been punched in the nose so many times I think his face has lost its nerve endings."

Brent chuckles. "Nothing can keep ol' Mr. Mel down.

Remember him charging through a barbed-wire fence when we were kids? Who knew the yard he was stealing apples from had a pit bull?"

I smile in spite of myself. "There we were," I say, "waiting on the other side of the fence to catch his apples, and next thing you know . . ."

Brent laughs. "But dang if he didn't still have an armload of apples as he plowed through that fence."

"I kinda lost my appetite after he bled all over them," I say, and we chuckle some more.

"We couldn't have been more than six, and we still had enough sense to try to talk him out of stealing those apples," Brent says. "Does your dad even eat apples?"

"Drinks 'em, once the juice is fermented," I say with a laugh. "But the thrill is what he was after. He loves seeing what he can get away with."

Brent *mmm*s his sympathy. He knows the drill. If I can't do anything about my train wreck of a dad, I guess he figures the least we can do is laugh about him.

"I'm really glad everything's okay," Brent says.

"Thanks, dude. Thanks so much for calling."

"Yeah . . ." he says, his hesitant tone suggesting this conversation isn't over yet.

My eyes narrow. "Is something else up?"

Long pause. Then, "Listen, bro," Brent says, "I hate to add to your problems, but I thought you should know."

"What?"

He sighs. "I'm only mentioning it because you're my best friend."

"It's cool, Brent," I assure him. "You can tell me anything."

He exhales audibly, then says, "Craig Cooper was at Jocelyn's tonight. He and Brianne were pretty flirty."

I purse my lips. "Okay."

"Bro," Brent continues, his voice apologetic. "They left together holding hands. And as soon as they got on the front porch . . ."

"Yeah?" I mumble.

"Well, the door was still open, so we could see them, and . . . sorry, Ethan, but they were kissing."

TWENTY-FOUR

JADE

"Well, I guess I've filled my annoying-noise quota for the week."

Rob and I are sitting in the back seat of Victor's car, the perfect vantage point for me to notice Victor and Gia exchanging "the look."

The look is their reaction to just about anything Rob says, which is justifiable, considering that just about everything he says is smarmy and arrogant. They've exchanged about fifteen looks so far tonight.

What an awful idea a double date was.

I thought it would be fun for Rob and me to go out with Gia and Victor. But Rob's annoyingness has been in stark relief all evening. Victor's driving us home from a club where we checked out an emo band he wanted to see. The band was fierce, but Rob kept up a running commentary about their deficiencies. Victor and Gia were pretty preoccupied enjoying the band and igniting sparks with their lust gazes, but after two hours of comparing and contrasting, I've come to a few conclusions:

- Not everybody in high school considers their romances

merely tolerable. Victor and Gia seem downright giddy. They're politely discreet about PDAs, but their eye contact alone is just short of combustible, and they have this habit of laughing into their hands at private jokes. Nothing about this romance falls into the "good-enough" category.

- Rob and I are a squirrelier fit than I've been willing to admit, even to myself. Especially to myself. The presence of other people—particularly other people I actually have something in common with—makes our incompatibility as subtle as a neon sign.
- Playing boyfriend-girlfriend with Rob isn't making me forget Ethan.

The latter is the hardest conclusion to acknowledge.

So Rob and I are a piss-poor match, huh? Do I honestly think Ethan is a closer fit? And am I forgetting the "friend" category that Ethan has oh-so-graciously assigned to me?

Still, I keep replaying our last conversation over and over in my head. I've studiously avoided him since that day in the gym, but I can't help but scrutinize what we said, how we said it, what our words might have implied. And Rob's Outstanding Young Republican of the Year impression is seriously chapping my ass.

"I liked the music," I say.

"What?" Rob asks, genuinely confused.

Okay. I guess a bit of time has passed since Rob's annoying-noise quota comment.

So I repeat my sentiment:

"I liked the music."

"I'm sure they were good for what they do," Rob extemporizes. "And I'm not suggesting there isn't a place in art for non-melodious, head-banging alternatives to Mozart. It just seemed so derivative."

"The band writes their own stuff," Victor says as he drives.

"No!" Rob quips. "You mean that wasn't professionally written music? Who would have guessed?"

He laughs at himself—his fake-hearty laugh.

Gia turns around and exchanges "the look" with me. She's clearly lost the will to be subtle about her contempt for my boyfriend.

My boyfriend.

What a joke.

●　●　●　●　●

I collapse on my bed, still dressed in the jeans and sweater I wore to the concert. How exhausting it was to spend an entire evening trying to make Rob's and my relationship seem un-weird. In fact, I really need to debrief with Gia.

"Sorry Rob was such a prick tonight," I say when I call her.

"You don't have to apologize for him. But yeah, he is kind of a prick," Gia says on the other end of the phone, then morphs into a professor-ish Rob imitation: "Don't you think this music is awfully derivative?"

We laugh lightly.

"You're sure you two are a good fit?" she asks me.

"Yeah, we're getting married next week."

"Seriously. What are you doing with him if things aren't clicking?"

"Who knows." I kick off my shoes and press my knees into my chest.

"If you're not feeling it with Rob, you should break it off," Gia says. "Life's too short to hang around with people you have nothing in common with."

I sigh. "We have some things in common. He's really helped me on a couple of tests."

"Oh my god. You sound like you're talking about an accountant. If the best thing you can say about your boyfriend is that he's really helped you on a couple of tests, the buzzer has clearly sounded."

"But feelings can develop over time, right?"

"Not in my experience."

That's Gia, a cut-to-the-chase kinda girl.

"He and I are supposed to go to Clay's Halloween party next Saturday night," I say, fluffing my pillow. "That should be fun."

Gia coughs. "Going to a Halloween party with your tutor? Yeah, that sounds like a blast. Here's how I feel about parties: If I'm there with somebody I'm not in to, I wonder who I'm missing out on while I'm wasting time with him."

I bite my bottom lip. "Do you want to go with us? You and Victor?"

"I thought I talked you out of going."

"I'm giving Rob a fair chance," I say definitively. "I mean, look where all my nitpicking has gotten me so far." Yes. Of course, my real rationale is my little secret: The best antidote to my Ethan obsession is Rob, flaws and all.

"Come with us," I repeat.

Gia sighs. "Is he gonna rag on our music again?"

"Not a chance. I'm bringing along a Celine Dion CD. Easy listening for everybody."

She laughs, then turns somber. "Jade, be honest: You're still hung up on Ethan, aren't you?"

Uh-oh. Maybe my little secret isn't so secret after all.

But I *tsk* impatiently, intent on maintaining my current strategy of hiding all my true feelings from Gia. She doesn't need to know about Ethan. She doesn't need to know about my mom. She doesn't need to know about college. Well, not yet, anyway. One day, when I no longer have a knot in my stomach, maybe I can hit the reset button and get real with her again. But today's not that day.

"Hey, did you hear he and Brianne broke up?"

I sit up straighter. "What?"

"That's what I heard," Gia says. "I think Brianne's dating Craig Cooper now."

My brow furrows.

"Not that you'd care," Gia says slowly. "Right?"

I shake my head, trying to jostle the confusion from my mind. "I *don't* care," I assure her, then start speed-talking before she can argue: "I don't care about any guys right now, including Rob. He just happens to be somebody to go out with. Why would I want to obsess about guys? Like I don't have enough on my plate."

"That's an excellent point," Gia says. "We can totally reinvent ourselves in college, so that's where we should be putting your efforts right now. We need to narrow down which schools we're applying to."

I already have. The one that's six miles down the street.

I *mmm* noncommittally.

"Jade, I'm getting weird vibes from you about college lately," Gia says. "I'm getting weird vibes from you about everything."

Yeah.

Weird is the story of my life these days.

I hear a knock on my bedroom door. "Gotta go," I tell Gia, who reluctantly cuts me loose.

As I end the call, Sydney walks into my bedroom and bounds onto my bed.

"Whatcha doing up so late?" I ask, tugging lightly on her ponytail.

"You have *got* to hear this," she says, grinning.

"Yes?"

"Well," she says, clasping her hands, "you know I told you how I've been following your advice, hanging around with Alicia when she's being nice, but walking away when she's not? Pretending she's Petra?"

I laugh. "Excellent," I say, rolling my hand for more details.

"Well, when I started walking away—like going to a

different table at lunch or whatever—Casey and Charlotte started coming with me!"

"Classic!"

"Then Luisa started coming with us," she continues, bouncing lightly on her knees, "then we just kinda made it our regular table. So we haven't been sitting with Rhee and Alicia at all."

"Ooh, eat your hearts out, Rhee and Alicia!"

"And the best part . . ."

"It gets *better*?"

"Yeah! Now, Rhee and Alicia are stopping by our table, just to say hi. And when they stopped by today, Rhee invited us all to her birthday party next weekend, and we were like, 'Um, sounds fun, but can we let you know later? We might have this other thing.' And Rhee and Alicia were trying to hide it, but you could tell they were all, like, 'What?!?'"

Sydney's good mood is contagious, but I can't help seeing a red flag. "Okay, this is all cool," I tell her. "But I don't want to see *you* turning into a mean girl. Rhee's still new. She may not even know Alicia's been dissing you. So if you don't want to go to her party, that's fine. But be nice about it. And no games."

"Oh, totally," Sydney assures me, her pixie face earnest. "We're always nice."

"Good," I say, nodding sharply. "And, uh, girlfriend?"

"Yeah?"

"High-fives all around."

We do this ritual of hand-slapping, interrupted only when I hear my phone ping.

"Keep up the good work," I tell Sydney as she heads out the door. "But be nice!"

"I will," she calls, closing the door behind her.

I'm still smiling as I read my text. But my smile doesn't last long.

I'm finally freed up for lunch!

Oh god.

It's my mom.

• • • • •

ETHAN

Brent and I are the last ones walking off the field, swabbing our faces and necks with terrycloth towels as we head for our cars.

Today's practice was extra brutal. Coach Davis is so psyched by our recent wins that he's basically threatening homicide if we break the streak. I've been at school since seven this morning, overseeing an early-morning worship service at the flagpole and chairing a Student Government Association meeting before rushing off to my first-period class. Seven hours and three tests later, it was straight to football practice, which didn't wind down until six. My calves are screaming from lunges as Brent and I limp toward the setting sun.

"Ethan?"

I glance to my left and see Brianne, wearing shorts and holding pom-poms from her cheerleading practice.

"Hi," I call. I keep walking.

I can't say I wasn't hurt when she and Craig hooked up. Yes, I was relieved more than anything (it's clearer every day that it's time for a clean break), but I was still hurt. Bree's sent me a blizzard of texts since Jocelyn's party (**DO NOT believe any rumors! Craig and I are JUST FRIENDS! CALL ME!!!**) but I haven't responded, particularly in light of the cozy photos of the two of them that keep popping up on my social media feed.

But I'm not going to be rude to her. No games.

"Ethan, can we talk?"

Sigh. Brent and I exchange looks, and I finally nod and motion for him to go ahead without me. He hesitates, but then resumes walking to his car, tossing Brianne a light wave.

"What's up?" I ask Brianne tersely as she approaches me.

"Just missing you." Her blue eyes fill with tears.

"Yeah," I say, rubbing the back of my neck and gazing past her. "But I think this is for the best."

"No, it's not." She folds her arms to ward off a chilly breeze.

"Maybe we can talk later, Bree? It's been a really long—"

"I only did it to make you jealous!" Her moist eyes lock with mine. "I know, I'm stupid. I'm immature. I'm everything you accuse me of being."

I shake my head. "I've never accused you of anything."

A tear rolls down her cheek. "Maybe not in words," she says, her voice shaky. "But I know you judge me. And why shouldn't you? Everything you think is true."

I take a deep breath and blow out through puffed-up cheeks.

"So I thought, you know, 'Screw it,'" Brianne continues. "'He thinks I'm a flake? I'll *act* like a flake.'"

Her face wrinkles as a fresh wave of tears floods her eyes. "But you didn't even care!" she sobs. "You didn't give a shit!"

The lights in the school parking lot flicker on in the dusk. "I do care," I say, and I mean it, though I wonder why I'm the one suddenly on the defensive. No one's tagged any photos of *me* nuzzling random girls. Still, I hate to see Brianne cry. And she's right. I've spent weeks trying to push her away.

"Ethan, let's start over," Brianne pleads. "The past few weeks have been awful, but we've had two great years to-gether." Her brows weave into an inverted *V*. "I love you."

I consider her words, then say, "You and Craig—"

"There is no me and Craig! I couldn't care less about him! He knows that. He knows I can't stop thinking about you."

I chew my bottom lip. The truth is, we have had two good years. Not perfect. But good enough. Maybe that's the most anybody can hope for. And moments like these are when our "good enough" feels the best, moments when Bree is real and vulnerable.

"Please give me one more chance," she says softly. "Please give us one more chance. Aren't we worth one more chance?" She weaves her brows hopefully.

I shift my weight and press the terrycloth towel against the back of my neck.

"Clay's Halloween party is coming up," she tells me, her voice sounding lighter. "I've got a killer Marilyn Monroe costume."

She cocks her head and smiles shyly. "And I could really use some help in calculus."

I smile in spite of myself.

Brianne traces the dimple in my cheek with her index finger, and I don't pull away. Then she pulls the finger away and points it skyward. "One more chance?"

Crickets chirp as a long moment passes.

I surprise even myself when I hear my response: "One more chance."

TWENTY-FIVE

JADE

Mr. Finch is yammering about *Beowulf* as I use my notebook to lazily sketch a Daisy Buchanan flapper outfit. Gia and Victor finally agreed to go to the Halloween party with us, and since Rob is dressing as Jay Gatsby, I'm uncharacteristically in fashion designer mode. Plus, *Beowulf* is boring me out of my skull.

"Think it's cute?" I whisper to Gia, surreptitiously trying to slip her the sketch.

She shoots me a what-the-hell expression before hastily refusing to take it. I'm not sure if her reaction is a reference to my costume choice, my reminder of a party she doesn't even want to go to, my sudden affinity for fashion design, or my blatant disregard of all things *Beowulf.*

"Jade?"

I gulp as Mr. Finch calls my name.

"Yes, sir?"

"Did you happen to hear my question?"

"Um . . ."

The bell rings.

Whew.

But I'm not off the hook yet.

"Jade, can you see me after class?"

"Sure."

Gia shoots me another what-the-hell glance as she gathers her books and rises from her seat.

I tense, wondering what's up. Mr. Finch knows I'm usually on the ball, even if Grendel is the topic du jour. He's not mad about one little infraction, is he?

I approach his desk sheepishly as everyone else files out the door.

"Mr. Finch, I am so sorry I wasn't paying—"

He waves his hand to silence me.

"You're forgiven. This time," he says.

I smile, relieved.

"But I do have an issue with you."

I twist my fingers together. "Yes?"

"Yesterday," he says, "was the deadline for college application essays."

"Um . . . wasn't that assignment optional?"

Annoyance flashes in his eyes. "Jade, I know you're a good writer, but don't you think it's a little arrogant to assume your essay is so good that no second set of eyes is needed? Especially when that second set of eyes belongs to your English Lit teacher? This is a very important part of your—"

"I didn't write an essay." I squirm a little as my eyes fall.

Mr. Finch blinks several times in a row. "You didn't write one?"

I shake my head. "I'll be staying home next year, either working or taking a few courses at Tolliver Community College. No application essay needed."

He's blinking faster than ever. "Tolliver Community College?"

I nod.

"What are you talking about, Jade? If money is an issue, you know you'll qualify for scholarships."

I consider my words carefully, then say, "I just feel that staying home next year is the right decision for me."

He pauses, searching my eyes. "Your father?"

I shrug. "It's just right for me. That's all."

"Jade, I can't imagine this is okay with your—"

"It's my decision. And it's cool. Really. I've given it a lot of thought."

The third-period class is starting to fill the room. "Let's talk some more when I have more time," Mr. Finch says, and I nod noncommittally.

There's really nothing left to say.

I thank him for his concern, then walk into the hall, where I see Rob.

"Hi," I say.

"Hi."

"Hey, good news: Gia and Victor are coming to the Halloween party with us."

He clears his throat, then nods.

"Got your white linen suit ready? Maybe some gel to slick back your hair?"

"Well, I . . . um . . ." More throat-clearing. "Let's talk later. I'm late for my class."

He disappears into the crowd before I can respond.

That's weird.

Oh, well. I guess I can handle spending an evening with Jay Gatsby. Gatsby was a tool, too, right? If Rob is pretentious at the party, he'll just be in character, that's all.

Yes. I can handle one more date.

Then we'll see what happens after that.

● ● ● ● ●

I hear the power drills before I even pull into my driveway.

The construction crew has clearly arrived. Between Dad's seizures and increasingly shaky gait, he and Lena decided the house needs to be wheelchair-accessible. That makes perfect sense. My dad, barely in his forties and the picture of health before this god-awful diagnosis, now needs a handicap-accessible home. I get it. I just hate it.

As I park my car, I see open doors, flying sawdust, torn-down walls and other evidence of a home under assault.

That's what it feels like. Yes, intellectually, I know this is a good thing—that a couple of weeks from now, the house will once again look pristine . . . just not the same. It'll never look the same again. The doors will be wider, steps will be replaced with ramps and we will have fully morphed into our new world of Dad as Invalid. Dad as Dying. Dad as Deceased. Innocence as Shattered. Childhood as Shot to Hell. Future as Suckfest.

I push the thoughts away as I walk in the door, nodding politely at a couple of guys in dirty shirts and hardhats.

"Dad?" I call.

"Back here," he answers from the den. "Watch your step."

I join him in the den and lean over to kiss his cheek, which is puffy from steroid treatments.

"How was school?" he asks, setting a book aside.

"Fine."

"Hey, Mom told me she's making you a Great Gatsby costume for a Halloween party this weekend. That sounds like fun!"

Sigh. When Dad adds that much enthusiasm to his intonation, we both know he's trying too hard.

"So you're going with Rob?"

I nod. "Yeah. We'll ride with Gia and Victor."

"That sounds awesome!"

More overly emoted sentences. Ugh.

"How long will the demolition derby be here?" I ask Dad, aiming for a breezy tone.

"Just a few days. They promised to finish up every day by dinnertime, so you should barely even know they're here."

Right. Keep dreaming, Dad. Keep pretending our lives are normal. Keep up the charade that if you play your cards right, your kids might not even notice this pesky brain cancer.

"Hey, by the way, I really like Rob," Dad says. "He seems so focused."

Okay, that's definitely the most benign word possible to describe someone you really don't like. Not that Dad actually dislikes anybody. It's just . . . Rob's buttoned-up conservatism isn't exactly the most natural fit.

I smile. "He's okay."

"Hey, Jade," he says, "when you were talking to me the other day about how Mom and I got together . . . was it Rob you were thinking about?"

I purse my lips.

No. As a matter of fact, it wasn't. I was actually thinking about some guy that I was stupidly obsessing over until I finally caught the bullet train back to reality. And again with the "Mom" language?

"Nah," I respond. "I was just curious about you two."

Dad looks unconvinced, but he smiles at me.

"Well," I say, "I better get some homework done. You need anything?"

"Me? No!"

I smile and head for my bedroom, shutting the door behind me. I hear Dad asking the construction crew in his cheeriest voice to please finish up and call it a day.

I settle on my bed and pull out my *Beowulf* notes, jotting answers to questions on a worksheet about the previous three chapters.

I'm about halfway through when my phone rings. "Hello?"

Throat-clearing. "Uh, Jade?" More throat-clearing.

"Hi, Rob. What's up?" I say, setting aside my notes.

"Not much, not much. Uh . . . you were mentioning the Halloween party earlier today?"

"Yeah?"

"Right. Well, here's the thing."

The thing? There's a thing?

"Looks like I won't be able to make it after all," Rob says.

I take a moment to process this. "Oh."

"So sorry," he rushes on. "It's just I have some relatives coming in from out of town, and my mother is ridiculously on my case about joining in on all the family stuff, and—"

"That's cool," I say. "No problem."

"I just feel terrible," he says.

"No, really. I understand."

Pause.

"Well, since Gia and Victor are going, I suppose you'll go with them?"

Oh, goody! Time to reprise my role as a third wheel. And what could possibly be cooler than Daisy Buchanan minus Jay Gatsby? Yeah. Sign me up.

"Nah," I tell him. "I've actually got some family stuff going on, too. In fact, I was just about to call and let you know I couldn't make it."

Christ, I'm a crappy liar.

"Well, hey," Rob says, "at least we'll *both* be miserable."

"Yeah."

More throat-clearing.

"Well, uh, I better be—"

"Right, me, too," I say. "I've got . . . laundry and stuff."

"Right. Well, see ya."

"See ya."

I end the call and peer at my phone. What the hell?

I should feel great about this, right? I was already dreading the party.

Still. Rob blowing *me* off? Seriously, what the hell?!

Oh, well. Like I said, problem solved, right? I didn't want to go to the stupid party anyway, and this will make it easier to make a clean break. Yeah. Time for Rob to be in my rear-view mirror.

My phone rings and I roll my eyes. No, Rob, I am not giving you another chance to slice and dice my ego.

But as I glance at the screen, I see it's not Rob calling back. It's my mom.

My stomach clenches as I silence the ringer. I never responded to her text trying to reschedule the lunch date she blew off. She'd sent a flurry of follow-ups, trying to talk me into meeting her at the same restaurant in Columbia. I considered responding that I'd definitely be there—as soon as hell froze over—but opted for crickets instead. A couple of days have passed since I've heard from her.

I'm still squeezing my phone, still staring at the screen, when a text pops up. **Okay, here's the deal: I am taking you out for dinner whether you like it or not! And this time, I'M coming to YOU!!!**

What is it with this woman's fixation with exclamation marks?

More dots are dribbling onto the screen. She's still typing. My phone pings when she's done.

Meet me tomorrow at seven p.m. at Taco Town. My GPS says it's a seven-minute drive from your house, so NO EXCUSES!!!!! I CAN'T WAIT TO SEE MY BABY GIRL!!!!

Oh my god, she's coming here? Does that mean that if I don't go, she'll show up on our doorstep? Over my dead body! I'll be damned if I let her upset my dad. My heart is pounding against my shirt. Should I tell Dad what's going on? Should I tell Lena? Can I stick to the script of ignoring her texts? I hate Mom for making me such a nervous wreck, yet the thought of her being a seven-minute drive away . . .

"Jade?"

I look toward my door and see Lena knocking her way in.

"Hi," I say, setting my phone face down, my heart still thumping wildly.

Lena smiles and sits on the foot of my bed, running a hand through her hair.

"Jade, I got a call from Mr. Finch a little while ago."

Damn.

"He said you didn't turn in an assignment—a college application essay," she continues.

Oh, hooray! One more dollop of stress! I actually wonder if my heart will explode.

"Right," I respond as coolly as possible.

Lena gives me the same incredulous look I got from Mr. Finch earlier today.

"The assignment was optional," I assure her. "Extra

credit. And I already have an A plus in that class. It's no big deal."

Her jaw drops. "No big deal that my incredibly smart daughter, the one who's been talking about medical school since she was four, is apparently deciding to skip college?"

Her daughter, huh? She and Dad are definitely doubling down on the make-believe.

"Nobody said anything about skipping college," I say.

"Then why didn't you write the essay?"

I shrug. "I've just narrowed down the field. That's good, right? Go ahead and pinpoint where I want to go without wasting a lot of time and money applying to a dozen different colleges?"

Lena's eyes search mine. "What college do you have in mind that doesn't require an admission essay?"

Oh, geez. Can't we just keep this conversation generic?

"Tolliver Community College," I mumble.

"What!"

I close my eyes. "Lena, chill!"

She stiffens. "You are not going to Tolliver Community College."

"It is no big deal," I say evenly. "Doesn't it make sense to get my core credits out of the way at an inexpensive college?"

"Money? That's what this is about?"

Among other things, yeah.

"Dad had to close his practice, and I'm guessing cancer treatment isn't cheap," I say. "I know I'm not supposed to care about those things, but money's got to come from somewhere, right? With some scholarship help, I can easily manage my tuition and expenses at Tolliver with my gym salary."

Lena opens her mouth to respond, but I present my palm.

"Forget it. I'm not taking your money. It's just not gonna happen. You've got two other kids to worry about, and—"

Lena opens her mouth again. I present my palm again.

"—and besides, I *want* to be home next year. I don't want to miss any time with Dad."

There. I said it. I'd have preferred waiting until the buzzer sounded on application deadlines before having this conversation, but Mr. Finch shot down that option by calling Lena.

She glances at my open bedroom door, then walks over to shut it and rejoins me on my bed.

"Jade, I want to make a few things very clear."

I open my mouth, but now, she's the one presenting her palm.

"One," she says. "Money in this household is your dad's and my concern, not yours. We are fine. We've got insurance, we've got our savings, we've got our investments—we are fine. If we weren't fine, I'd owe it to you all to sit down and have a discussion about it. Then we could figure out the best way to move forward. But we are fine. The money you earn at the gym is your spending money, not your college tuition money."

My mouth has flapped open a couple of times during this speech, but her palm has silenced me both times.

"Two: I know you want to spend as much time as possible with your dad. But you can't put your life on hold in the process. That's the last thing either of us want."

Her eyes turn misty. "Nothing will give him more pleasure," she says, her voice trembling, "than watching you launch your dreams." She pauses, then adds, "And nothing would give him more pain than thinking he was standing in your way."

Now, my eyes are misty, too.

"I don't want to stay home just for Dad's sake," I say. "I want to stay home for mine."

Lena shakes her head. "If I really believed that, it would be one thing. But I don't. You'll have plenty of time with your dad and me on weekends and holidays. But you know as well as I do that college is when you are going to start kicking some major ass in this world."

I laugh through my tears.

"You're bigger than this town, bigger than your school," she tells me. "Your dreams are bigger."

I rest a fingernail on my bottom lip. "My dream is to turn back the clock. My dream is for Dad to be okay."

Lena nods and entwines our fingers as a lock of her silky, black hair falls on our hands. "Dad's lived his dreams. All he cares about now is making sure you guys have the chance to do what you want to do. If swiping cards at the Regal Gym for the next forty years is what you want out of life," I laugh, and she smiles, "then that's what your dad and I want for you, too."

She looks me deeply in the eye. "But that's not what you want out of life."

I swallow hard to dislodge the lump in my throat.

"So," Lena says, her tone lighter, "looks like you have a college application essay to write."

She pauses, then nods smartly and walks out of my room, closing the door behind her.

I take a deep breath and watch my ceiling fan oscillate. I appreciate Lena for saying all the right things—we really do have our moments, she and I—but deep down, I don't know.

Maybe swiping cards the rest of my life has real potential.

TWENTY-SIX

ETHAN

Ethan Garrett, please report to the front desk. Ethan Garrett . . .

I narrow my eyes in puzzlement as my name is called over the school intercom. What's up?

I glance at Brianne in the desk next to mine and shrug in response to her confused expression.

I stand up, then walk out of the room, down the hall, and toward the front desk. A police officer is waiting for me. His expression is friendly, but my mind is racing. Is Dad in trouble again? Is Grandma in the hospital, or worse? As I approach him, I see someone else heading our way from another hallway. Jade. What in the world?

"Thanks so much to both of you for meeting me," the officer tells us. "Sorry to pull you out of class."

Jade looks as clueless as I am, but the officer quickly fills us in as he flashes his badge.

"I need to ask you both a favor. Could you accompany me to the station? We think we may have the Regal Gym burglar in custody and would like you to try to identify him in a lineup."

Whoa.

"After all this time?" Jade asks.

The officer nods. "Robbing you at gunpoint and holding you against your will are federal offenses. We've pursued this case very aggressively."

I nod, swallowing hard.

"And we received a tip that promises to advance the case considerably," he continues. "But an ID in a lineup—or better yet, two—would really move things along."

I catch Jade's stunned eyes.

"Can you come with me to the station? It shouldn't take more than a few minutes."

Um . . .

"Do our parents know about this?" Jade asks.

"You're certainly free to call them," the officer says. "You're both over eighteen, so it's not necessary on our end, but if it would make you more comfortable . . ."

"No, no," Jade says, more to herself than to him. "Dad's getting chemo."

"But you can still call and let them know what's going on," I say, desperate to help alleviate her anxiety.

"No," Jade responds. "They've got enough going on."

The officer looks at me. "Would you like to call your parents?"

"No, sir, that's not necessary," I say. "I'm ready when you are."

He nods, then thanks the school secretary and leads us out the door. His squad car is parked right out front.

"Your limo awaits," he quips, opening the back door for us.

As we slide inside, Jade's eyes widen. A pane of glass separates the front and back seats, and our doors don't have handles. We secure our seat belts, then I reach over and take her hand.

"You okay?"

Jade nods, but her hand is trembling. "Don't worry," I tell her. "I'll be with you every step of the way."

It's as our eyes lock that it all comes flooding back: Jade's petrified expression as she realized I was going to try to take down the robber pointing a gun in her face; her look of crushing despair when I failed; her trembling hands as we were shoved into a room, wondering if we would live or die.

I squeeze her hand tighter. Gosh, it feels good. But that's because of the circumstances, right? We're kinda like foxhole buddies, or at least what I imagine foxhole buddies would be like: the only people on earth who truly get each other, the ones who have walked through fire together.

The police officer picks up his radio occasionally and exchanges scratchy conversation with a dispatcher.

"You know how you can't help thinking about jumping when you're on top of a really tall building?" Jade asks me conspiratorially.

"Sure," I say playfully.

"Well, something about that pane of glass makes me want to try to kick it out."

We stifle our snickers. "Let's not and say we did?" I suggest.

She tosses me a sly smile. "At least there aren't any jellyfish back here."

I nod gamely, then cock an eyebrow. "But there *are* a couple of belly buttons."

"Stop it!" she moans. "I knew I shouldn't have told you! Now I'll have to kill you."

"Shh!" I say, still laughing, pressing an index finger against my lips. "It's not the best idea to murder somebody in a police car."

We glance at the driver, who's clearly oblivious.

Jade gazes out her window, squeezing my hand tighter. "What do you think it'll be like?" she says softly. "Seeing him again, I mean."

Trees pass by in a blur.

"I don't know," I say somberly. "I hope I can feel compassion for him."

"Yeah, well, while you're doing that, I'll be imagining kicking him in the balls. Work for you?"

We sputter with laughter again. "Works for me."

The officer turns into the police station and parks the car. Jade and I unfasten our seat belts as he walks around to our doors and lets us out.

I smooth my polo shirt as the officer leads us inside. Jade folds her arms, shivering slightly.

"We'll take you in one at a time," the police officer says. Jade's eyes widen as her arms fall to her side.

"No," I tell him, more intensely than I intended. "I mean . . . I told Jade I wouldn't leave her."

I reach for her hand again, and we grip each other tightly.

The officer glances at Jade's panicked face and places a hand on her shoulder. "We need your feedback to be as objective as possible," he says in a kind voice. "We don't want you to influence each other. But I'll be with each of you during the lineup, and the men on the other side of the glass won't see or hear you at all."

Still. I can't stand the thought of Jade dealing with this alone. I still see the robber's clear blue eyes in my nightmares. I remember contemplating, when I was staring at them, that those eyes might be the last thing I ever saw. I know Jade felt the same way. No. I don't want her in his presence without me there beside her.

"How about if we withhold our feedback until we leave the room," I suggest to the officer, "then give it one at a time outside of each other's presence?"

But Jade is nervously waving away my idea before I've finished my question. "It's okay, Ethan," she says. "I'll be okay."

She smiles at me, then adds, "Thank you, though."

Our eyes stay locked for a long moment. Gosh, her eyes are beautiful.

"Ready?" the officer asks her, and she nods bravely.

Good. She's going first. I don't want this to be any more drawn out for her than necessary.

Our eyes are still locked as the officer begins leading her down the hall. "So do not fear, for I am with you," I recite in my head, hoping the verse washes over Jade. "I will go before you and make the rough places smooth."

I call to her just as they round a corner and she slips out of sight:

"Don't worry, Jade," I say. "I'm right here waiting for you."

● ● ● ● ●

I impulsively sweep Jade into my arms as she walks out of the police station, joining me under the awning where we wait for our ride back to the school.

"Oh, Jade, they got him!" I say, hugging her so tightly that I lift her off the ground. "They got him!"

As I put her back on her feet, she pulls away and peers at me frantically. "How can you be sure?" she asks, her voice shaky.

"The scar! Remember the scar?"

Her brows pull together. "I'm sure he's not the only guy in the world with a scar over his eye."

"He was the only guy in the lineup with one," I say.

"But it's not a given that one of those guys in the lineup was the one who robbed us!"

I shake my head in surprise. That scar? That little *V* over his eyebrow? Surely that image is as seared into her brain as it is in mine. "I'd have known him even without the scar," I tell her. "I'll never forget those eyes."

She nibbles a nail. "I think so, too. But if I can't be absolutely sure . . ."

Her eyes grow misty, and I take her hands. "It's okay, it's okay," I say. "I told the officer I was sure. I am sure. And I stand by that. If they need my testimony, I'll be more than happy to give it. But all you can do is be honest. If your honest answer is that you're not sure, then you did the right thing by saying that."

Her mouth is a thin line. "I told him I was *almost* sure," she says. "But, Ethan, to risk sending the wrong man to prison? I could never forgive myself."

"I understand," I murmur, folding her back into my arms. I truly am surprised by her reaction—I, for one, was elated that there was not a shred of doubt in my mind—but I meant what I said: All Jade owes anyone is honesty.

The squad car pulls up under the awning and Jade and I resume our familiar spots: a back seat with no inside door handles and a pane of glass separating us from the front of the car. We're back in our own little world again, just like we were in the aerobics room.

"I want to be sure," Jade tells me as we pull out of the parking lot.

"But if you're not, you're not," I respond. "I respect you for owning that."

It's just now that I realize we're holding hands again.

"But you're okay?" I ask her. "It didn't shake you up to see him again? I mean, assuming he's who we think he is."

She nods. "Looking into those eyes, I thought I might be sick," she says. "Which should have been a pretty good indication they got the right guy. But, Ethan, if there's even a sliver of a chance that I'm wrong . . ."

"Absolutely," I tell her. "I just want you to be okay. That's all I care about."

I squeeze her hand tighter, and her lashes flicker as she stares at me.

"How about you?" she asks me.

My brow furrows. "What do you mean?"

She pauses, then says softly, "Are you okay? I heard you and Brianne broke up."

It takes a second to process what she's saying—my mind is still peeling off in a thousand directions—but when I absorb the words, I nod.

"Yeah."

I don't know why I said that. I guess it just seemed like the least-complicated response.

"I'm sorry," she says, and my stomach clenches.

"It's okay." I swallow hard and avert my gaze. Why can't I be honest with her? Why can't I tell her we've gotten back together? Why am I still holding Jade's hand?

I momentarily justify my dishonesty by reminding myself that Brianne's and my relationship status is really no one's business but our own. Or that our resumed relationship status is still entirely conditional. Or that my relationship status has nothing to do with the fact that I can't take my mind off Jade.

"I really am sorry," Jade repeats, and I still can't look her in the eye.

What a coward I am.

● ● ● ● ●

JADE

I drum my fingers anxiously on the laminated tabletop.

The aroma of chili powder wafts through the air as a waitress walks past me carrying sizzling fajitas in cast-iron skillets. Another waitress follows her with a pitcher of beer, and cheerful voices emanate from the booths around me.

Yes, I'm here. Yes, I'm an idiot.

Part of the reason I was such a ball of nerves at the police station earlier today was that I knew I was meeting Mom for dinner four hours later at Taco Town. Nothing stressful about my day.

So here I am.

Fine. Whatever. What do I have to lose? Mom is coming to me, after all. This is no skin off my nose. Hell, I might have chosen to eat here tonight even if she hadn't texted me. I'm grabbing a bite to eat at Taco Town, just like I have a thousand times before. Granted, this is the only time I've been sitting at a table by myself. But not for long. Because Mom is coming.

Right?

Every time a waitress passes by, I bury my face in the menu as if I'm totally fascinated by the entree selections I have to choose from. Burritos *and* rice? Beef *and* chicken fajitas? Whoa! Such a fascinating menu. So much information to absorb.

I sip my ice water through a straw and glance anxiously around the restaurant. It's only 7:05. Yes, I've been here ten minutes, but arriving five minutes early seemed courteous, not desperate. Right?

I pull my phone out of my purse and check for texts. Nothing.

Ethan texted about an hour ago, making sure I was okay. That was sweet. I didn't utter a word to him, or anyone else for that matter, about tonight's dinner date with my mother. I'm perilously close to forming an ulcer as it is, so I figure some things are better left unsaid. Still, it's clear Ethan's been thinking about me since my meltdown at the police station. He was so protective and caring. That really meant a lot.

God, I can't believe that it's really true: he and Brianne broke up. That blows my mind, after all the time they've been together. It's hard to picture one without the other. They're such a unit. (Where have I heard that before? Ugh.)

Sure, I heard rumors that Brianne was stepping out on Ethan, but that kind of gossip has been circulating since the two of them started dating. I really thought they'd weather the storm, particularly since Ethan is such a good guy.

Yeah. Such a good guy.

I drum my fingers on the table some more and glance at the time on my phone: 7:11.

"Still waiting on your guest?"

I jump a little in my booth and look up at the waitress. "Yes," I say.

Still waiting.

I've been waiting for Mom for approximately twelve years, to be exact, fifteen if you count the moment she packed her bags.

I check again to make sure I haven't missed any texts. Nope.

I decide to play a couple of apps on my phone to pass the time. The last thing I want to do is look frantic and needy when Mom arrives. I'm determined to play it cool, just like I've rehearsed in my mind since I was six years old.

Happy voices chatter all around me: families with little kids, teenagers munching chips and salsa, college-age kids sharing a pitcher of margaritas, and I wonder if my heart will crumble right here on the spot.

Because guess what? It's 7:24 now and Mom is clearly not coming.

I take another sip of water, then manage to smile when the waitress breezes past me one more time.

What the hell was I thinking? What an utter fool I am. The woman I don't call Mom is home right now sewing me a Halloween costume, and the loser I do call Mom is standing me up. Again. When will I learn? And when will I stop caring?

"Can I refill your water?"

I glance up at the waitress and shake my head. "Actually, I won't be ordering after all," I tell her, setting my menu aside. "Sorry."

She smiles sweetly, and I leave her a five-dollar tip for wasting the table space. I sling my purse over my shoulder, glance around the restaurant one last time, then head for the exit.

● ● ● ● ●

"So, wanna get some takeout?"

I draw in a quick breath, then clutch my racing heart as I see Pierce walking up to me as I step into the Taco Town parking lot.

"Pierce, what are you doing here?"

He shrugs. "Just hanging out."

I start crying and he hugs me.

Leaves rustle lazily in nearby trees.

"I got a private Facebook message asking if I would join you two," he says, rubbing my back in circles. "I didn't think she'd show, but I wanted to be here for you."

I sniffle into his chest. "What a moron I am," I blubber.

"Nah," he says, sounding just like my dad, who always defaults to casual when tensions are running high. "Hey, I showed, too."

I pull away enough to look him in the eye. "But you were just waiting outside for me," I say, my breaths jagged.

"You weren't stupid enough to request a booth for two and spend half an hour staring at a menu."

He considers my words, then shrugs again. "I may have come inside if she'd shown up," he says. "I can't deny my curiosity. Who wouldn't be curious?"

I shake my head, sniffling some more. "It's not just curiosity on my part," I say miserably. "I feel this crazy need for closure sometimes."

Pierce nods as a breeze buffets my cheek, and I warm to the subject. "It's like I've walked into an empty room when I was expecting a surprise party," I continue, "and I want to scream, 'What the hell?' How pathetic am I?"

Pierce smiles at me as a few customers drift in and out of the restaurant a few yards away. Normal customers. Customers coming here because they're hungry for tacos, not some flaky mother's crumbs of attention.

"The good news is that"—Pierce gives a gasp of mock surprise—"we have a mom! Whoa, we lucked out! All we have to do is go home to her."

I smile through my tears. "Lena's the only mom you've ever known," I remind him. "I have the unfortunate distinction of remembering the jerk who gave birth to us."

"I remember more than you think," Pierce says in a playful tone. "That time you stole my pacifier when I was two weeks old, for instance? Clear as day."

I laugh again.

"I don't think I'd have even answered her texts," I say wistfully, "if it hadn't been for Dad's diagnosis. I mean . . .

will I still be Lena's kid after he dies? I know you will, what with your boatload of charisma."

He smiles his charismatic smile.

"But considering that I've been something of a brat through the years," I continue, "who knows if she'll still want me around?"

"Yeah," Pierce agrees. "You're a pain in the ass. Can I divorce you, too?"

I pretend to slug him, and he reels dramatically in response with spot-on timing, making me laugh some more.

"Let's go home to our real mom and I'll talk her into setting up a cot for you in the basement," he says.

He drapes an arm around my shoulder and leads me to my car, a gentle breeze blowing.

"Oh, by the way . . ."

"Yeah?" I ask him.

"I heard the cops picked you up this afternoon? Something about the robbery?"

"Oh, yeah. Hey, did you know the back seats of cop cars don't have handles inside? Crazy, right?"

"Yeah, that's what I'm curious about: the cop car. Tell me what happened, numbskull."

Our sneakers pad on the asphalt as we continue walking. "They brought Ethan and me to the station to ID guys in a lineup," I respond. "Isn't that, like, so *CSI*?"

"Was he in the lineup?" Pierce asks. "The guy who robbed you?"

I shudder and fold my arms together. "I think so. Ethan

ID'd him, and the police apparently have some DNA evidence, so it looks like they got him."

"Now, that's the best news I've heard in a while," Pierce says.

"Right? If it hadn't been for this crappy trip to Taco Town, it probably would have qualified as the most newsworthy part of my day."

"Can I stop by the station and rough him up?" Pierce quips.

"Yeah, that's totally allowed."

Pierce opens my car door for me, then gives me a two-finger wave as I buckle up.

I watch him head to his car through my rearview mirror, and it's just as I'm about to start the ignition that I hear my cell phone ping. I glance at the screen.

Baby Girl, I am SO SORRY I won't be able to–

I delete the text without finishing it.

Then I block Mom's number on my phone.

I take a deep breath.

This is the lightest I've felt all day.

TWENTY-SEVEN

JADE

"Jade? Is that you?"

I smile over at Clay Hamilton as Gia and I walk into his house.

Gia leans in close and whispers, "Told ya."

My Daisy Buchanan costume, complete with a flapper dress, doe-eyed makeup, and finger-curl blonde wig, is causing more of a stir than I anticipated.

"You don't even look like the same person!" Clay says.

Good. Anonymity would suit me just fine tonight.

I had no intention of going to the party, but Gia finally wore me down. She's noticed that Rob has been studiously avoiding me all week—he's embarrassed about having to cancel our date to work the family circuit, I guess—so she's definitely on pity patrol again.

I told her over and over again that I didn't want to go, but she wouldn't take no for an answer, and, well, Lena had already made me the costume.

So I found myself once again in the back seat of Victor's cluttered, musty-smelling car. I'm starting to feel like their child.

But this isn't so bad, I guess. Lena and Sydney had fun doing my makeup (everything short of a spatula was involved), and Victor and Gia look kick-ass in their Bonnie and Clyde costumes. Plus, Clay's house is oozing with Halloweenishness: "Monster Mash" is filling the air, and orange-and-black decorations cover almost every square inch of his house. And from the looks of things, there are plenty of other dateless people here, so I don't feel hideously loser-like or conspicuous.

"Beer?" Clay asks me, and before I can decline, he's planting it in my hand. Oh, well. Holding the bottle will give me something to do with my fingers besides fidget.

"You really do look amazing," he tells me before floating off to the next guest.

"Hey, if you get plastered tonight, you're on your own," Gia tells me with a smirk.

I twirl my pearls with my free hand, and in my best East Egg accent ask her playfully, "Who wants to go to town?"

I kick my shin back, Charleston style, and Gia laughs.

I turn toward someone who's suddenly touching my arm. It's a guy I barely know named Keith, dressed as Spiderman with the mask pulled away from his face.

"Score!" he says. "I found myself a dance partner!"

"Whoa!" I protest, but he's already pulling me toward the middle of the greatroom, where a few people are doing Frankenstein moves to the music.

I hand my beer to Gia and let myself get pulled along. I laugh as we start dancing, comforted that the song doesn't exactly beg for graceful moves. Keith shifts his weight from side to side, banging his head rhythmically. I do the couple of hip-hop moves I know, which conveniently kinda lend themselves to Frankenstein's hunched shoulders and stiff arms.

"Damn!" Keith says, his eyes twinkling. "You've got some moves, girl!"

A couple of nearby dancers are cheering me on, too, and I really start hamming it up. What do you know: All it took was a Daisy Buchanan costume to bring out my inner party girl.

We dance to a couple more silly novelty songs and I find myself relaxing more and more. Keith's short and wiry, but he's got some moves himself.

"More refreshment is definitely in order," Keith says as a song winds down. "Can I get you a beer?"

"I've already got one somewhere," I say, seeking out Gia.

When I spot her, I tell Keith I'll catch him later, then head her way.

"You were a maniac out there!" Gia tells me.

"Yeah, well, it's not easy being fabulous."

I take my beer from her, then smile at a girl named Elyse, dressed like a mouse, as she heads my way.

That's weird: Why has Elyse just stopped in her tracks?

"Hi," I tell her, glancing around self-consciously to try to figure out why she looks so stunned.

"Jade!" she says, her jaw gaping. "I thought you . . . I heard you weren't coming tonight."

What? Why would Elyse care whether I was coming? I barely know her.

Oh. That's why.

Rob, dressed like a tomcat, is following her.

He has a stupid, silly grin on his face, and he's kind of dancing in our direction, which I guess means he doesn't recognize me in my costume. Yet.

He's singing heartily to the dance music, but then stops abruptly and turns yellow. Now he recognizes me.

"Jade."

I stare at him.

An orgy of throat-clearing ensues before he manages to spit out, "Jade! Hi!"

I raise my beer to him ever-so-subtly without changing my expression.

Elyse is keeping her mouse head bowed, peeking up occasionally to gauge the reading on the awkward meter.

"I thought you couldn't make it tonight!" Rob says, committed to jolly.

"Mmm."

"It's the damndest thing," he says, followed by more throat-clearing. "My relatives—remember I told you some relatives were coming into town?" He simulates pulling a trigger at his head. "Well, at the last minute—the very last minute, like, maybe an hour ago—they canceled! Can you believe it? And since you said you were busy with family stuff yourself, I thought, 'Oh, what the hell.'"

I wonder how flattered Elyse is by this every-man-for-himself rendition of Rob's story.

"How convenient you had matching costumes," Gia observes dryly.

"Wasn't that something?" Rob gushes, pushing past everyone's wooden stares. "That was the clincher, really. When Elyse asked me at the very last minute if I wanted to go, I was like, 'No way!' But when she mentioned she had a mouse costume . . . well, of course I immediately thought of my cat costume from last year."

I guess our glares at last are doing the trick. Finally, this jackass is sputtering out.

There's really nothing left for him to do but clear his throat. Even the stupid grin has disappeared from his face.

Elyse, her mouse head still bowed, starts inching backwards, and Rob follows her lead. He tries to spit out a couple more inane pleasantries, but Gia's raised middle finger, positioned to look like she's casually scratching her nose, stops him short. At that point, the cat and mouse scamper away in double time.

"Asshole," Gia mutters, seething.

I shake my head and take a swig of my beer. "Don't sweat it. It's not like I give a shit."

"Totally," she says too enthusiastically. "He is doing you a favor. You two were an epic mismatch. Not that anyone would be a good match for that know-it-all blowhard. Hey, you know what? You and Keith should dance some more.

You were rockin' it! I think he's in the kitchen. Do you want me to . . .?"

I turn to face her directly. "I want you to chill," I say softly but firmly. "Please?"

Gia holds my gaze for a second, then nods.

I walk over to the couch, take a seat, and polish off my beer, at which point somebody offers me another. And hey, what the hell. That pledge I made never to make a fool of myself again with alcohol? Well, the fool ship has sailed. Besides, life's a crap shoot. Dad has taken great care of himself his whole life—running marathons, playing tennis, eating fiber, the whole nine yards. A lot of good it's done him.

My stomach tightens at the thought. Well, you know what, then? I won't think about it anymore.

At some point during beer number two, several people come up and tell me what a weasel Rob is. I nod politely. A few others overcompensate, telling me how positively gorgeous I look tonight. More polite nods all around.

I think it's during beer number three that Keith asks me to dance some more.

"Only if I can take my beer with me," I say, then my beer and I rejoin the dance floor.

● ● ● ● ●

"I'm cutting you off."

It's spoil-sport Gia, snatching beer number four out of my hand as Keith and I return to the couch after a few dances.

I stick my tongue out at Gia but let her take it. I was just about to start elaborating on the physics associated with my dance moves, which reminds me of the time I decided to research how to add a word to the dictionary, which reminds me that I'm apparently the world's most pretentious drunk.

Pretentious. Superior. Maybe Rob and I were a good match after all. I laugh ruefully in spite of myself. Here I was deciding I was much too good for him, and he doesn't even give me the satisfaction of dumping him. Just like a certain birth mother who comes to mind right about now.

Oh well. At least I'm not a chronic throat-clearer.

I'm just not entirely clear what I *am*.

"You are hot," Keith says, growling in my ear. "Hey, Clay's parents are supposed to be gone all night. Wanna go find some privacy?"

Yeah, great idea. The last time I hooked up with somebody at a party it went fabulously.

"I'm good," I say.

"C'mon," Keith whines, nuzzling my ear with his nose.

"I'm good," I repeat, this time with an edge in my voice.

"I thought you liked me," he purrs, nibbling my earlobe.

I scoot farther away from him. "Watch it, will ya? You're gonna tear my wig off."

He scoots closer, still messing with my ear. "If you say so."

I spin around to face him and bore my eyes into his.

"Can you please not go all creepy on me? We had a perfectly fun time dancing. Let's just leave it at that."

He stares at me a moment, then jerks back against the couch.

"No wonder," he mutters.

"No wonder what?"

He glares at me from the corner of his eye. "No wonder Rob dumped you. Let's see, how long did that last? Three weeks, maybe four? I'm surprised he made it that long."

I've got to admit, this stings enough that for once in my life, I have no quip to fire back. I consider standing up and walking away but don't want to give him the satisfaction.

"What did you do on your dates?" Keith says, his voice dripping with contempt. "Take him to a meat locker?"

Okay, now I'm just curious. "A meat locker?" I ask him.

"'Cause your heart is made of ice."

"Ah. You know, an insult is kinda like a joke: If you have to explain it . . ."

Keith narrows his eyes. "Rob told me he wanted to dump you after the first date, but he felt bad about your dad."

My jaw drops.

"But sick dad or no, you're still an A-one bitch."

Somebody leans over from behind the couch. "Hey, wanna do me a favor, buddy?"

Keith and I both glance over our shoulders.

It's Ethan.

Resting his elbows on the top of the couch, Ethan moves

to within an inch of Keith's ear. "Wanna make yourself scarce before I break your legs?"

Keith gulps and stares straight ahead. He looks like the kid in kindergarten who can't quite make it to the bathroom on time.

"Off you go," Ethan tells him in the steadiest of voices. "Get your ass off the couch, and if I see you within a yard of Jade for the rest of the night, I'll give you a lift home. And when I'm finished lifting you, certain body parts will be missing. Are we clear?"

Keith considers this message, then *hmph*s. "Whatever," he mutters, still staring straight ahead, then pops off the couch like a slice of bread coming out of a toaster. As he disappears into the crowd, Ethan walks around the couch and sits next to me.

"Thanks," I say, smiling and feeling my cheeks grow warm. "I could have handled him, though, I promise."

"I think my mother's miniature poodle could handle him," Ethan says, and I laugh, nervously fingering the long beads around my neck. "So who are you supposed to be?"

I look at him searchingly. What does he mean? Is this some kind of existential question? Is he intuiting my ever-growing identity crisis? Is he challenging me to finally be comfortable in my own skin and my own personhood?

Oh. *Oh.*

"I'm supposed to be Daisy Buchanan. No costume for you?" I ask, surveying his shorts and T-shirt.

He waves a hand through the air with his aw-shucks smile. "Costume parties aren't really my thing."

"Then why are you here?" I ask him.

He glances away, and a warm, tingly feeling surges through my body. Because I'm here? He's here because he wanted to see me? I can't deny how amazing that feels, particularly in light of how caring and tender he was at the police station. True, I'm a little mortified that he, along with the rest of the high school, know in real time that Rob has dumped me. But maybe that's the best thing that could have happened tonight. Maybe Ethan and I really *do* stand a chance. And now that he and Brianne have broken up . . .

"Have you been doing okay?" he asks me, his Brussels-sprouts eyes searching mine.

"Yeah," I say, nodding. "Rob and I eloped Friday during study hall so, you know, the love life's going well."

His eyes twinkle. "What did you ever see in that guy in the first place?"

I shrug, then lock eyes with him. "What did you see in Brianne? I'm really curious. I'm not trying to start anything. I just don't get it, unless hotness cancels out every other annoying characteristic."

He bristles, and I bite my bottom lip.

"Sorry," I say.

"It's not about Brianne," he says, twisting his fingers into pretzels. "It's about me. I made a commitment to her. I want to be the kind of guy who honors his commitments."

"Yeah, but if you weren't compatible . . . "

His eyes flicker toward mine. "I made a commitment."

A moment passes, and Ethan says, "Hey, Jade?"

"Yeah?"

"That day at the gym? I'm really sorry if I hurt your feelings. That thing about telling you I had room for you in my life as a friend—"

"Forget it," I say and look at him sheepishly. "And I'm sorry, too. That crack about you tossing me crumbs? You've never been anything but nice to me. I'm learning the hard way that isn't so easy to come by."

He looks like he's bouncing words around in his head. Finally, he says, "Rob told me you defended me when he was calling me a Jesus freak or whatever."

My eyebrows knit together. "Why would he have told you that?"

Ethan shakes his head.

"Seriously," I persist. "Why in the world would he tell you that? I didn't know you two even talked."

Ethan shrugs, glancing at me warily before staring at his lap. "He told me he was breaking up with you because you weren't really into him. He said your heart wasn't in the relationship because . . ."

"Yes?" I prod.

His eyes meet mine. "Because you were thinking about me."

My eyebrows arch. "I never told him that!"

Ethan nods. "I know. I mean, he told me you never said it. He just said he sensed it."

I'm really too dumbfounded to speak.

Ethan inches his face closer to mine, his eyes earnest, and says, "There's one other thing I need to tell you."

I hold his gaze. "Yeah?"

He takes a deep breath. "When I told you in the police car that Brianne and I had broken up—"

"Gee, don't you two look cozy."

Ethan and I glance up and see Brianne, dressed like Marilyn Monroe. Ethan blushes.

"Hi, Brianne," I say.

She crosses her arms and surveys us coolly.

"Jade and I were just talking," Ethan says.

Clay, the party host, comes over and drapes his arm over Brianne's shoulder.

"Hell-ooo, gorgeous," he tells her, then looks at me.

"Impressive, Garrett," he tells Ethan. "You've got Marilyn Monroe on one arm and the Gatsby chick on the other."

I'm too busy churning in my own discomfort to notice Ethan's and Brianne's expressions, but a pall suddenly falls over the room.

"I was just giving you a hard time, man," Clay says, aiming for breezy. "I mean, two beautiful girls? Score, right?"

Still no break in the tension.

"Hey, man, sorry if I'm stepping in it," Clay says. "I just thought you were . . . Say, who *are* you here with tonight?"

The moment lingers as all eyes fall on Ethan, who is staring at his hands.

"Brianne, of course," he mutters.

Of course.

I stand up, smoothing my flapper dress. "Gonna get some air," I say under my breath.

As I start to walk outside, Gia catches my eye from across the room. "Ya okay?" she mouths, and I nod, clenching my fists.

I open the front door and smile politely to a small gathering on the porch. Oh, goody: Rob and Elyse are among them. A guy sweeps his arm toward one of the porch chairs, but I beg off. "Just getting a little air," I say, then fold my arms and walk toward the driveway. The evening is crisp and cool, with stars twinkling in a velvety, blue-black sky.

I walk toward the street, then take a random right and keep going.

"Jade!"

I turn around and see Ethan, standing at the edge of the driveway. "Where are you going?" he asks.

"Taking a walk." I keep moving but hear his sneakers gaining on me.

"I didn't lie to you!" he says. "Brianne and I really did break up. It's just, well, we—"

"Whatever," I say, throwing a hand in the air and continuing to walk away.

"Would you just wait?" Ethan says.

"Go back to your girlfriend," I call without turning around or slowing my stride. "Or your ex-girlfriend. Or your ex-ex-girlfriend, or whichever version you'd like me to believe."

I hear his sneakers thudding in my direction. "I can't

believe you're going to do this again!" he sputters, catching up with me.

"Do what?"

"Act like this again!"

I stop and look at him. "Like what?"

"Like you're mad, or I'm doing something wrong, or you're expecting something from me."

I gaze at him. "Don't flatter yourself, Ethan."

"See? I can't do anything without pissing you off! It's making me crazy, because I really, really want to be your friend."

I consider his words. "In the immortal words of Mick Jagger," I finally say, "you can't always get what you want."

He clenches his fists, beads of perspiration dotting his forehead. "Why not? Why can't we be friends?"

I hesitate, but then forge ahead: "I think what you want, what you really, really want, is to be the gosh-darn nicest guy anybody's ever met."

He juts out his jaw. "What does that mean?"

"That's what you're committed to: your good-guy reputation."

He runs a hand through his hair. "And that's a crime? Yes, I want to be a nice guy. I take my faith seriously. I want to set a good example."

"So we're all looking to you as our moral compass?" I say. "Nothing superior about that."

"You're putting words in my mouth!"

I rest a fingertip on my bottom lip. "If there's a god," I

say, "do you know what I think he wants? I think he wants you to be true to yourself."

"That's why I'm trying to do," he says through gritted teeth.

"And I'm not talking about picking one girl over another: Marilyn versus Daisy, or what-the-hell-ever. I'm talking about making real choices based on what you really feel and owning your decisions." I shake my head slowly. "You know what's ironic? I used to think I was the one you were tossing crumbs to. Now I realize it's Brianne."

He squeezes his eyes shut.

"You're not doing her any favors, you know," I continue. "I actually feel kinda sorry for her. She deserves a real guy, Ethan, not a paper cutout or a martyr. No wonder she's so damn insecure."

He frowns and glares.

"Want some advice?" I say. "Quit trying so hard. Quit trying so hard to impress everybody, or be an example to everybody, or save everybody."

His eyes flicker toward mine and I hold his gaze.

"Save yourself, Ethan."

TWENTY-EIGHT

JADE

"Something wrong, Jade?"

I listlessly poke my peas with my fork. "Nah," I tell my dad.

I couldn't sleep after last night's Halloween party, each mortifying moment playing on an endless loop in my mind with high-definition precision. Today, a Sunday, is actually Halloween; but Dad was concerned the construction work at our house might present safety hazards, so we're leaving the porch lights off this year. All the same, we can hear trick-or-treaters nearby as we eat our dinner, shrieking and squealing and laughing as they run from house to house like Pierce and I did just a few years ago.

Now Lena, Dad, Pierce, and I are sitting gloomily inside, pushing peas around our plates, ignoring the occasional lights-are-off-but-might-as-well-give-it-a-try doorbell ring. Sydney's outside trick-or-treating in the Hermione Granger Gryffindor costume Lena made for her, and Dad's too weak from today's chemo to do more than sip his water. This time last year, we'd decorated the house in a mad-scientist theme. Dad was Frankenstein and Lena was his bride, with a mile-high black wig streaked with white. They were serving lemonade on the porch to the trick-or-treaters and their parents. That was last year. Tonight, Dad can barely muster the energy to sit up. I feel like I went straight to hell without passing go.

I know that's over-dramatic. I keep trying to follow Dad's lead—smile, count your blessings, make lemonade out of lemons—but the knot in the pit of my stomach never seems to loosen. I've given serious consideration to Lena's admonition to proceed with my original college plans for Dad's sake, but in the same breath that I'm exhilarated by the prospect of getting out of the house, I have the suffocating sensation of being away from Dad when he needs me most.

"Are you and Rob studying for midterms together next week?" Lena asks.

Pierce averts his eyes. News has certainly trickled his way by now about Rob's date last night with Elyse. Pierce wouldn't touch this subject with a pole. Our typical vibe is to crack wise, and he doesn't have the heart to make light of his sister being the biggest loser/laughingstock in school, particularly on the heels of our birth mom's epic diss.

"Nope," I tell Lena simply.

Ding-dong.

Dad grips his fork tighter. "I don't understand why parents don't tell their kids to stay away from the unlighted houses," he says.

I know the random doorbell rings are bothering him

more than anybody—stark reminders that all the fake cheeriness in the world can't conceal the fact that joy and festivity no longer live here. The lemonade stand has closed for good.

"Actually, my stomach's a little upset," I say after a while, no longer able to bear my family's pained eyes and pinched mouths. "And I've got some studying to do. Mind if I excuse myself early?"

Lena and Dad exchange anxious glances but murmur their consent.

"Call me when you're finished so I can wash the dishes, Lena," I say, and she promises she will, although I know she won't.

I go in my room and shut the door, the laughter of trick-or-treaters punctuating the air outside my window.

My cell phone rings and I glance at the screen. Gia.

Sigh.

I've already ignored a handful of her calls and texts today, but I owe it to her to answer the phone. She was so great last night, rushing to my side after my come-to-Jesus lecture with Ethan in the middle of the street. She pulled me back toward Clay's house, shooing Ethan away and insisting she and Victor would cut their date short and take me right home. What a goddess I must have looked like in the musty, cluttered back seat of Victor's car as we drove away, all done up like Daisy Buchanan with nowhere to go. Gia tried to follow me inside when they got to my house, but I waved her back into the car. Funny how many times I've waved her away lately. Maybe it's time I stopped doing that.

"Are you okay?" she asks when I answer the phone.

My bottom lip trembles. "I'm a mess," I whisper.

"Well, I knew that."

I manage the tiniest of smiles in spite of myself.

"Gia, I'm so sorry I've been such a crappy friend," I say, flopping onto my bed and hugging a pillow against my chest. "Is it a halfway decent excuse that my life has been horrible lately?"

"Hey, you were the bitchin'-est babe at that party last night," she says gently.

"Good times," I quip, and she laughs lightly.

"Gia," I continue, "I've got all kinds of crap to get you caught up on."

"Ooh, I love all kinds of crap," she says.

"You don't know the half of it."

"Wanna give me a hint?"

I twirl a lock of hair in my finger. "Um . . . random correspondence from a long-lost mother is involved," I say.

"Oh wow."

"And a guy I'm secretly hung up on who I started to believe might be secretly hung up on me, too, until I figured out he lied to me about breaking up with his girlfriend."

"Oh, Jade."

"And trying to decide if a certain stepmother—not mentioning any names—might decide to bail on me after my dad dies because I'm an epically ungrateful brat."

"Jade," Gia coos sympathetically.

"And trying to figure out how to break it to the world's best BFF that I'm opting for Tolliver Community College next year to stay close to my dad."

"I'm coming over right now," Gia says, her voice steady as always.

I smile. "Thank you for not hating me," I say.

"I didn't say that. I just said I'm coming over."

I bite my lip lightly, smiling. "Considering I've been bottling up this conversation for weeks now, could we delay it for maybe just one more day?" I ask. "All I want to do right now is sleep."

Gia takes a deep breath. "Okay. But you owe me a shit-load of details."

"One shitload of details coming right up," I say, my lashes fluttering.

"Do you promise?"

I'm still smiling, buffeted by the warmth of her voice. "I promise."

● ● ● ● ●

"Help! Help!"

My lashes flicker and I jolt into consciousness. When did I nod off? I'm still wearing my shorts, and my school books are strewn around me, but I feel like I've been sleeping for hours. I glance at the clock: Ten-fifty. Wow. It's not even eleven o'clock yet, and I rarely go to sleep before midnight.

"Help!"

I bolt out of my bed, sending my textbooks flying. Dad is calling me from his bedroom.

I run into his room and flip on the light.

Dad is lying face-down on the bedroom floor, trying to push himself up on his arms while alternately screaming for help and gasping for air. His loose pajamas swallow his ever-shrinking frame.

"Lena!" I scream at the top of my lungs, then fall to my knees at Dad's side.

"It's okay," I tell him, turning him from his stomach to his back, then easing him back upright. His mouth and the floor are stained with vomit.

"I . . . couldn't make it to the bathroom . . ." he says. "I think I broke my ankle when I fell."

I try to lift him in my arms but can't support his weight. What do I do? What do I do? What do I do?

I hear Lena, Pierce, and Sydney running up the stairs. When they bound into the room, Pierce drops to the floor, inadvertently barreling me aside, and scoops Dad in his arms. Lena kneels by their side.

"I'll call nine-one-one," I say numbly.

"We can get to the hospital faster if I drive us there," Pierce says, then speaks directly to Dad. "If I lift you up and put your arm around my shoulder, do you think you can make it to the car?"

Dad nods weakly, wincing in pain.

Lena steps aside to make room for Pierce, who painstakingly helps Dad to his feet. Lena rushes to the other side, and Dad drapes one arm around each of their shoulders. I catch Sydney's eye and see her shaking in her Manga nightgown. I grab her hand and run out of the room with her, opening doors wide as Pierce and Lena inch Dad through the house.

"Open the car door!" Pierce calls to me after I reach the porch.

I run to the car and follow his instructions. Pierce and Lena gently lead Dad to the car, then ease him into the passenger seat.

"I can drive," I mumble, but Pierce is already shooing Lena, Sydney, and me to the back seat. Sydney is gulping down sobs.

The car squeals out of the driveway and dings relentlessly, reminding us Dad's seatbelt is unbuckled.

Dad turns in his seat to smile wanly at us, reaching to pat Sydney on the leg.

"I'm fine," he says. "I'm fine. I'm so sorry I scared you."

Sydney buries her head in Lena's arms and weeps softly.

"It's okay, baby," Dad repeats to her. "Everything's gonna be okay."

TWENTY-NINE

JADE

"So you missed the cafeteria food, huh?"

We all laugh too loudly at Dr. Brecken's joke—a sign of hours' worth of accumulated stress.

Dr. Brecken winks at us. "Just can't keep your dad away from that strawberry Jell-O," she teases.

Our stint in the emergency room stretched for hours (Grandma picked up Sydney once Dad was settled) so Lena, Pierce, and I are watching the sun rise with zero sleep, other than a few catnaps in boxy vinyl chairs.

At least Dad has been admitted now and is finally comfortable in a hospital bed.

Dr. Brecken is telling us all kinds of cheery things; there's lots they can do for Dad, she assures us—increase the dosage of his nausea medicine, give him an electric wheelchair while his ankle heals, send him home with a monitor (like a baby monitor, she helpfully clarifies)—all kinds of things.

"No matter how much you like our food," she tells Dad, "I'm anticipating you'll be home by dinnertime tomorrow."

Dad thanks her effusively, and we all join in gamely,

as the doctor wraps things up. On to the next patient. She can be as cheery as she wants, because no matter how good-hearted she is, the fact is that she can walk out the door and leave this goddamn disease behind. We can't.

"Speaking of leaving," Lena tells Pierce and me, "I've got to get you two to school."

"Honey, don't make them go today," Dad says. "They haven't slept all night."

"Well . . . we can talk about that a little later. Right now, how about a trip to the cafeteria for breakfast? You, of course, will get room service," Lena tells Dad.

"You two go ahead," I tell Lena and Pierce. "I'll be down in a little while."

"Ya sure?" Lena asks, and I nod.

When they leave, I close the door behind them, then walk over to Dad's bed, twisting my fingers together.

"Dad, I want you to know something," I say, plunging right in before I lose my nerve.

"What is it, honey?"

I lean close to his face and rest my hand on his shaved head. "When you've had enough of this—I know we're not there yet, but when we are—I want you to let me know. I won't let the doctors do anything to you that you don't want done. I will do whatever it takes, whatever you want, to keep you from suffering."

Dad reads my eyes warily.

"Honey . . ."

"I mean it," I say firmly.

Dad blinks several times.

"Oh, Jade."

A clock on the wall ticks methodically. *Tick . . . tick . . . tick . . . tick . . .*

Dad considers my words, then says, "I am truly grateful for every day I have on this earth. Granted, I hate burdening my family—that drives me nuts—but I know you guys can take it."

I smile.

"I didn't raise any wusses, you know. And I know you can not only take it, but you can learn from it. And you'll take that wisdom and compassion into the world and use it to help other people."

I smile sadly. "No pressure there."

Dad's weary eyes twinkle. "No. No pressure. You don't have to do extraordinary things to live an extraordinary life. Just take your wisdom and compassion wherever you go. The extraordinary part will follow."

A tear rolls down my cheek, and Dad reaches over and wipes it away. "Believe it or not," he tells me, "there are still lots of things I'd rather do than die."

I wistfully think back to my night with Ethan in the aerobics room, then our remix a few weeks later in the neurologist's waiting room. Let's play a new game: things we'd rather do than die.

"Are you afraid to die?" I ask Dad, realizing too late that I'm afraid of his answer.

"No," he says simply, and my heart floods with relief.

I can stand almost anything, but I couldn't bear for my father to be afraid.

"Do you think there's really a heaven?" I ask him.

"My idea of heaven," Dad says, "is being able to connect with the people I love—with my children, and your children, and their children—and guide them spiritually. That's it. That's all I want. And I've still got that here on earth. I get to connect with you and guide you. And for however much longer I have on earth, I get the bonus of being able to touch you and talk to you and laugh with you and nag you."

We both laugh through a new wave of tears.

Dad strokes my hair. "We'll get through this together, honey. I promise."

● ● ● ● ●

"Brianne?"

Her eyes flicker toward me as the hospital's elevator doors close behind her. "Hi," Brianne responds grudgingly, then adds, "What are you doing here?"

"Um . . . my dad. We had to take him to the emergency room last night, and they admitted him this morning. I was just going to the cafeteria to grab some breakfast."

"Oh," she says, lowering her head and pulling a lock of hair behind her ear. "I'm sorry about your dad."

"Thanks. How about you? Why are you here?"

A flash of surprise crosses her face. "You haven't heard?"

My eyebrows knit together. "Heard what?"

"Um, I guess he wouldn't mind me telling you."

The elevator dings and the doors open on the first floor. Brianne and I step out and start walking down the hall together. "Ethan's dad crashed his car last night; wrapped it around a tree."

I gasp slightly and stop in my tracks. "Oh, no! Is he alright?"

"He's in intensive care," Brianne says. "It's really bad."

I swallow hard. "Are you headed for the cafeteria, too?" I finally manage to ask her.

She shakes her head as we resume walking. "I'm leaving now, going to school. I just wanted to stop by on the way and let Ethan know that I was, well, you know."

I nod. "Do you think he'd mind if I dropped by and said hello?"

She looks at me from the corner of her eye as we continue walking.

"Like I have anything to say about it," she murmurs.

"What do you mean?"

We reach an intersecting hallway. I'll take a left to go to the cafeteria. Brianne will take a right to leave the hospital. We linger while she considers my question.

"You know he broke up with me last night," she says.

I gasp again. "I didn't know."

Brianne shrugs and shifts her weight, her face hardening even as her eyes mist up. "Whatever," she says, crossing her arms.

"Brianne, I promise there's nothing going on between Ethan and me. I had no idea."

She snorts a little, but then her face crinkles. She dips her chin down so I won't see her tears.

"I'm so sorry," I say, contemplating touching her arm but not quite able to do it.

Brianne looks up, her eyes shimmering. "I guess it was stupid of me to come see him. It's time that I—"

"No, no," I murmur. "I'm sure he's really grateful you came."

She shrugs. "It's just that I know how he feels, you know? My mom's an alcoholic, too, so . . ."

I swallow hard. "I didn't know. I'm really sorry."

She flips a lock of blonde hair over her shoulder. "It's all good. At least my mother's never been in intensive care. So far."

I stand there motionless, clueless how to react.

"I really am sorry about your dad, Jade," she says.

"Thank you," I respond, thinking I should say more but not finding the words.

"Well," Brianne says, "I guess I'll see you around."

I offer a slight wave as Brianne heads toward the exit.

I'm frozen in my spot for a few seconds, feeling like I've been sucker-punched. Ethan broke up with her? Whoa. I never intended that to happen . . . did I?

What exactly *did* I intend with my self-righteous speech at the Halloween party? And why was I so smug about Brianne in the first place? Of course she was jealous of me; she should have been. She could see what I wasn't willing to admit to myself: that I'm totally falling for Ethan.

Was. I totally *was* falling for him. Has all this damage finally snapped me out of my ridiculous crush? Maybe they were a great couple, Ethan and Brianne. Everybody thought so. Here I was, dismissing her as a superficial twit and arrogantly assuming I knew anything about her.

I didn't know shit.

THIRTY

ETHAN

I choke down a sip of weak coffee, wince, and push cold scrambled eggs listlessly around my plate with a plastic fork.

I was still awake at one a.m. when the call came that Dad was in the emergency room. Brianne had kept me on the phone for two hours trying to talk me out of our breakup. I was almost relieved when Uncle Byron's call forced me off the line. I threw on some jeans and a T-shirt, brushed my teeth, and drove Mom to the hospital, my wipers flapping intermittently against chilly November drizzle. We've been here ever since, gazing down at Dad's purplish face and listening to the steady lull of a dozen different beeps. This seven a.m. coffee break in the hospital cafeteria is the first time I've stepped away since we got here. Mom hasn't left his side at all.

I'm still a little shaky from Brianne's visit—yes, the breakup is final this time, but I still hate to see her hurt—so even though the coffee tastes like kerosene, it's helping to calm my nerves.

"Ethan."

I look up and see Pastor Rick.

I stand up and offer a handshake that morphs into a hug. I swallow a lump in my throat.

"I came as soon as I heard," he says. "I'm so sorry."

I nod. "Thanks so much for stopping by."

"Sure, sure," he responds gently, and I wave him into the seat across from mine.

"I wasn't sure when we drove here last night whether Mom and I would be headed for a hospital room or the morgue," I tell Pastor Rick as we settle into our seats.

"So what happened?" he asks.

I squeeze the bridge of my nose wearily. "Car accident," I say. "Just Dad and a tree, thank God. My uncle called sometime after midnight, said it was really bad. Go figure, though. Looks like he's cheated death one more time."

"I'd like to go pray with him—pray for him—if that's okay," Pastor Rick says, and I nod eagerly.

"Of course. Thank you so much."

He holds my gaze, seeming to bounce some thoughts around in his head.

"Ethan," he finally says, "the last few conversations we've had have really stuck with me. I've given your concerns a lot of thought, and I don't think I did them justice earlier."

I peer at him anxiously. "No, no, Pastor Rick—"

"It was kind of ironic," he says, lightly rubbing his beard. "When you told me you were concerned about your relationship with Brianne, I counseled you to own your true feelings—to be honest with everyone involved, including yourself."

"Yeah?"

"But before that, you'd stopped by my office to express some doubts you were having."

"Pastor Rick, I was just having a bad day," I say, feeling my neck grow warm. "I didn't mean to make you think—"

"As I recall," Pastor Rick continues, leaning into his elbows, "I quoted the Book of James: 'The one who doubts is like a wave in the sea, blown and tossed by the wind.'"

My eyes drop. "I agree with that," I say softly. "How strong can someone's faith really be if they get knocked off balance any time someone rags on their beliefs?"

I feel disloyal even as I say it. Jade never ragged on my beliefs. She just challenged me, that's all. But I really need my faith right now. I don't want to be blown and tossed by the wind. I want to feel the one thing I never felt before I opened my heart to Jesus: steady on my feet.

"I agree, too," Pastor Rick says with a light chuckle. "Good thing, what with me being a pastor and all."

I laugh back.

"But the thing is," he continues slowly, "I have doubts, too."

I study his eyes. "Really?"

He nods. "Really. Time for me to own how I really feel, right? Ethan, my mother committed suicide when I was seventeen."

I gasp. "Oh my gosh!"

"My brother died of leukemia when he was three. I barely remember him, but Mom was never the same. She felt like she'd done everything right—she *had* done everything right—yet she had to deal with this? A doctor prescribed some pills for her anxiety, and she basically got hooked. One day while I was at school, she swallowed the whole bottle. I'm the one who found her."

"Pastor Rick, I had no idea—"

"So where's the meaning in that?"

Utensils clatter lightly around us as Pastor Rick's face pinches at the memory.

"You think I haven't asked myself that question a million times?" he continues, sadness flooding his eyes. "See, Ethan, the thing is we all have doubts. And it doesn't mean your faith is weak. It means you're human."

I pitch forward slightly. "I'm so sorry for what you've been through."

Pastor Rick folds his hands together on the table. "I think James was wise to use the analogy of waves in the sea," he says, "Overcoming doubts isn't about being saved from turbulent waters. It's about learning how to swim through the waves, even the rough ones. I decided the day my mother died that I wanted to devote the rest of my life to teaching people how to swim."

I nod, my chin trembling.

"So just like we need to own our feelings about earthly matters," he says, "we need to own our doubts about God.

It's when you resist your feelings that they take on a life of their own."

I nod again. If life has taught me nothing else in the past few weeks, it's taught me that.

"God can handle your doubts," Pastor Rick says. "He'll see you through the turbulent waters."

Soft chatter continues unfolding at the tables around us.

"Oh, and Ethan, one more thing."

"Yes?"

Pastor Rick rests a hand on my forearm. "We're not our parents, Ethan," he says quietly. "I'm not my mother. You're not your father. I know how hard you've tried to lead your dad to God, and as long as there's a breath in his body, it's not too late. But relieve yourself of the burden of trying to change his heart. God's got this."

I swallow hard. I love Pastor Rick for knowing how badly I needed to hear that.

"Hey, any updates on you and Brianne?" Pastor Rick asks gently. "What's up with that?"

I smile wanly. "Interesting timing. I broke up with her last night. I hate hurting her, but I think it was the right thing to do." Jade's right. I'm not doing Brianne any favors by tossing her crumbs.

"Well," Pastor Rick says, "there are very few people on earth whose instincts I trust more than yours."

I blink back a sudden wave of tears.

I don't know that I've ever appreciated a compliment more.

• • • • •

JADE

The elevator doors open, and I walk into the intensive-care unit. I pass a waiting room where I hear muffled cries, then press a button to access a locked door.

"Yes?" a voice asks over the intercom.

"I'm here to visit a Mr. Garrett? If that's okay?"

The disembodied voice buzzes me through.

Once I enter, I look around at a unit unlike any I've ever seen in a hospital. No rooms here, just a central nursing station ringed by areas with transparent panels. Doorways lead to each area, but there's no door, just an open space that health care providers can burst through at a moment's notice. The patients behind those transparent walls are clearly visible from the nurses' station, and several moans emerge from the beds. Some of the patients look gray, some deathly pale. Intravenous lines hang from their arms. A few visitors hover fretfully by their sides. Beeps, buzzes, flashing lights and pages punctate the air.

This unit is strictly business. Every moment, every action, every reaction is potentially a matter of life and death. There's no idle chatter at the nurses' station, no privacy, no niceties, no jokes about strawberry Jell-O on this unit.

I immediately feel like a fraud, and wish I hadn't come. This is where some people are spending the last moments of their lives, where priests are giving last rites, where loved ones are dabbing their eyes with tissues. Who am I to be here? I don't even know the man I'm visiting, not counting the time I screamed at him on a football field.

I want to leave, to slink away as inconspicuously as possible, but I assume the door will have to be unlocked for me again, and I feel terrible for putting people to all this trouble.

"Can I help you?" a nurse asks.

"Uh . . . I'm not really a . . . I mean, I'm just a . . ."

"Who are you here to see?" she prods.

"Um . . . Mr. Garrett?"

A petite lady in a sweatshirt and sweat pants suddenly rushes to my side. "Hi, Jade," she says.

I nod, feeling my face flush. "Hi," I say to Ethan's mom. "I heard about the accident and wanted to stop by and say how sorry I was."

"How sweet of you, darlin'," she says, seemingly intent on making me feel less out of place.

"I just feel terrible for you, Mrs.—I mean Ms.—"

"Call me Carla." She smiles. "Would you like to see him?"

"Uh . . ."

But she's already leading me to one of the beds, through the doorway and on the other side of a transparent wall.

Ethan's father lies on the bed, unconscious and motionless, a myriad of machinery making various calculations: his blood pressure, his heart rate, his oxygen intake. Cuts and bruises cover his face and neck.

"He was thrown clear from the car," Mrs. Garrett whispers. "A good thirty feet."

I nod, peering at him. "I'm so sorry," I tell her.

"Thank you. We've been divorced for years now, but, well, you know, he's my son's daddy, and he really doesn't have anybody else. I mean, there's his mama, but she's gettin' on in years."

"It's great that you're here for him."

Carla nods. "He never was much of a husband or father," she says. "He's had a drinking problem since he was, oh, I don't know, probably fourteen years old. But he does the best he can, you know? He doesn't know how to be any different. His daddy and granddaddy were both alcoholics, too. He just doesn't know any better. Breaks my heart for Ethan. I always tried to encourage them to be close. I still bring him food, clean up a little. Some people call that enabling, but what can I say? He gave me my son. I'll always love him for that."

I nod. "Where is Ethan?" I ask.

"Downstairs, gettin' some breakfast."

"That's where I was headed when I heard the news," I say. "I just came right up here instead."

"That's very kind."

Then she puts two and two together.

"You were already here?" she clarifies. "So you have somebody in the hospital, too?"

I nod. "My dad. He has glioblastoma. That's cancer of the—"

Carla nods solemnly. "I know what it is. Lost a friend to it. I read about your daddy in the newspaper. I'm just so sorry, darlin'."

I offer a weak smile. "Thanks. He fell last night and . . ."

She takes my hand and squeezes it. "Then you need to get back to your daddy," she says.

"Oh, he's much better now. In fact, he's probably coming home tomorrow."

"I'll be praying for him."

"Thank you. Thank you so much."

She hugs me and I walk out. Next stop: cafeteria.

● ○ ● ○ ●

"Hi."

Ethan and the man at his table glance up from their coffee. Ethan does a double-take.

"Jade. What are you doing here?"

I take the empty seat next to the man's and smile at him nervously.

"Jade," Ethan says, "this is my pastor."

"Nice to meet you, Reverend—"

"Rick. It's Rick," he says, then smiles and shakes my hand.

"Jade Fulton," I say.

"Yes. I know your dad. We've worked on several fundraisers together over the years. Jade, I'm so sorry about his cancer."

I nod. "Thank you. That's why I'm here. We brought

him to the emergency room last night. It was a little scary, but he'll be okay."

Right. Dad will never be okay again.

"May I drop by his room and say hello?" the pastor asks.

I smile. "He'd really appreciate that," I reply.

"Jade, I'm so sorry," Ethan says.

"Thanks. And, hey, I just heard about your dad," I say. "I went up and saw him. I hope that's okay."

"Of course."

"Speaking of," Pastor Rick says. "I'm headed that way myself. Then I'll check in on your dad, Jade."

"Thank you. Thanks so much."

"Pastor Rick, I'm so grateful you came," Ethan says.

He shrugs. "That's what I do. God bless you both."

We all wave lightly as he walks away.

Ethan leans into the table. "How'd you hear about my dad?"

"I ran into Brianne." I lean closer and furrow my brow. "Ethan, you broke up with her?"

"Yeah."

"Because of what I said?" I ask in a frantic whisper. "Ethan, I was just being my typical big-mouth self. I didn't expect you to break up with her!"

He taps an index finger absently against his coffee cup. "You were right."

"I was stupid!" I say, still whispering. "Look, I have my hands full screwing up my own life; don't let me screw up yours."

Ethan rubs the light stubble on his chin. "It's like you said: I wasn't being fair to her."

I moan and drop my face in my hands. "No, no, no. What I said wasn't about you; it was about me. It was about my own stupid insecurity. I don't know where I get off telling you what to do, because—"

"Here's the thing," Ethan says, his eyes resting on the breakfast he's pushing around on his plate. "It's not fair to waste somebody's time when your heart's not in it. You're right: how arrogant of me to think I was doing Brianne a favor. Lucky girl, she gets me. Woo-hoo."

I shake my head, exasperated. "Your heart was in it. You do really care about—"

"It's not fair to waste Brianne's time," Ethan continues in the same tone of voice, "when all I can think about when I'm with her is . . ."

I lean closer. "Yes?"

"Is a girl who has a thing about belly buttons."

I try to make eye contact, but he won't let me.

He shrugs. "So that's what's up with that."

He spears a piece of scrambled egg on his fork and pops it in his mouth.

"Ethan," I say.

He chews and swallows, then stares into space. "You know that thing you said about me wanting to convince everybody I'm the ultimate good guy?"

I squeeze my eyes shut and slowly shake my head. "I didn't know what I was talking—"

"You were pretty close, but you didn't quite nail it." He's pushing his food around again with his fork.

"What do you mean?" I ask.

"I honestly don't think I'm trying to convince other people of anything. I think I'm trying to convince myself that I'm not my dad."

I consider his words, then impulsively reach across the table and cup my hand over his.

"So that's lesson one from the assignment you gave me," Ethan says, finally meeting my eyes.

"Assignment?"

"To be true to myself."

"Oh."

"I guess being true to myself starts with being honest with myself," he continues. "So, yeah, I think I'm finally starting to get that I have to focus on who I want to be rather than who I don't want to be."

I raise an eyebrow. "And lesson two?"

His eyes drop again. "Lesson two is admitting to myself that I'm in love with you."

THIRTY-ONE

JADE

All around us, people are going through the motions of life in a hospital. Doctors in white coats, nurses in scrubs, people with bloodshot eyes—they're mechanically carrying their trays to a table, or chewing a tasteless meal, or staring blankly into space as they pick at their food, or strapping their purse over a shoulder and heading out of the cafeteria.

Even those sharing a table are mostly quiet; the snatches of conversations I overhear as I sit in stunned silence are rote and concise: "Don't forget to bring Mom's glasses back when you go home to take a shower," "The test results should be back in a couple of hours," "I missed the doctor this morning, but the nurse says he should be back in the afternoon," "I've called Aunt June; can you call Aunt Barbara?"

Faces are dazed or resigned. Everybody looks tired. Theoretically, some people in a hospital are happy—those having babies, for instance—but those people are less likely to visit the hospital cafeteria. The happy people zip down the street for takeout wearing an "It's a Boy!" button, then smuggle a nice meal to their wives' bedside. Those people have appetites.

The dazed people are milling about as Ethan tells me he loves me. I freeze for a moment, wondering if my heart is even beating. I realize my mouth has dropped and forced myself to shut it.

I ask, "Where do we go from here?"

Ethan shrugs. "We don't have to go anywhere. I'm just trying to be honest."

"But what does that mean?"

A look of hurt flashes in his eyes. "Chill, Jade. You don't have to do anything. This is my issue, not yours."

I bristle. "You know I feel the same way," I say.

He holds my gaze. "I know that, do I?"

"Duh."

I study the confusion on his face, then say, "Well, Brianne sure knows."

His eyes widen. "You two talked?"

I roll my eyes. "We didn't have to talk. She knew how I felt from the moment she found us locked in the aerobics room together. That's why she put me on notice. Maybe she's smarter than both of us put together. Or maybe everybody's smarter than us. Even Preppy Rob figured that one out."

For the first time since I've sat down, we both smile—guarded smiles, for sure, but smiles nonetheless.

A silver-haired lady walks past us with a tray and beams down at us. We smile back and offer tepid waves.

Ethan's face turns somber again. "I never wanted to hurt Brianne," he says.

I nod. "I don't want to hurt her, either. She must really care about you. I mean, she spent hours looking for you the night we were robbed, and she came here this morning, even though you'd just broken up with her."

"She's not a bad person," Ethan says softly. "She's got her stuff, just like all of us do. But, you know, I'm her friend, not her savior."

I bite my bottom lip. "Do you love her?"

He holds my gaze. "I love you."

He thinks for a moment, then says, "I really thought I loved her, until I got to know you. Who'd have figured: the Christian and the atheist."

I wrinkle my nose. "I told you, I'm not an atheist. I'm a . . . wonderer. A figure-outer."

More people ease past us with their trays.

"But we are awfully different in a lot of ways," I say slowly.

I glance at his tray. "I mean, those eggs you're eating? They look disgusting."

Ethan's lopsided grin slides up his face.

"Seriously," I continue, poker-faced, "I just don't know if I could be with a guy who likes watery scrambled eggs."

Ethan's eyes glisten. "Come to my church with me sometime, just once. Even if we're all full of crap, we have a good time, and we're there for each other, you know?"

I smile and extend my hand. Ethan shakes it.

"Deal," I say. "And, hey, you can come with me to Lena's church sometime. The Catholics may just win you over with their spontaneity."

We sputter with laughter.

"Hey," I continue, "let's go to lots of churches—like a fact-finding tour. We can even throw in a temple, and a mosque."

"I actually love that idea," Ethan says.

"Oh, just because you want to convert everybody," I tease, and he laughs some more.

It feels so good to see him laugh.

"But mostly," I say, "let's just concentrate on being friends for a while. No pressure. I mean, we started our relationship with a gun shoved in our faces. How about if we lighten it up and take things slow?"

"I think," he says, "that sounds like the best idea I've heard all day."

THIRTY-TWO

JADE

I hear giggles as I climb the stairs.

It's only eight o'clock, but considering I had no sleep last night, I'm headed for bed. Lena and Sydney said they were, too, but whatever last-minute conversation they started up has clearly given them a second wind.

I head for the source of the laughter and see them cuddling on Dad and Lena's king-size bed. And then—what the hell—I make a running leap and tumble into the covers with them.

"Aw, group hug," Lena says as our arms entwine.

Lena didn't sleep last night either, of course, but she managed to make dinner, oversee homework and call Dad's nurse for one last check-in before calling it a night.

"What did the nurse say?" I ask her.

"Daddy's sleeping peacefully," Lena responds. "He'll probably be home by this time tomorrow."

"Yay!" Sydney says, hoisting her arms in the air, at which point I tickle her armpits. She wriggles away, laughing, then reaches for my armpits.

"Payback!"

"You wish!" I say, clamping my arms against my side.

"Hey, I have a better idea," Lena tells Sydney. "You know what your sister really hates?"

"What?" Sydney asks.

I eye Lena skittishly and echo, "Yeah, what?"

Lena gets a glimmer in her eye, then grins and says, "A belly button attack!"

She and Sydney shriek with laughter as their fingers aim for my navel. I howl in protest, rolling myself into a ball.

"You touch, you die!" I wail, and they laugh some more before backing off.

I wait a moment before uncoiling myself, peering at them suspiciously. "How did you know about my deal with belly buttons?" I ask Lena, genuinely curious.

She drops her jaw. "Seriously?"

"Yeah, seriously," I say through more laughter.

"I've known you hated belly buttons ever since you refused a Cabbage Patch doll on the grounds that she had one," she says.

We're all still laughing.

"I don't remember that," I say, staring lazily at the ceiling fan.

"As I recall, you were particularly grossed out because it was an outie," Lena continues.

"That's a perfectly acceptable reason to reject one's offspring," I say, our grins pasted to our faces.

Which makes me wonder . . .

Did Pierce tell Lena about Mom? I dunno. If so, Lena's waiting for me to come to her about it. And maybe I will. On the other hand, it suddenly seems way unimportant.

"Bedtime, kiddo," Lena tells Sydney, who moans in protest.

"C'mon," Lena prods. "You've got a big day tomorrow. You get to show off your science project."

"Oh, is it that egg shell thing to see what stains your teeth?" I ask, recalling the voluminous cartons of materials I've noticed accumulating in the kitchen.

"Yep," Sydney says. "Alicia and I are partners."

I wince teasingly. "How's that going?"

"Okay," Syd says. "She's been a lot nicer to me lately."

"Only because you're teaching her how to avoid gray teeth," I say faux-solemnly, and we laugh some more.

"Because she's sticking up for herself," Lena says, nodding smartly while tousling Sydney's hair. "Our little pipsqueak's turning out to be a tiger."

"Well," Sydney says, "I've supplied all the eggs for the project, so if we make an A, Alicia owes me—"

"—an omelet?" I respond.

"—a quiche?" Lena suggests.

"Well, *some* kind of breakfast," Sydney says, and we nod in agreement that this is the least she can do.

"Don't forget to brush your teeth before you go to bed," I tell her. "If you're lecturing everybody about teeth, you can rest assured they're all gonna be staring at yours."

"Excellent point," Lena says. "Now, scat."

Sydney climbs off the bed, her silky nightgown brushing against my leg, then blows a kiss as she heads out the door.

The ceiling fan clicks rhythmically as I continue staring at it.

"I love that Syd is sticking up for herself. I really can't stand it when people are mean to her," I tell Lena, who *mmm*s in agreement.

"I can't stand it when people are mean to you," she says, and I turn my head to study her eyes.

Okay, who exactly might she be talking about? Mom? Rob? I'm finding out these days that she knows more than I give her credit for knowing.

"I'm a tiger, too," I assure her.

She wraps her arms around me and squeezes. "I know you are," she says in my ear, and I swallow hard.

"Lena, that costume you made me—nobody could believe how incredible it was," I tell her.

She dangles a lock of my hair in her hand. "I'm so glad."

"Which made it slightly—just slightly—less horrible," I continue, "that all kinds of humiliating things were happening to me when I was wearing it."

She smiles knowingly. (Yeah. She knows plenty.) "But just like Syd is getting better at rolling with the punches," she says, "so is my big girl."

I wrinkle my nose. "My day actually got weirdly better this morning."

She cocks an eyebrow. "Go on."

I laugh. "Maybe you don't get to know *everything*."

"Oh, I have my sources."

"Nope. Moms aren't supposed to know everything."

Our eyes lock as the moment lingers in the air.

Lena finally says softly, "As long as my girl is happy. That's all I need to know."

The fan keeps clicking away.

"So happiness is an option?" I ask wistfully.

"Uh, duh," Lena says, stroking my hair again. "I guess sleep is an option, too. Think we ought to give that a try?"

I nod.

"Why not. But first, I've got an essay to write."

THIRTY-THREE

JADE

I approach Mr. Finch's desk shyly as our English Lit class wraps up the next day.

"Yes?" he asks.

"I need to ask a favor."

He smiles. "Ask away."

"Well, first of all, you know I've never turned in an assignment late ever, right?"

He taps a pencil playfully against his chin. "Why am I thinking a first time is rolling around?"

"It's really your fault," I say. "Brilliant move, calling my mom about the college application essay."

My mom. Yeah. It rolled right off my tongue.

"I thought so," Mr. Finch says. "Did she knock some sense into your head?"

I nod. "Guess so. Would you mind reading what I wrote?"

Mr. Finch winks at me. "Late or not," he says, "nothing would give me more pleasure."

• • • • •

Dear Admissions Committee Chairperson:

I'm very conflicted about sharing with you that my father is dying.

I'm conflicted because a) I desperately wish it weren't true, b) I cringe at the thought of receiving your pity vote, and c) the truth is that the reasons I think I would make an excellent addition to your student body really haven't changed substantially since before my father's diagnosis.

Well, that's not entirely true. On the days that I'm brave enough to admit it, even to myself, I realize that not a fiber of my being has gone untouched by my father's glioblastoma, the worst kind of brain cancer. The fact that this disease is destroying his mind and body almost literally takes my breath away sometimes. I love him so much that I feel like my own muscles are withering, my own diaphragm is weakening, my own life is slipping away. Not a day goes by anymore that I don't ruminate on the fragility or meaning of life.

So yes, I think my contributions to your college will be even stronger because of my newfound empathy and perspective.

But for the most part, I think my most compelling contributions will be those that I possessed before my father's disease invaded our lives. I fervently request your consideration of my application because I am simply ravenous for knowledge. Since my stepmother read *Madeleine* to me as a child, encouraging me to inhabit the protagonist's point of view as an orphan in a French convent, I have devoured every book I came across, then hungrily sought out the next one.

What's more, I don't simply read those books; I think about them, reflect on them, apply them to my existing knowledge base, then use them to broaden my perspective. My parents have always encouraged me to think critically—a challenge at times, when the path of least resistance, and the path of optimal approval, often seem to require taking things on faith.

I have faith: faith that beauty and wisdom will emerge from my father's last days on earth, no matter how weakened his body becomes; faith that his spirit will continue to love, guide, and support me even after he has drawn his last breath; faith that I can overcome my grief and make the world a brighter, happier place no matter how deep the hole in my heart.

So, yes, I am a person of faith. But mostly, I am a person of curiosity. Everything I learn makes me want to learn more. Every answer I obtain leads to more questions. Every assumption leads to scrutiny.

I learned this at my father's knee, and I will carry that hunger for knowledge into my college experience. I considered staying at home next year, and the year(s) after that if necessary, so I could spend as much time with my father as possible. But my father, more than anyone else, knows that I yearn not just for a college education, but for the whole college experience. I want to immerse myself in a hotbed of question-asking. I want to meet as many different people, from as many different backgrounds, as possible. I want to live independently, to challenge myself to stand on my own two feet as my parents have prepared me to do.

I want to do this while also holding my father's hand, literally and figuratively, during his last days on earth. I want him to feel my love, support, comfort, and faith.

But I still need things from him, too. Mostly, I need him to feel proud of me. I know nothing will give him more pride than seeing me launch my life with optimism. Quenching my thirst for knowledge—and refilling that cup over and over throughout my life—is my path to optimism. It is my path to faith.

It is my father's legacy. I will devote my life to honoring that legacy to the best of my ability.

Thank you for considering my application. I would be privileged to join your study body.

Sincerely,

Jade Fulton

THIRTY-FOUR

JADE

"I'll take 'Tooth or Consequences' for four hundred, Alex."

Pierce (AKA Alex Trebek) clears his throat ceremoniously and reads Dad the answer: "The Tooth Fairy took an unexpected sabbatical the night this Fulton child sank a tooth into a Happy Meal after a soccer game."

"Aw, that's too easy," Dad says, then dutifully answers in the form of a question. "Who is Jade?"

We all laugh and clap lightly.

"She never let Mom and me forget how she checked under her pillow the next day and came up dry," Dad adds, his eyes shining.

"I'm still traumatized to this day," I say, pouting.

"Pierce had just had his tonsils out!" Lena whines, and when I drown her out with *boo*s, she protests, "Aw, gimme a break!"

"In your dreams," I mutter playfully.

"I made up for it when Jade spent the night at my house that weekend," Grandma tells Lena.

"A ten-dollar bill!" I tell the others. "Score!"

Lena rolls her eyes. "One little Tooth Fairy fail, and here comes Grandma, ridiculously overcompensating."

"That's what grandmas are for," Grandma replies, patting me on the knee.

Dad's cancer has progressed so fast that our heads have spun, but Christmas morning was actually un-awful. Pierce wheeled Dad to the couch at daybreak and he watched us open presents, smiling cheerfully. He's the one who suggested our presents to him: taking turns sharing memories around the Christmas tree as we sipped hot chocolate. A couple of the memories were tear-jerkers, but most were funny, and Dad seemed content as he snuggled under the afghan that Lena, Sydney, and I spent the past two weeks crocheting for him. The vibe has lasted all day, and as the sun is setting, we're back in the family room, where Dad's "gift" has morphed into an impromptu game of Fulton Family Jeopardy.

Christmas night has always been game night at our house, and it feels great to keep the tradition going.

The savory scent of Lena's Christmas kaldereta (another tradition) still lingers in the air as Dad, our sole contestant, answers the questions.

"Has anybody noticed how many of the questions involve Jade?" Sydney observes, raising an eyebrow.

I shrug. "Can I help it if my life is the most interesting?"

"And have you noticed the questions about me are the ones Dad keeps missing?" Pierce grouses.

Everybody laughs.

We've been committed to good cheer all day, and kudos to everyone—especially Grandma, the ultimate crybaby—for soldiering through. But there's no denying what everyone is wondering: Will this be Dad's last Christmas?

I guess my sadness shows on my face. Ethan, who came for dinner and is gamely joining in on Fulton Family Jeopardy, squeezes my hand. He's had an unconventional Christmas, too—his dad moved into the guest bedroom after being discharged from the hospital a few weeks ago, and his mom has segued seamlessly into the role of caretaker. As Ethan points out, she never really abandoned that role in the first place, and now, at least she has the advantage of a sober, compliant patient. Who knows how long that will last (it helps that his dad can't sneak out to a bar or liquor store anymore) but the family is taking one day at a time, just like we are.

Pierce rattles off a few more questions (none of which are about me, for the record), and after the game winds down, Ethan and I walk out to the porch while Pierce and Lena help Dad to bed. The weather is unseasonably warm. It's only nine p.m. or so, but the street is already quiet. Christmas lights twinkle in the dark.

"We did it," Ethan says as we settle on the porch swing. "We made it through Christmas."

I was at his house the night before, eating chili with his mom, dad, grandmother, and Uncle Byron. Ethan's been hesitant to bring me around, worried about what he calls "leakage"—dribs and drabs of racist remarks that everybody in his family insists aren't racist. But they were definitely on their best behavior—his mom is really sweet—and, what do you know: His dad, the biggest dribber-drabber of all, concluded after I smoked him at poker that I am officially "pretty cool." I'll take it.

"Yeah," I say, a light breeze blowing through my hair. "We made it through Christmas."

Ethan puts an arm around me and presses me closer. "Today was great. The dinner, the jokes, the game. Your dad looked like he was in heaven."

He stops short for a sensitivity check, but I squeeze his knee to let him know it's okay.

"Thanks for coming," I say. "Everything's easier when you're by my side."

He leans in and kisses me. I kiss him back, massaging the curls on the back of his neck.

We meant what we said that morning in the hospital cafeteria about the whole friendship thing. But a couple of weeks into that plan, Ethan explained that if he didn't kiss me soon, he might have to join the Peace Corps. Plus, we'd just learned that the guy who robbed us entered a guilty plea, giving us something to celebrate. So, yeah. Things have progressed.

"Hey," Ethan says as we pull apart, "I got you a little something."

"You already gave me my present!" I scold, dangling my new bracelet in front of him.

"Yeah, just one other little thing."

I pluck a framed photo from his hand, the back facing up, as my mind races with curiosity. Ethan and I have been careful about not taking photos of the two of us together; no telling whose Facebook page they'll turn up on. Brianne already has another boyfriend, but considering all the drama we've already inadvertently generated, we're intent on keeping a low profile and tamping down the gossip to a dull roar. Still, Ethan is so sentimental that he probably snapped my picture when I wasn't looking. Or maybe it's his senior photo. Or maybe just a snapshot of a beautiful sunset.

I turn over the frame and sputter with laughter.

It's a close-up of his navel.

"You are sick!" I say, sputtering with laughter.

He laughs too, then takes back the picture frame and slides the navel shot from the back of the glass. He hands the frame back to me, this time with the real picture in it.

I peer at it for a couple of minutes, blinking back tears. It's a picture of my dad holding me when I was around three, my curls tumbling down my shoulders as I beam from ear to ear. Dad is beaming, too, gazing into my eyes.

"Where'd you get this?" I whisper.

"Your mom," he says, and I love that his words need no clarification. I know exactly which mom he's talking about: the one who helped me crochet an afghan for my dad. The one who remembers when I bit into a Happy Meal and left behind a tooth. The one whose Christmas kaldereta aroma is still wafting through the air. The only mom who matters.

On the bottom of the photo, Ethan has printed a quotation: "It is always darkest just before the day dawneth."

"You remembered Dad's quotations," I say, and he gives his "aw, shucks" smile. God, how I've grown to love that smile.

As I wipe a tear from my cheek, I notice Grandma peering through the blinds with a worried expression.

"Are you two okay?" she calls through the window.

"We're good," I call back, then repeat it for good measure.

"We're good."

THIRTY-FIVE

ETHAN
SIX MONTHS LATER

"We're coming, we're coming!"

I wave over to Jade, adjust the tassel on my mortarboard and push the wheelchair toward her.

"Let's get both our families together," I call.

"Just us first," Jade says.

We position the wheelchair in the center as Jade, my mom, and I gather behind it. Pierce jogs a couple of paces toward us, then readies his phone to snap the shot.

"Smile and say, 'World's most boring commencement address,'" he says, and our faces broaden into smiles.

"Your brother's so funny," my mom tells Jade.

"Don't encourage him," she replies. "Okay, now just you three," she tells me, stepping aside so Pierce can take a picture of my family.

"Now everybody!" my mom insists when Pierce is finished. She starts waving Jade's family over. We all pile in behind the wheelchair: Jade, me, Lena, my mom, both of our grandmothers, Pierce, and Sydney.

"Closer, closer," says the random guy Pierce handed his phone to.

He cups his hand to the group to the right of the wheel-chair. "A little closer."

We jostle a bit more, then Camera Guy says, "Great! Great! Everybody smile."

Click.

Gia and Victor drift over and start photobombing. "We can use these to paper our dorm room," Gia tells Jade, and she sticks out her tongue playfully for the next shot.

Then, Jade leans over the wheelchair and kisses my dad on the cheek.

"Thanks for being such a good sport," she tells him, and he smiles at her. Dad should probably be on his feet by now; he isn't paralyzed, and if he'd just stick with his rehab, he could be walking with a cane. But he doesn't seem to be in any hurry, and Mom and I are trying not to nag. As long as he's sober, we can deal with him. The old guy's got to be stubborn about something, right?

"That was perfect," Camera Guy tells Pierce as he hands him back his phone. "Just perfect."

● ● ● ●

JADE

We all know it's not perfect. Nothing will ever be perfect again. Of course, the truth is that it never was. But try telling that to my memories.

Dad's last moments were beautiful. He'd spent a couple of weeks on morphine, barely able to open his eyes. But he was home, in his own bed, with no tubes or needles. And right before he died (on Easter morning, no less, when tulips, hydrangeas, and azaleas were springing from our backyard garden) he woke up and gazed at us all around his bedside—me, Lena, Pierce, Sydney, and Grandma. He said, "I love you," clear as day, and he gave us the sweetest, most contented smile I'd ever seen. Then he closed his eyes and drifted away.

I swallow to dislodge the lump in my throat and force another smile on my face as I cajole Lena into stepping into the frame for a selfie.

After I snap the picture, I look at it on the screen of my phone and smile at the late-afternoon sunbeams shining down on us in streaks. Our faces are ringed in warmth and light, and I know, as firmly as I've ever known anything before in my life, that Dad is right here with us.

ACKNOWLEDGMENTS

When I submitted my initial draft of *Things I'd Rather Do Than Die*, Flux's brilliant managing editor, Mari Kesselring, gently suggested that I was half done. The story was told solely from Jade's point of view, and Mari lobbied for equal time for Ethan. If I was going to write a book about polar opposites, shouldn't I accord comparable ink to both sides?

Mari suggested that I alternate points of view with each scene—a he-said, she-said structure. I went back to the drawing board, relishing the challenge.

Enter Kelsy Thompson, the editor assigned to my story. I'd worked with Kelsy previously on *All the Wrong Chords* and marveled at her dedication, diligence, kindness, and overall mad skills. I couldn't wait to work with her again.

And what a gift she became to my story. When I submitted my first revision, I'd basically added new scenes to my original manuscript, letting Jade live and breathe the story, then adding Ethan's perspective in tacked-on additions. I didn't realize it at the time, but Ethan's scenes felt flat and passive, like afterthoughts. It was Kelsy who prodded me to detach myself from the original manuscript and create something altogether new, giving Ethan his own story, his own arc, his own pulse.

I am immensely grateful to both of these inestimable talents for glimpsing Ethan's full potential when I did not, and for challenging and inspiring me to unleash it. Thank you, Mari and Kelsy. I am so honored to work with you.

Thanks also to my unofficial (yet invaluable and indispensable) editor—my Jules. Your unerring instincts, sharp eye, and pitch-perfect ear for dialogue are among the many gifts that enhance my craft day by day, scene by scene, book by book.

Ironically, my editors' "show-don't-tell" mantra was one I'd been living all my life. My wonderful parents, Gregory and Jane Hurley, walked the walk in every conceivable way while teaching me to live a life guided by love, not fear. Thank you, Mom (rest in peace) and Dad.

Thanks also to the rest of my amazing, insanely adored, and unsparingly supportive family and friends.

Finally, a most heartfelt thanks to Joy LaShea Mobley, the beautiful little girl in a sunny yellow dress who invited a frightened and overwhelmed classmate to play jackstones on her (my) first day at a new school. I'll love you forever.

ABOUT THE AUTHOR

Christine Hurley Deriso is an award-winning young adult author who loves putting interesting characters in character-defining situations. Her novels include *All the Wrong Chords, Then I Met My Sister, Thirty Sunsets*, and *Tragedy Girl*. Visit her at www.chderiso.com.